For Sue Kenyon, who makes it all possible.

HER PERFECT HUSBAND

BE CAREFUL WHAT YOU WISH FOR

SUSAN WILKINS

PROLOGUE

She's slipping away now. Losing consciousness. Her lungs are screaming for air. She can't breathe. His forearm is across her throat, bearing down and compressing her windpipe. Her body jackknifes with terror.

No! This is not happening.

But the fear is real. Adrenaline is flooding her veins.

No. She's dreaming; it's the fever dream again.

Her heart pounds. Trapped in the instant before waking.

She gasps.

As she surfaces, the horror ebbs and recedes.

Just a bad dream. It will pass.

She opens her eyes. A shiver runs through her; goosebumps, although she's bathed in sweat. The dread never goes. It's visceral.

Embedded in the memories; the tracks left in her brain. No way to scrub them out. They're etched too deep.

Ever since she can remember. The same recurring dream.

She inhales. Deep breaths to slow her thumping pulse.

Dark outside.

A faint orange glimmer edges between the curtain and the wall.

She places a hand on her heart to soothe herself.

Relax. Breathe. All fine.

But something's not right.

A smell?

There's definitely a smell. The musky scent of male sweat?

Someone's in the room.

A shadowy spectre glides in front of the curtain. Or did she imagine it?

Panic shoots through her.

It's not part of the nightmare.

This is real.

He's here in her bedroom.

It's him.

1

_____

'And in conclusion, I'd like you to raise your glasses and drink a toast to the happy couple.'

Sophie Latham, resplendent in white lace, looks up at her father as he speaks.

Poor old bear.

He doesn't approve, but he's doing his best. He's wearing that terrible morning suit her mother made him buy for Nick's wedding. The waistcoat strains across his paunch. He's put on a good few pounds since her brother got married.

Sophie glances across at her new husband. His suit fits those broad shoulders like a glove. Looking at him sends a shiver right through her. Jet black hair swept back from his magnificent forehead, and those stunning blue eyes. He's a Celt. His ancestors fought with broadswords. He could swing a broadsword round his head, no problem.

He turns and smiles at her. She adores his face. But it's not just the looks. He gets her, he totally gets her. She's the luckiest woman in the world. And to think that three months ago they hadn't even met.

She knows her family's views. Deirdre Latham never

minces her words.

'You're marrying your personal trainer? Don't be so bloody ridiculous! Are you really that desperate?'

'Mum, you're being a snob.'

'I'm being a realist. Okay, I understand. You're thirty-nine, you want kids, the clock's ticking. But you're a successful businesswoman, Soph. You call yourself a feminist. Go to a clinic, get a sperm donor.'

Her father watched them argue. He doesn't fuss like her mother and he's always on her side. But even he looked dubious.

'What do you even know about him?' Her mother added.

'I know I love him and he loves me. Isn't that the best reason to get married?'

Okay, his touch sends a sexual charge zinging right through her. But how do you tell your mother that?

The guests are all getting to their feet. The sides of the marquee flap in the breeze; it's blowing in straight off the North Sea. It feels as if the entire edifice could take off, canvas billowing like the tall Viking ships that once harried this coast.

The choice of her parents' back garden in the small Norfolk market town of Holt was a last minute compromise. It became a question of what was available. A London venue would have been preferable.

There's a scraping of chairs and a rustling of dresses.

Roger Latham holds his champagne flute aloft.

'Sophie and Ollie,' he says.

The guests repeat in unison, 'Sophie and Ollie.' Glasses chink.

Ollie turns to her, raises her hand to his lips, kisses it and mouths *I love you.*

Out of the corner of her eye, she notices her brother. He's

giving her his supercilious look. Lawyer Nick, always Mum's favourite. He's the family man with two gorgeous little tots, the bridesmaid and pageboy who followed her down the aisle. She and Nick have been competing since they were kids themselves. But she's still ahead on points. He's only an associate at his firm. It'll be years before he makes partner.

When she graduated from uni, she ignored parental advice and went backpacking round the world for three years. She took risks and had adventures; sailed close to the wind a few times. Some nasty scrapes, but she doesn't dwell on that. Roger and Deirdre despaired of her. All that expensive private schooling. They expected her to have a professional career. Something solid, like accountancy or law. Sophie thought no way.

She met her business partner, Claire, in a hostel in Sydney. Claire loves to bake. When Sophie told her parents she was opening a coffee shop, Deirdre threw up her hands in horror. How would that ever make money? But Sophie had a plan. Her parents think she's rash and impulsive, but Sophie always has a plan. You figure out what you want and you make it happen.

Now she's CEO of one of the coolest upmarket coffee chains in London. Beans organically sourced, a mouthwatering array of cakes and pastries, a tempting deli counter, *Sophie and Claire's Place* soon became the most popular hangout in Shoreditch. Ten years down the road, Sophie has equity investors hammering at her door. And when the price is right, she'll sell.

As the guests settle back down, Ollie gets to his feet. He's such a big, tough guy, but his hand is shaking. He clears his throat. She gives him a reassuring smile. He's nervous. This isn't his thing. People will judge him. He's five years younger than her. And she's the one with the money.

'Well,' says Ollie.

'Speak up!' someone shouts from the back.

'Sorry. Umm, thank you everyone for coming, and thanks to Roger for a great speech. I expect that many of you are pretty surprised to be sitting here today. But I can tell you, you're not as surprised as me.'

A ripple of polite laughter runs through the marquee. Sophie reaches out and squeezes his hand. She wishes she could just do this for him, but that wouldn't be fair.

He takes a sip of champagne and then continues.

'The day I met Sophie, she was rather grumpy. She was late for her session, but somehow she blamed me. So I started her off with an easy circuit. And while I watched her, I realised that I'd never met a woman quite like this before. I think we can all agree that she is amazing. And, well, I guess the rest is history.'

Sophie can see Nick smirking to himself and shaking his head. Deirdre has too much dignity to indulge in such childish behaviour. She has a big smile on her face and a big pink hat on her head.

'And I'd just like to say, thank you Sophie Latham, for making me the happiest man alive.'

The applause is enthusiastic. It's hardly surprising. A meal prepared by a Michelin-starred chef and copious amounts of champagne should be enough to warm up any crowd.

Ollie sits down. 'Was that all right?' he whispers.

He could've recited the phone book for all she cares.

'It was perfect,' she says. 'Short but heartfelt. They'll appreciate that, because now they can all relax and get pissed.'

He laughs. He has such a dazzling smile. And she hopes that the babies she'll soon be having will look just like him.

2

Kristin sits in a high-backed leather armchair in the waiting room. Places like this make her twitchy. You'd think she'd be used to it by now. But she isn't.

Front it out.

The room is light and airy, on the sixth floor with a panoramic view of the Thames and the London skyline. Ged says the hospital is named after some dead king. It's one of the best in London, mega expensive; they treat royalty.

A nurse in a crisp white uniform appears. She looks West African, beautiful, but way too chunky to be a model.

She gives Kristin a polite smile. But the eyes remain frosty.

'Lady Sullivan,' she says, 'we're ready for you now.'

Kristin knows she's being judged. She's seen that look before. It says *who d'you think you are, girl? Nothing but a skinny whore who caught a rich man's eye?*

Part of Kristin wants to say yes, but we could be sisters. My mother was from the shores of Galway, but my father was an African Prince. That's the story she was told when she was little. Obviously, it was a lie. Her childhood was full of lies.

She stands up, smoothing her Gucci crepe de chine tunic. Still, she worries about the rounding of her belly. Will people think she's getting fat? Pregnancy is normal, of course it is. But models aren't normal.

The nurse marches off down the corridor, leaving Kristin to follow. Although she's pushing twenty-nine, she remains gamine, weighing no more than she did as a teenager. Leggy with soulful amber eyes like Bambi. Often she's felt like Bambi. Fleeing through the forest from the hunters, their dogs snapping at her heel and their sharp arrows piercing her flesh. She knows they want to destroy her just as they destroyed her mother.

She started making porn videos when she was fourteen. It was a favour to help a mate, that's what her stepfather told her. But she was lucky. A photographer saw her, and he knew. He told her she could be legit and still make money. And he wasn't wrong. He created a portfolio for her, showcasing those amazing looks. The eyes, the raven hair, the cheek-bones. She looked "exotic", he said. She was smart; growing up a mixed race kid, she knew what he meant. At school, the racism was casual; accept it and laugh it off, or else get battered. Not much of a choice.

The portfolio got her signed to a top modelling agency. They decided her unique selling point was mysterious and fragile. In fact, she was simply shit scared. She had her first magazine cover at eighteen. She knows her career, her staggering fame, her status as an icon, depends on being the beautiful blank canvas onto which men can paint their secret fantasies. And not just men. She plays the game and gives them what they want. It still feels like her only option.

The nurse is standing by an open door and waiting.

'You can leave your outer garments and shoes in here.

Any jewellery or phones will be quite safe,' she says. 'And then slip into the gown. Would you like any help?'

What Kristin would like is for Ged to be there. He knows how to deal with these people. But, as usual, he's busy.

The nurse is staring at her, waiting for a reply.

'I'm fine,' she says. 'Thank you.'

'Press the bell when you're ready.'

She had her first scan at seven weeks. Ged insisted; he said he wanted to confirm the dates. And he came with her for that.

This is number two. She knows the drill. Drink a glass of water half an hour before and they don't let you wee. You lay on the couch, cold gel on the tummy. It'll be fine. Nothing to be nervous about.

The trouble is, she is nervous. She doesn't want a baby. Never has. Her mum had four kids by as many men, and it wrecked her. Nearly bled to death twice.

But she keeps telling herself it's different nowadays. And she's with Ged. He's her safe haven. He's twice her age. But that doesn't matter. Older men are easier to manage. Give them regular blow jobs and they're happy.

There'll be nannies and once the little bastard's born, they can get on with it. No shitty nappies for her.

As she lies on the examination couch, the consultant comes in. Ged had a word, told him how frightened she is. She gets lots of personal attention as a result.

'How are you, Lady Sullivan?' he says in that plummy voice. He wears blue theatre scrubs, as if he's about to cut her open. And his arms are hairy like an ape. How can that be hygienic?

'I still keep being sick,' she says.

'We'll see if we can give you something for that.'

He can give her an abortion. That's what she'd prefer. But

she knows that Ged would go batshit crazy if she even mentioned it.

He's been married twice before. He has three grown-up daughters. She knows what they think of her. When he's not around, they treat her like an idiot. The bimbo model. Dad's trophy wife. She plays along. It's easier.

'Would you like to know what you're having?' says the consultant.

She nods. She doesn't care. But Ged will ask.

'It's a little boy.'

She smiles. That'll put their noses out of joint.

Two of the daughters have provided Ged with grandsons. But Kristin knows he wants a boy of his own.

As she dresses after the scan, her phone pings.

She glances at it. A couple of pictures. She reads the message.

So here we are. The happy couple! I can't wait for you to meet her, babes. I know you'll get on.

She stares at the picture and sighs. Nice dress. It looks like a posh do. He can't have paid for it.

He's added three kisses and several emojis. And it's signed Ollie.

Ollie? WTF?

That must be what he calls himself nowadays.

3

Deirdre Latham has never been a conventional mother, but she did imagine she and her daughter would plan the wedding together. A lovely stone church. Norfolk's full of them. Not that the Lathams are religious, it's more a question of tradition. Roses round the lychgate, a nice choir with hymns, sunshine. Late June would've been ideal.

Of course, Sophie had other ideas. She insisted she couldn't wait months for a suitable venue for the reception to be available. She wanted to do it now. At one point, she was talking about a beach in the Bahamas. Fortunately, Roger talked her out of that. He came up with the idea of the marquee in the garden. In late August? Crazy. It was obvious it'd rain.

The whole thing was ridiculous. It felt rushed. Even so, it must've cost a small fortune. The chef and his team, who'd taken over the Lathams' kitchen, came from London. The DJ. Famous, apparently, though Deirdre had never heard of him. Sophie said she could afford it; she didn't expect her parents to pay.

Deirdre felt excluded. Was her daughter punishing her because of what she said about Ollie?

She looks down the table at her new son-in-law. There's something about him that disturbs her. But it's hard to say what. He's always polite, perhaps a bit shy. He sits back and watches things. To Deirdre, he seems to be waiting and calculating. There's a tension about him, a wariness. Why doesn't Sophie notice it?

She confided her misgivings to Nick, and he said they should hire a private detective. But Roger vetoed that, said Sophie would go mad if she ever found out. They had to respect their daughter's choice.

And Sophie is besotted. Foolishly so.

Most people seem to think Ollie is handsome. But Deirdre can't see it. Those startling blue eyes make his face hard. And men with bulging muscles and tattoos. That's never been to her taste.

She feels someone touch her hand and realises her husband is smiling at her.

'You all right?' says Roger.

'Not really,' she says.

'Sophie's a clever girl. And she's thirty-nine, she's not young and naïve. She made him sign a watertight pre-nup. It'll be fine.'

'I just want her to be happy.'

Roger laughs. 'She looks pretty happy to me. She's worked bloody hard for the last ten years. Now she wants babies, maybe a house in the country and a couple of dogs.'

Babies certainly. But a house in the country? Deirdre doubts it. Sophie is obsessed with London. Loves the metropolitan life. She's bought a rundown old Victorian pile in Hackney and is having it ripped apart and rebuilt.

She sighs. 'But will he look after her?'

'You have to give it a chance. Try to get to know him, Dee.'

Roger's probably right. He often is when it comes to their daughter. Deirdre's own upbringing was tough; it's muted her maternal instincts and shaped her view of the world. She saw no point in mollycoddling her children. She left that to her husband.

Her own parents weren't well off; her father was an insurance salesman. And a lousy one at that. They moved frequently between small towns in the Midlands and the North. He had an abrasive manner and liked a drink. He also took the view that educating girls was a waste of time.

She left school at sixteen and trained as a shorthand typist. She jettisoned her regional accent, learned to talk posh and went to work for a small engineering firm in Norwich, and that's where she met Roger Latham. He was a different sort of man, the sort who bought you flowers and opened doors. The sort who didn't treat you as his skivvy and certainly never thought that you needed a clout.

Deirdre married him before she was twenty. She had no idea if she loved him. He took over the engineering business from his father, and was never going to set the world on fire. But through their years together she has become extremely fond of him. Isn't that love?

He provided a beautiful home away from the mean, narrow streets of terraced houses, where she grew up. And when she got fed up with being a housewife, he supported her ambition to go into local politics. In her small pond, she's a big fish. She's worked her way up, run most of the main committees and been chair of the County Council twice. A tireless fundraiser for the Party, rumour has it she could be in line for a seat in the Lords. What would her long-dead father make of that, miserable bastard that he was?

She watches Ollie get up from the table, kiss Sophie on the back of the head and walk over to the bar. She stands up herself and moves to intercept him. As a politician she's had plenty of experience of working the room, casually bumping into someone.

'Ollie!' she says with a big smile. He's huge. Like a bloody gorilla. She hates having to look up at him.

He beams. 'Just got myself a beer,' he says. 'To be honest, I don't much like champagne.'

'I agree. Give me a nice glass of red any day.'

'Can I get you one?'

'No, I'm fine.' She steels herself. 'It's good to have a chance to talk to you.'

He chuckles. 'Yeah, you must think all this has happened in a bit of a rush.'

'When my daughter makes her mind up, she doesn't hang about.'

'Everyone says she's very much like you.'

'Oh, I don't know about that.'

Flattery; rather obvious.

He's looking straight at her. Those cold blue eyes.

'I'm sorry that none of your family could make it,' she says.

'Me too. I was hoping my younger sister would come. But she's very busy. I've just sent her some pictures. She and Sophie will get on really well.'

'I don't think I knew you had a sister.'

'People sometimes have a funny reaction. So I keep it quiet.'

'Do they? Why?'

He sighs. 'She's quite well known. She's a model. Kristin Kelly. We don't have the same name.'

Kristin who?

He seems to read her blank expression.

'Sorry,' she says. 'I'm not really into fashion…'

He jumps right in. 'Course not. Why would you be? She's married to Gerald Sullivan. You've might've heard of him.'

What?

The disbelief must show on her face. It's hard for it not to.

This is even more ridiculous.

'Oh yes, of course,' she says. 'But Sophie never mentioned any of this.'

Does she even know? Surely she'd have said? Sir Gerald Sullivan!

He's grinning like the cat who got the cream. It's their first joust. And the sly bastard knows he's won.

4

Ollie drops his bombshell on the third day of their honeymoon.

Sophie raises her sunglasses and stares at him in disbelief.

'Kristin Kelly is your sister? You mean the supermodel?'

They're on the beach, on sun loungers, at a private island resort in the Seychelles. The expanse of the Indian Ocean stretches out towards the far horizon, waves gently lapping. The barefoot waiter has just brought two daiquiris.

'Why on earth didn't you tell me?' she says.

He sighs. His brow is furrowed. He has that look on his face; she's seen it before. Inside this big tough guy, there's a nervous little boy. And at times he seems lost.

'I wanted to tell you,' he says. 'But everything has happened so fast, and it never seemed like the right time. And then, I ended up mentioning it to your mum at the wedding. I thought she might have said something to you.'

Sophie would like to have eavesdropped on that conversation. She can imagine it; Deirdre being snobbish and Ollie deciding to assert himself.

'Hang on,' she says. 'Didn't Kristin Kelly marry Sir Gerald Sullivan?'

It was all over the tabloids about six months ago. Billionaire industrialist and she's his third wife.

Ollie nods. He's looking sheepish.

Sophie laughs and claps her hands.

'And did you *mention* that to my mother?'

'I might have,' he says.

She reaches over and takes his hand. 'You're a dark horse, Ollie Harmon. So you've figured out how to put the mother-in-law in her place? Very clever.'

'I thought you'd be upset.'

'Why? It's great. Serves Deirdre right. She's not exactly welcomed you into the family, has she?'

Sophie hasn't spoken to her mother since the wedding. They flew out from Heathrow at seven am the next morning. There were family farewells after the reception. A slew of good luck texts. But Deirdre was keeping her distance. They'd had a bust up two days before. Deirdre was still insisting it was a mistake. And Sophie had let rip. It was an epic row. Her passing shot was, *if you can't be happy for me, don't come.*

The old man had smoothed things over, as he usually does.

She gazes at her husband. It feels odd, thinking of him as that. He's made no secret of the fact he had a tough upbringing, in and out of foster care. But she respects him all the more for making something of himself. Even if being a personal trainer doesn't match her mother's stupid notions of a suitable match.

'Listen, Ol,' she says. 'I'm your wife. You can tell me anything. I'm not going to judge you or your past.'

He looks at her and smiles. Those blue eyes never cease to amaze her.

'The first thing I want you to know,' he says, 'is that I've never lied to you.'

'I never thought you had.'

'Me and Kristin, it's a complicated story. She's my half sister, different fathers. I'm six years older than her, and I've tried to look after her, to be a proper big brother. But she's had such a messed up life. Fame, but at a price.'

'I'm sure it's not been easy for either of you,' she says. 'I want to know about your life, of course I do. But you can tell me as much or as little as you want, when you want.'

'I want to tell you everything,' he says. 'But it may take a while.'

She raises her glass, takes a sip of the daiquiri.

'Well, here we are in this beautiful place. We've got all the time in the world.'

He picks up his glass too and takes a sip. His gaze drifts off towards the horizon, where azure blue turns into a line of dark navy.

'My mum came from the west of Ireland,' he says. 'She was eighteen when she got pregnant with me. Her father gave her a wad of cash and sent her to London to have an abortion. But she didn't go through with it. She kept the money and never went back.'

Sophie watches him; his chin juts and there's a fierceness in his face. Is it anger at his grandfather? Or pain? Probably both.

'I suppose you could say she was a bit of a hippy, my mother,' he says. 'She lived in squats in the winter and then in the summer she went on the road. My earliest memory is being in the back of an old converted ambulance. It had a wood burner that smoked all the time. And loads of rugs and this little dog that used to lick my face.'

Sophie listens. It doesn't sound so bad. Unconventional perhaps. But there's nothing wrong with that.

'Problem was,' says Ollie. 'Too much of the time, they were just wasted. That's how they made a living; she and the blokes she lived with, they were drug dealers. Every now and then they'd get busted, and then the social would come along. I'd get dumped in a foster home. I was in and out of those places, and I was in and out of schools. Then she'd get her shit together, and they'd send me back. And we'd be on the road again, with a new man.'

'Did you have other siblings besides Kristin?' says Sophie.

'We ended up four of us in all,' he says. 'I'm the oldest, Kristin is second youngest.

'Are you in contact with any of the others?'

'Not really. We lost touch over the years. My brother got adopted. Ended up in Canada. Our baby sister was fostered, disappeared into some new family, but we never saw her again. I suppose I was jealous. Me and Kristin, why did we get left? We were the rejects.'

Sophie realises he has tears in his eyes. It's tough for him to rehash all this. She grabs his hand and kisses it.

'Thank you for telling me all this,' she says.

He shrugs. 'At school, I got bullied. I was always the odd one out, the new kid in the class. Got called stupid because I'd missed so much school that I was always behind. Never learnt to read until I was a teenager. Once I got my first wage packet, I joined a gym and got into weight training as a way of protecting myself. Got fed up with being picked on, I suppose.'

'You've done brilliantly,' says Sophie. 'To cope with all

that as a kid and to make something of your life. You should be proud. I'm proud of you.'

'Are you? You don't think I'm just a yob with a good body?'

'Don't be stupid. Of course I don't.' She smiles. 'Not that I don't appreciate the body.'

He grins. Leans over and kisses her.

'You're the best thing that's ever happened to me.'

'So tell me about Kristin,' she says.

'I did my best to look out for her. But I wasn't always around. My mum got this new bloke, and he didn't like me. My mum was a total junkie by then. She just zoned out. And he did stuff to Kristin, if you get what I mean.'

'He raped her?'

Ollie nods.

'The trouble is,' he says. 'she can't take care of herself. Never has been able to. Blokes take advantage of that. They use her, either professionally or sexually. And she can't say no to them.'

Sophie feels her indignation rising. For her new sister. For all women. 'That's terrible,' she says.

All she has in her head is a vague image of Kristin from a perfume ad. But already a plan is forming in her mind. Ollie has tried his best to protect his sister, but now there are two of them.

She can see the pain in his eyes. This riles her even more.

'And that's why I haven't been in touch with her much,' he says. 'She got married. And he's made it clear he doesn't want me around. He doesn't like me.'

'I've heard of him,' says Sophie. 'CEO of some big conglomerate. Mining and oil?'

'He's twice her age and, okay, he's rich and respectable. But he's no different from the rest. I tried to tell her that.

She's got a career of her own as a model. And she could get into acting. Why does she need someone like him?'

'She wouldn't listen to you?' says Sophie

'No, she wouldn't. She lives on her nerves. Has loads of panic attacks. I don't think she's happy. In fact, I'm sure of it.'

'Do you think he abuses her?'

'Maybe. He controls her. She has to ask his permission about everything. I invited her to the wedding. But she said that he was too busy to come. So she couldn't.'

'Well,' says Sophie, 'I want to meet my new sister-in-law. And I don't care who her bloody husband is. He's not going to stop me doing that.'

5

Sophie's schedule, in the week after their return from honeymoon, is impossible. Her business partner, Claire, has been in charge. Claire may be a genius in the kitchen, but with everything else, she's flaky. Only together do they make a winning combination.

The office is informal but cramped, and located in an old textile workroom above their flagship shop in Shoreditch High Street. Sophie knows they need somewhere bigger; it's on her to-do list. But being back in the buzz of work is energising.

By the third week in the Seychelles, she was bored. They'd swum, snorkelled, and jet-skied. They'd chilled out and worked out and had sex. That was the best part. But, if she was honest, she'd had enough blue sky, blue sea and unremitting sunshine. Her brain was nattering, and she was ready to get back to work. She was missing London and even looking forward to a bit of rain.

The first day is rammed with back-to-back meetings. Plans to open two new shops, a row with one of their suppliers to be sorted, and a lunch with the account manager at a new ad agency that Sophie's thinking of hiring.

If she's going to get pregnant soon, she needs to get the business in a strong place so she can coast for a bit.

She's dispatched Ollie to see how the builders are getting on at their new house. He phones her to say that there are additional structural problems.

'I'm a bit confused,' he says. 'The builder, he reckons we'll need extra RSJ beams right across the new kitchen. I think you need to come and look.'

'Why?' Sophie's still triaging her emails.

'Well, it means going over budget. That's what he says.'

'When you say you're confused, what do you mean? You think he's trying to pull a fast one? Rip us off?'

'Oh no. He showed me. It's clear they're necessary.'

'Then you decide. You're there.'

'I could send you a video.'

'Ollie, I haven't got time. You sort it out.'

There's a moment's silence. Then he says 'Okay. If you're sure.'

Why wouldn't she be sure?

She feels a certain irritation. How long will it take him to get used to the fact that they're partners now?

More silence.

Then he says, 'Oh, yeah. And I spoke to Kristin. She's invited us to dinner.'

'Great. When?'

'Tonight.'

Sophie tries not to huff down the phone. 'Tonight? You're kidding?'

'She says Ged's really busy.'

'So am I.'

'Sorry, Soph. She says it's all they can do.'

'Well, where do they live?'

'They've got an estate near Newmarket. Ged keeps horses.'

'Newmarket? Seriously? That must be at least an hour and a half's drive. Nearer two. How's that going to work? I've got meetings until six.'

'We just need to be at Battersea Heliport by half-seven. We'll get picked up.'

Sophie digests this.

Having made a tremendous fuss about meeting these people, there's little she can say.

The interior of the helicopter is a plush cocoon with tan leather armchairs and a complimentary bar. But for most of the journey, she and Ollie are like big kids, peering out of the window at familiar landmarks, the skyscrapers of the City, then the London suburbs giving way to farmland.

According to Ollie, his sister apologised for the short notice and wanted to be helpful. So she arranged this online, using her private account; a sort of Uber for helicopters. It's how they travel.

Sophie is determined not to be intimidated by the casualness of this, or their super-rich lifestyle.

After a thirty-minute ride, the helicopter comes in above the treetops, passes a red-brick farmhouse, and drops down towards a neat tarmac circle at the back of the property.

The house is large, ultra modern and sleek, with a slanting zinc roof and acres of plate glass that reflect the evening sunshine; it looks like something off *Grand Designs*.

She checks her watch and gives her husband a mischievous grin. 'Dinner at eight,' she says. 'I hope the chef has prepared something nice.'

He smiles back at her. 'I've no idea. They've never invited me before.' He seems nervous. She squeezes his hand.

'C'mon, let's do this. Be confident, big guy. It's only your sister.'

As they get out, Kristin appears on the terrace and waves.

Sophie's first impression of her new sister-in-law is of a tall wraith with hunched shoulders, her luscious dark hair pulled back in a simple ponytail. She's wearing a beige shift dress, basically a sack. On her, it looks amazing.

Then he joins her. About the same height, grey hair shaved up the sides, a neat beard; he's lean and athletic, sixty three, although he looks ten years younger. He has a phone in his hand, which he slots into the pocket of his faded denim shirt.

Sophie feels overdressed. She rushed home to change. She grabbed the first thing that came to hand. What her mother would have described as a cocktail dress. Now she remembers why she never wears it.

They walk up a short path towards the elevated terrace. Sir Gerald Sullivan gazes down at them as they approach; he's checking them over.

She's done her homework too. He's a grammar school boy from the Midlands, who trained as a geologist, went into the oil industry and had a meteoric rise to the top. He's CEO of a company trading in oil and petroleum products, and in the news for toxic waste dumping.

Sophie has to climb six steps to come level with them. Ollie follows.

When she gets to the top, their host is holding out his hand.

'I'm Ged. Welcome and congratulations.'

She shakes his hand, meets his gaze, and smiles. 'Sophie.'

Kristin steps forward and draws her into an awkward hug.

'I'm so pleased to meet you,' she whispers. 'I'm Kristin.'

'You have a lovely house,' says Sophie.

'Ged likes to be near his horses.'

'Racehorses, I gather. Well, Newmarket is the place for it.'

Ged and Ollie are shaking hands.

'Do come inside,' says Kristin. Her voice is small and soft, like a nervous teenager. 'I'm sorry we couldn't make the wedding.'

'I know you're busy people. We probably didn't give you enough warning.'

'No. My brother texted me the week before.'

'He could've given you more notice than that,' says Sophie.

Ollie steps forward and gives Kristin a hug.

'Hey, babes,' he says. His voice is gentle, pleading almost.

She smiles but doesn't make eye contact.

Ollie's right about one thing: his sister is a jangling bag of nerves.

Ged leads them in through the open doorway, across the triple height atrium, which contains an orange tree, and into another room with a long dining table. It could accommodate twenty people, but at the far end it's laid just for four.

'Drinks?' says Ged. 'I think we should at least drink a toast to your wedding. Is champagne okay?'

'Isn't it always okay?' says Sophie. She's trying to be engaging. But Ged gives her a tepid smile.

His eyes are shrewd and appraising. Sophie gets the feeling he's a man who knows how powerful he is, but is choosing to be friendly.

From nowhere, a young lad in a blue butcher's apron appears. He already has a bottle of Cristal wrapped in a cloth.

He extracts the cork with a small *phut!* and fills the flutes on the table.

Everyone stands round and watches. The tension is unmistakable, but Sophie can't decide where it's coming from. Ollie seems uncomfortable. He's looking at Kristin, but she still continues to avoid his eye. Ged has a quick glance at his phone.

'Just three glasses,' he says. Then he smiles at his wife. 'What would you like, darling?'

'Oh, just a Perrier or something,' says Kristin.

Ged picks up two of the flutes and hands Sophie and Ollie one each. 'Actually,' he says. 'We have a reason to celebrate, too. We're expecting. That's why Kristin isn't drinking.'

Kristin is staring at her impeccably manicured nails. But the look of horror that spreads across Ollie's face grabs Sophie's attention. He makes no attempt to hide it.

Ged doesn't seem to notice. He's raising his own glass.

'Kristin's just had her second scan,' he says. 'It's going to be a boy. My first son. I already have three girls.'

'Oh well, congratulations,' says Sophie, with as much enthusiasm as she can muster. She raises her own glass.

Ollie continues to glare at his sister. For a terrible moment Sophie fears he's going to say something. But he doesn't.

The lad in the apron brings a glass of fizzy water on a tray. Kristin picks it up and raises it.

She paints on a smile. Her hand shakes.

'But first we should drink to you two,' she says. 'I never thought I'd see my brother married. But it's lovely to meet you Sophie. And I wish you both all the very best.'

'Yes, indeed,' says Ged.

Sophie glances at Ollie. His jaw is quivering. Anger? Distress? It's hard to tell, although his eyes are teary.

'Thank you,' he says with a curt nod.

6

The helicopter is booked to collect them at ten. And Sophie is relieved. She's exhausted. She expected it might be a little uncomfortable at first. But the whole evening has been a trial.

Kristin ate next to nothing, and Ged kept glancing at her.

'Can I get Andreas to make you something different?' he said. 'How about an omelette?'

Kristin grimaced and shook her head.

'You must have some protein. For the baby.'

'I keep feeling sick.'

Sophie sensed a battle of wills going on. She suspected that if they hadn't been there, Ged would have been more forceful.

Ollie said nothing. He kept his gaze focused on his plate.

And the food was faultless. Beautifully presented and prepared by someone who took pride in their work.

'Your chef is very good,' said Sophie.

Ged smiled. 'You're in the catering business yourself, aren't you? I expect you know more about these things than me.'

It sounded like a compliment, but it felt patronising. He

paid people to provide his food, people like Sophie, and he didn't give it much thought. He expected it to be the best.

Sophie was glad they hadn't turned up to the wedding. She wasn't even sure why Ged had agreed to this. He was going through the motions, being polite. It was more like an awkward business lunch than a family dinner. She could see that what Ollie had told her about Ged was true. He controlled everything. He didn't quite snap his fingers to summon the boy who served them. But he made a gesture, a motion with his hand which was a more subtle version of that.

Perhaps he was trying to control them too? Is that why they'd been invited? He didn't want any hassle from his wife's relatives.

The tension throughout the meal was horrible, although it didn't seem to concern Ged. The problem was the brother and sister weren't talking to each other.

Ollie was in a sulk, which wasn't like him at all. As each course was served, he shovelled it down and finished way before anyone else. In contrast, Kristin pushed her food around the plate with a fork. They exchanged moody glances like a couple of teenagers.

It was left to Sophie to keep the conversation going. She did her best. She asked Ged about his racehorses. He answered in boring detail. The trophies they'd won, the jockeys who'd ridden for him. His opinion about trainers and how much leeway to give them.

At first, she avoided anything relating to his business. Asking him about the accusations of toxic waste dumping and the impending corruption investigation in the US seemed tactless. Although Sophie suspected it wouldn't have bothered him. He showed no sign of wanting their good opinion or anyone else's.

They got on to politics. Ged had firm views on everything. He talked about members of the government as if he knew them and judged them to be idiots. By this time, Sophie was fed up. She wanted an end to this bullshit.

'What about climate change?' she said. 'Your industry has a lot to answer for?'

A spark of interest flickered into Ged's eye. Did he prefer a bit of conflict?

'My dear Sophie,' he said. 'Here's the problem. Politicians are shallow creatures who only care about what the voters think. But the voters don't think and they don't like their boring little lives disrupted. So governments can never be real agents of change. Industry must solve the problems through technological innovation. Research costs money. And it takes time.'

'Sounds like an excuse for doing nothing.'

'Untrue. We're doing plenty. But that depends on us continuing to make a healthy profit.'

'So we all sit back and rely on a few smart billionaires?'

He laughed. 'You could do worse.'

Kristin got up from the table, whispered 'Excuse me.' And hurried out of the room.

'Is she okay?' said Sophie.

Ollie stood up. 'I'll go and check.'

Ged seemed about to speak, then he changed his mind and shrugged.

Ollie followed his sister.

Sophie could hear the murmur of voices. But Ged started to explain carbon capture and how carbon dioxide can be stored deep underground in geological formations.

She watched his face. Chin tilted upwards, he was staring into the middle distance. It didn't matter to him who he was talking to. To him, she was just some woman. He expected her to listen. His arrogance and sense of superiority were nauseating.

It was becoming clear to Sophie that her new sister-in-law shouldn't be married to this man. She was beautiful and fragile, like a rare butterfly that some horrible little boy had trapped in a jar.

Once they're settled in their seats and the helicopter is lifting off, Sophie turns to her husband.

'What the hell was that about?' she says. 'I've never seen you like that before.'

Ollie shrugs. 'I was angry.'

'Yeah, I got that. I think everyone did.'

He shakes his head. He has a sorrowful look.

'Kristin should not be pregnant. And he knows that.'

'Okay. Why not?'

He puts his face in his hands. 'It's dangerous for her, Soph. A few years ago, way before she got tangled up with him, she had a miscarriage, and it was bad. She was really sick. The doctors told her she couldn't have any kids. She should never get pregnant again.'

'Does he know that?'

'Of course he knows.'

'Well, maybe not, Ollie. She gets in a new relationship. Perhaps she was reluctant to tell him. Or she went to another gynaecologist, got some different advice.'

He's shaking his head. 'She just told me she doesn't want it. And he knows that. But he's bullied her into it. I told you, Kristin finds it hard to stand up for herself. You can see what it's like.'

'Yeah. I can. She's obviously a very nervous person. What else did she say to you?'

'She knew I was mad. And she knew why. I told her she should have a termination. It's not too late. But she said Ged would never allow that. Especially now he knows it's a boy.'

'If it was on medical grounds, he'd have to accept it. The doctors treating her would advise her.'

'That's just it. He's got some private consultant. That's who she has to see. And she's explained to this doctor how frightened she is. But he's just dismissed it. More or less told her not to be silly. But it's not silly. For Chrissake, she could die!'

Sophie reaches out and takes his hand.

'Don't panic. Let's think about this. We need to get her examined by another doctor.'

'How? He won't let her.'

'You give up too easily. We'll find a way. My gynaecologist is great. She could help Kristin.'

'You think so?' His eyes are moist, but now they're filling with hope.

'Yeah. I do. We just have to make it happen.'

7

Kristin sits on the terrace wrapped in a pashmina shawl, staring out into the darkness. Below her a line of sunken lights traces the outline of the formal part of the garden. The colours of some of the late summer flowers are discernible — red dahlias waving their tall heads — under the shadow of a row of newly planted hornbeams. Day or night she loves the tranquility of this place; and the fact it's totally private. No paps with their ladders and long prying lenses. It's a safe haven.

The idea of her brother getting married had seemed outlandish at first. And Sophie is not what she was expecting. Nothing like it.

She's slim enough, medium height, but no one would call her pretty. Her face has no symmetry. The mouth is lopsided when she smiles and she has a long, rather boney nose. Her hair is blonde and well cut in a chin-length bob. Her taste in clothes is good; she knows what suits her. However, the thing that strikes Kristin the most is her confidence. She's comfortable in herself, in her own skin; the fact she's almost ugly doesn't seem to hamper her one bit.

How?

Kristin can't imagine feeling like that. She's been bullied and berated about her body for as long as she can remember.

Ged comes out of the house; he's checking his phone.

'How are you doing?' he says. 'Any better?'

'Yeah. I'm okay.'

'I've asked Andreas to make you a smoothie. You like those. At least get some nutrients in your stomach.'

Why does he have to be so irritating?

'Oh, for God's sake, Ged,' she snaps. 'Stop going on. I'll eat when I'm ready. The bloody baby's not going to starve to death, and nor am I.'

He squats down in front of her and takes her hand.

'Darling, I'm just trying to take care of you. No need to freak out.'

She leans forward and rests her head on his shoulder.

'I know,' she sighs. 'I don't mean to be such a grouch. But look at me. Fat as a beached whale. It's gross.'

He strokes her hair. 'It's not. You're hardly showing.'

'Is that what you really think?'

'Yes. And pregnancy just makes you more beautiful.'

'Does it?'

'Yes. Cheer up. I think tonight went well, don't you?'

She huffs. 'No. He's such an arse, my brother. I knew it was a mistake to invite them.'

'I liked her. Strikes me he's fallen on his feet.'

'She's very confident. Very outspoken.'

'Krissy, women like her have to be.' He cradles her hand. 'She doesn't have your natural advantages. No bloke's going to look at her twice, are they? So she needs a big personality. That's the only way she'll hook someone. And she's smart enough to realise that.'

'I wouldn't call her ugly. That's unfair.'

'She's okay, but more of a Saturday night shag when you're too pissed to care.' He laughs.

She smiles. 'You're so rude.'

He stands up and goes back to his phone. 'But I've been checking her company out. I never realised there was so much money in coffee and cakes. She's done well for herself. I admire that.'

Kristin stands up and pulls the shawl round herself. 'How is it I get married and then, six months later, he does the same? I mean, don't you think that's weird?'

Ged sighs. 'Darling, you need to let go of this. Don't let him get under your skin. We keep them at arm's length, we keep it polite.'

It's irritating him now. He has a short fuse. But she's not ready to back off.

'I think he's trying to make a point,' she says.

He shakes his head; now he's exasperated. 'You don't owe him anything. You can't always be feeling guilty. Forget about it.'

The warning glance. There it is.

He's done with this conversation.

She inhales. 'Sorry. You're right.'

He pats her shoulder. 'Just trying to take care of you. Let's go in, shall we?'

She nods.

Suddenly there's a piercing electronic wail. Kristin jumps out of her skin. On the wall above their heads, the alarm is flashing red.

'What the fuck…' mumbles Ged.

A moment later, his phone rings. He answers it.

'What's the bloody hell is going on, Raoul?'

As he listens, she sees disbelief cross his face.

'What?' he repeats.

Kristin's anxiety is going into overdrive. She hates stuff like this. 'What is it?' she says. 'What's happening?'

Ged raises an index finger to silence her. His jaw ripples with anger and he clenches his fist. 'Okay, I'm coming down.'

He hangs up, takes Kristin's elbow. 'Darling, you need to go back in the house. Lock the door behind you.'

She's shaking. She clutches his hand. 'No, I don't feel safe. Stay with me!'

'You'll be perfectly safe in the house. It's just some bloody hooligans, climate protestors they call themselves. They've climbed over the perimeter fence and strung up some stupid banner.'

'Can't security deal with it? Do you have to go down there?'

'I'm just concerned about the horses. I don't want them spooked.'

'Please Ged! I'm scared.'

He takes both her hands in his and squeezes them. 'They're not after you, darling. It's a stunt. Something they can stick up on social media, so all the sandal-wearing, carrot-munching idiots'll get so excited they wet themselves. Now be a good girl. Go inside and let me deal with it. If you want company, go down to the kitchen and talk to Andreas. I'll be back before you know it.'

He leans forward and kisses her forehead. He's walking away. She's going to panic.

Breathe. BREATHE!

She manages a couple of deep breaths. This is what she's been taught. It works. She knows it does.

The panic is subsiding.

It'll be okay. It is okay.

She gets up and goes into the house. Ged's right. She should chat to Andreas. Leave her husband to sort it out. Everything will be fine.

8

Detective Sergeant Jo Boden is more cheerful when she's on days. Life feels normal when she can walk to work across the Cambridge Water Meadows. Early in the day, it's tourist free, and she only has to share it with the swans and other water-fowl, and a few joggers.

When she transferred from the Met, she missed London. Cambridge seemed small and provincial to her, and weird. On the one hand, a world-class university, high-tech industries and a vibrant student population; that's if you believed the marketing hype. On the other, a clash between the haves and have nots, the city and the countryside.

But as a member of the Cambridge-based unit of the tri-force Major Investigations Team, covering the counties of Bedfordshire, Cambridgeshire and Hertfordshire, she soon realised behind the picturesque facade, her new patch is full of contradictions.

She walks into the office well before seven and is surprised to see the boss's door already open. DCI Hepburn rarely appears until much later. This means something is going on.

She hovers outside. 'Morning, boss,' she says.

He looks up from his laptop.

'Oh, Jo. Good morning. Glad you're early. Come in.'

This sounds ominous.

Alistair Hepburn is brisk and professional; he also likes to be ahead of the game. He has a tight budget he has to juggle, and the team is permanently under strength.

'Do you know the Newmarket area?' he says.

It's east of Cambridge, maybe a half-hour drive, depending on the traffic.

'I went to the races there once,' she says. 'But surely that's Suffolk, not us.'

'Last night, there was a serious incident. To the west of Newmarket, nearer to Burwell. So it's just in Cambridgeshire. Lucky us. A bunch of climate change protesters broke into the estate of Sir Gerald Sullivan. He's a billionaire industrialist, and he keeps racehorses. It's not clear what happened, but one protester was seriously injured. She's in hospital with a fractured skull.'

'Over enthusiastic security?' says Jo.

'Could be. Uniform dealt with the matter last night. But CID have flagged it up to us. This girl is in a bad way. Bleed on the brain; she's still in surgery. Hospital says she might not make it. So I want you to get over there and find out what happened. I don't need to add, this will be sensitive and controversial.'

'Upset billionaire versus upset climate change protestors, and the media all over it?'

'Exactly. Pictures of it on social media already. Not a lot we can do about that. Who do you want to take?'

'Chakravorty and Mackie?'

'Okay. I gather that Sir Gerald himself wasn't at home at

the time. But his head of security is Raoul Kemp, and there should be CCTV.'

DC Scott Mackie drives, Boden sits beside him and DC Prisha Chakravorty rides in the back.

'Do you think we'll get any racing tips?' says Mackie. 'I like a bet.'

Boden ignores him, so does Chakravorty. She's scrolling social media on her phone.

'It's trending,' she says. 'We've got some grainy footage, lots of shouting and confusion. Can't see much.'

'Who's attacking who?' says Boden.

'Can't tell.'

'Y'know,' says Mackie. 'If a bunch of yobs broke into my place, I'd feel entitled to give them a smack.'

'Fracturing someone's skull is hardly a proportionate response, not unless she was seriously threatening that person,' says Boden.

'She could've been.'

'Okay, yeah, if she was armed,' says Boden.

'Come on, Scotty,' says Chakravorty. 'Big butch security guard against small female protester?'

'You come on, Prish,' he replies. 'I've policed some of these climate change demos. It's the little ones you have to watch out for. Like a snapping terrier, they can be vicious.'

'But you love a ruck,' says Chakravorty.

He pulls a face at her in the rearview mirror and wags a finger. 'Don't jump to conclusions. Isn't that right, Jo?'

Boden cracks a smile. She's become familiar with these two bickering. It lends a symmetry to her days. She also knows, when push comes to shove, they'll walk through fire for one another.

'Don't you care about the planet burning up because of fossil fuels?' says Chakravorty.

'Yeah, course I care, everyone does,' says Mackie.

'Everyone doesn't. And Sir Ged Sullivan has got very rich not caring at all,' says Chakravorty, with feeling.

'Okay,' says Boden. 'Time out. There's going to be lots of differing opinions on this. Which is why the boss wants to make some kind of statement to the media this afternoon, if possible. And why we need to work fast but focus on the facts. What happened, and where's the evidence to confirm it?'

9

Deirdre Latham gets off the Norfolk train at King's Cross. She's spending the day in London, attending a seminar for local councillors on planning issues, and she plans to squeeze in some shopping. What she's not expecting is to see her daughter. Since the wedding, they've had no contact.

'Two proud and stubborn women,' said her husband. 'Neither of you wants to be first to apologise.'

'What have I got to apologise for?' said Deirdre. 'I speak my mind. Sophie knows that.'

But when Deirdre sees Sophie hovering near the barrier, her heart soars. She strides towards her, chin held high.

'Well, I wasn't expecting to see you,' she says. 'I've got a very busy day.'

'Dad says the seminar doesn't start until eleven. There's time for me to buy you breakfast.' Sophie seems to hesitate, then she adds, 'and to tell you I'm sorry.'

Deirdre looks away; she doesn't want Sophie to see her tearing up. It's horrible when they fall out.

She envies her daughter; not her youth and education, but the fact she's grown up unscathed. Sophie has a father who adores her, not a bully who tormented and belittled her; she has a brother, who knows she's the smart one, not two thugs, who teased and groped her whenever they thought they could get away with it. Sophie's never had to make herself small. She probably can't even imagine what that's like.

Only when Deirdre became Mrs Roger Latham did she find a way to stand up for herself in the world. Her husband's status protects her. His class protects her. These things were necessary for her, but not for Sophie. And Deirdre is glad about that.

'I hope you know somewhere nice,' she says.

It turns out her daughter does, and she's booked.

The place is in Pancras Square, and once they've been escorted to their table and seated, Sophie leans forward and whispers. 'I'm snooping. There's a lease coming up three units away. I'm thinking of taking it. I reckon we can give this place a run for their money.'

'You're very sure of yourself,' says Deirdre. 'One of these days you're going to fall on your face, my girl.' She catches Sophie's disgruntled look. 'I'm teasing.'

Sophie cracks a smile and opens the menu. 'Look at the prices. Expensive. And the number of people in here. Not enough. They're struggling. And the coffee's not organic. And the servers look bored.'

'I wish you luck.'

'Do you?' says Sophie.

Deirdre's taken aback.

'Of course I do. Don't be ridiculous. You're my daughter. I've only ever wanted the best for you.' Why would she ever doubt that?

Sophie sighs. 'I just want you to get to know him. Then you'll understand.'

Deirdre notices the puckering between her daughter's

brows. Since she was a little girl, this has been her expression whenever she's anxious or in need.

Deirdre reaches out and grasps her hand. 'Don't be a soppy sausage. Of course I want to get to know him. Apart from anything else, Sir Gerald Sullivan is his brother-in-law. You know how much he donated to the party last year?'

'I dread to think.'

'Why didn't you tell me about all that?'

'Truth is, I didn't know.'

'How could you not know?'

Sophie sighs. She seems eager to skate over this. 'Well, actually, I met him. We went to dinner last night at his estate just outside Newmarket.'

'No! How exciting?'

'The most exciting part was the helicopter ride there and back.'

'I read in Tatler that he keeps racehorses.'

Sophie grimaces. 'Tatler! Really Mum?'

'They have it in the waiting room at the dentists. So how was it? And what's Ollie's sister like? Isn't she some kind of top model?'

'Her name is Kristin; she's very beautiful, obviously. But quiet and nervous. Worryingly so, if you ask me. And she's expecting a baby.'

'How lovely.'

'Not really. Because after a miscarriage a few years ago, she was told never to get pregnant again. She's told Ollie she doesn't want it.'

'Oh dear. But, y'know, if she's married to Ged Sullivan, I'm sure she's getting top-notch treatment. What they would've advised a few years ago…'

'I said that. Ollie's not convinced. He's worried about her.

And it looks to me like it could be quite an abusive relationship. He's twice her age, controls everything she does.'

'Surely not.'

'Mum, just because he's rich and successful, it doesn't make him a nice man. Some of these guys, the power goes to their heads. They're selfish narcissists and they treat women appallingly. Look at the big name cases there have been. That film producer and the TV guy.'

'I know. But not Ged. I've seen him interviewed on television. He's charming.'

Deirdre is already imagining all kinds of scenarios. Her next local fundraiser with Ged Sullivan as the surprise guest? That would be a coup.

'I've just had dinner with him. He didn't charm me.'

'You can be very judgemental, Sophie.'

'I know. And I don't want to be. But, if I'm honest, he gave me the creeps. Ollie insists Kristin has never been happy with him.'

'Y'know, brothers and sisters don't always see eye to eye. Look at you and Nick.'

'That's different. Okay, we've always been competitive. But in a good way.'

'Perhaps Ollie doesn't like the fact his sister's a very successful model, and he's a personal trainer?'

Sophie bristles. 'You're determined to think the worst of him, aren't you?'

'I'm not. I'm sorry.' She reaches out. 'Sophie, let's not fall out again. I'm not trying to upset you. And I'm sure when I know Ollie better, I'll see all the qualities in him you admire.'

Sophie gives her a curt nod and turns back to the menu. 'Let's order, shall we?'

10

———

Jo Boden lowers the car window. They've just pulled up at the tall, wrought-iron gates to the Sullivan estate. A uniformed officer is standing there. He steps forward.

Boden smiles at him and shows her warrant card. 'Morning.'

'Morning, Sarge.' As the gates swing open, he points up the tree-lined drive. 'Follow the drive. Take the right fork and you come to the stables and outbuildings, where you can park. That's where it all kicked off. We've done our best to secure the area. But, to be frank, it's been difficult.'

'Difficult how?' says Boden.

'It's a working stable. But there's nowhere to move the horses to, and without the staff, no one to handle them. Head of security's been kicking off. Saying they're worth a lot of money, we can't touch them.'

'Okay, thanks for the heads up,' says Boden.

'This should be fun,' says Mackie, as the car accelerates through the gates and up the drive.

They round a bend and get their first glimpse of the

house. It's large and modern, huge windows glittering in the morning sun.

'How the other half live,' says Mackie.

'How the less than one percent live,' says Chakravorty.

'Turn of phrase,' he replies.

Boden is pondering. 'You know what?' she says. 'Forget the stables, Scott. Drive up to the front door.'

'Yes!' says Mackie, fist punching the air.

He takes the left-hand fork.

The drive ends in a turning circle at the front of the house. There's a small granite rock spouting water set in a flowerbed in the middle. Mackie pulls up as close to the steps as he can get.

The countryside around is flat and wooded, but the house has been constructed on an elevated platform with a terrace all round. Boden wonders whether this is to give the occupants a view, or so they can feel superior.

She gets out of the car and walks up the steps. Chakravorty and Mackie follow. The front door is a solid steel slab. It gives an impression of impregnability. Before Boden can even search for a doorbell, it opens. A small Filipino woman in a smart black uniform appears.

Boden takes out her warrant card. 'Good morning,' she says. 'Is Sir Gerald at home?'

The woman hesitates. But a voice behind her says, 'It's alright, Maria, I'll deal with this.'

The door opens wide and Boden faces a tall, lean man in a tracksuit. Hair and beard are grey, his face is lined and tanned. He has a phone in his hand and peers at her over rimless reading glasses.

'Good morning, sir,' she says. 'I'm DS Boden and these are my colleagues, DC Mackie and DC Chakravorty.'

'Ged Sullivan,' he replies. 'And before you go any further

Sergeant, my head of security, Raoul Kemp, is dealing with this matter. He has an office in the stable yard. And I think your colleagues know this.'

'But you are the owner of this property, are you not, sir?' says Boden. 'So we just have a few questions, if you wouldn't mind.'

Sullivan meets her eye. He shakes his head and appears to chuckle to himself. 'Well, you'd better come in,' he says.

'Thank you, sir,' says Boden. She and Mackie exchange glances as they follow him into the house.

The hallway, if it can be called that, goes up three stories. The floor is polished concrete. Boden looks up to glass balconies above. For a second, she glimpses a figure. A woman? Whoever she is, she disappears.

They follow Sullivan through into a large, book-lined room. Many of the books are leather bound, sit on glass shelves, and appear to be for show. But there's a rectangular desk with three computer screens on it, displaying columns of figures. The Stock Market?

'As I'm sure you know,' says Boden, 'we're making enquiries about the incident that took place here late last night. I understand from my colleagues that climate protesters broke in and, in the confrontation that ensued, one protester was injured.'

Sullivan puts the phone on the desk and folds his arms. This is him, in his castle, but the body language is defensive.

He sighs. 'Y'know, I could ask, whose side are the police on? They trespassed on my property.'

'I appreciate that, sir. Did they do any damage?'

'Tried to hang up a bloody great banner on the roof of my stables. I have seven thoroughbred race horses, worth a great deal of money.'

'Were any of your horses injured?'

'No, but that's hardly the point. I've been the victim of these kinds of stunts before. And I know what you're going to say, it's civil trespass.'

'So the protestors broke in, then what happened?' says Boden.

'I don't know. I wasn't here. That's why you need to talk to Raoul. And, I should make it clear, I don't want your untrained officers touching the horses.'

'Can I ask where you were?'

He sighs again. 'In London. I returned early this morning.'

Boden notices a woman hovering in the doorway. Tall, willowy and beautiful, she looks familiar. An actress?

'What's going on?' she says in a small, nervous voice.

'Darling,' he replies. 'The police are here about last night.'

'It was scary,' says the woman. 'People just breaking into your home like that. Quite a shock.'

'Yes, well,' Sullivan interjects, 'it was fortunate that we weren't here.'

Boden notices the look that passes between the couple. It's momentary. The wife dips her head. She seems about to leave.

Then Boden says, 'I'm sure it's upsetting for you. But, perhaps your head of security told you, a girl was seriously injured. This means we have to investigate.'

The woman swivels round. She has huge eyes. Amber with flecks of green. 'What girl?' she says.

Sullivan walks towards her, takes her arm and guides her to a chair. 'I didn't want to upset you, darling. Apparently one of the protestors was injured.' He shoots an irritated glance at Boden. 'My wife is expecting. She hasn't been feeling well. Her doctors have told her to rest.'

Maybe no trips to London then, thinks Boden.

'Was she badly injured?' says the wife. She sounds concerned.

'She has a fractured skull and is still undergoing emergency surgery,' says Boden.

'Oh my God, that's terrible, Ged.' Turning to her husband, she has tears in her eyes.

'Yes, it is,' says Sullivan. 'And I've been telling the sergeant that in spite of the fact they were trespassing, we would not wish to see anyone hurt on our property.'

'God, no.' She glances at Boden. 'Will she be all right?'

'That I couldn't say.'

'Can I take you down to the security office?' says Sullivan. 'Raoul Kemp is the man you want to speak to. I'm sure he will answer all your questions.'

'I'm sure he will,' says Boden. 'But we'll find our own way. Thank you for your time, Sir Gerald.' She turns to the wife, meets her gaze directly. 'I hope you feel better, Lady Sullivan.'

11
***

Kristin remains in the study, while Ged escorts the police out. When he returns, he's steaming.

'Bloody cheek!' he says. 'They're all just little Hitlers. Stupid woman, walking in here, waving her badge about. Who do they think they are?'

'Ged, why did you say we were in London?'

He wags his finger at her. 'Quiet, darling. I need to call Raoul.'

She sits down in an armchair and folds her hands in her lap. Demure is not her natural state. But it's what her husband expects. She's learned it's best to comply.

When he returned to the house last night, she knew something bad had happened. He went straight to the bathroom and took a shower. He wouldn't speak to her or explain. This morning she looked in the laundry basket. The clothes he was wearing weren't there. They've disappeared.

Ged is ticking with impatience; he's not usually like this. Things don't phase him. Raoul isn't answering. Her husband tosses his phone on the desk. It clatters against the computer keyboard.

Keep your head down.

She says nothing. She waits.

He inhales. Puts his hands on his hips.

'Okay, listen to me,' he says. 'This could get complicated. So the story is, we weren't here, we were in London.'

'But what about my brother? He knows that—'

Ged curses under his breath.

He's forgotten about that.

'Right,' says her husband. 'You need to talk to him.'

'Me?' Her panic is rising. 'It would be far better if you did it.'

'For Chrissake, Krissy! He's your bloody brother. You call him, you tell him, in fact tell both of them not to speak about it. They did not come here and have dinner with us last night. Anyone asks, they deny it. Got it?'

Her hands are shaking. She hates it when he gets angry. When he's like this, there's no telling what will happen.

'But how will I explain—'

He looms over her. 'It's simple. You have the power. You don't have to explain. He won't want to upset you. All you're asking for is his discretion. I doubt he'll refuse.'

He's asking them to lie. And he doesn't know her brother.

Her stomach is fluttering, and she feels sick.

He picks up his phone. Trying Raoul again. No answer. It's winding him up. He's pacing like a caged beast, phone in hand.

She wonders what happened; there's no way she can ask. The police said a girl was badly hurt. A fractured skull?

Did he do something?

She bats the thought away. She can't go there.

He's scanning her. She adjusts the look on her face and gives him a smile.

He exhales, then smiles back. 'Darling, the last thing I

want is for you to worry. I'm sorry if I spoke harshly. I'm just annoyed about all this.'

Gently. Be the little wife.

'Of course you are. But it's fine.'

He shakes his head. 'It's the way the police behave. We're the victims here. These hooligans have invaded our property.'

'I know.'

'And the fact they've upset you, especially in your condition. It's unforgivable. And I won't have it.'

She swallows. The storm is passing. She knows her husband; quick to lose it, but he soon calms down.

'Don't worry,' she says. 'I'll speak to him. I think he was grateful even to be invited. So, you're right, it won't be a problem.'

'Good girl. I knew you'd understand. And I promise you, I've done nothing wrong. It's a lot of nonsense. But you know what the media's like.'

She knows. They smell blood, they go for the jugular.

Panic over. She gets up.

'I'll sort it out,' she says.

Ged's phone rings. He answers. 'What the bloody hell, Raoul? The police came up to the house. They've upset Lady Sullivan. I thought my instructions were clear. I pay you a lot of money to handle these things. Now do your job. Don't give me excuses—'

She heads for the door. As she walks out of the room, she can hear him continue to rant.

Better Raoul gets in the neck rather than her.

Deep breaths.

She decides to go and do some yoga before calling her brother.

12

Sophie Latham orders an Uber which picks her up at the side of King's Cross station.

Her morning has gone well. She extended the olive branch and has patched things up with her mother. She and Deirdre disagree about most things. Her mother's mixture of snobbery, occasional bigotry, and irritating criticism couched as maternal advice, is tedious in the extreme. But Sophie has lived with this all her life and ignores it.

The row over the wedding is their most serious bust-up for some time. Deirdre was out of line; she was horrible about Ollie. But Sophie lost her temper and was more scathing than she intended. Dad contacted her several times, saying how upset her mother was, and pleading with her to sort it out. And now it's sorted. She can tick it off her to-do list.

The cab drops her outside their new place in Hackney. The three-story Victorian property is encased in scaffolding. There's a skip in the front garden, and most of the interior has been stripped back to the bare brick. But there doesn't seem to be any sign of the builders. Usually, at least one truck is parked in the narrow driveway next to the house.

She mounts the steps to the front door and finds it ajar.

'Hello?' she calls.

A head pops round the corner, and she beams. Ollie.

'Oh,' he says. 'I wasn't expecting to see you. I thought you were really busy today.'

She walks into his arms and kisses him. 'Well,' she says. 'I am. But you seemed anxious yesterday. Wanted me to come and look. So here I am. Where are the builders?'

He huffs. 'Giving me bloody grief,' he says. 'These RSJs for the kitchen will take three days to arrive. In the meantime, they can do nothing. Or so they said. So I said, we're not paying you to sit around and drink tea for three days. That's not in the contract. Come back when you've got the RSJs.' He gives her a sheepish look. 'I hope that's all right. You said sort it out. So I did. They weren't happy. But I thought it was best to be tough.'

She grins and kisses him again. 'Absolutely. That's what I would've done.'

He smiles. 'I'm learning,' he says. 'But then I have a great teacher.'

She moves in for another kiss. It's long and lingering.

He's such a good kisser.

This is the advantage of a speedy wedding that her mother doesn't appreciate. He's her husband, but she still wants to rip his clothes off every time he touches her. She wonders how long this level of desire and passion will last. Once they have kids, it'll wane. But for now, she intends to make the most of it.

He pulls away and sighs. 'I should get back to the gym. I've got clients this afternoon.'

Sophie runs her finger along his forearm. 'Pity this place is so mucky,' she says. 'Wouldn't it be great to check out our new bedroom?'

He laughs. 'Soph, it's a building site. We'd end up covered in brick dust.'

'You don't fancy hot sex on naked floorboards then?'

He laughs again. 'You want splinters in your backside?'

'Probably not.'

He moves away. And she has a sense of something else going on. She's still learning his moods. And he can be moody. Things seem to change quickly with him.

'You all right?' she says.

He looks at her, slots his hands in his pockets and shrugs. 'Actually, I just talked to Kristin. She's upset.'

'About what? I thought we had an okay evening.'

It wasn't okay. It was bloody hard work. And listening to Ged drone on was a pain. But she did it for Ollie.

'I'm not sure what it's about,' he says. 'After we left last night, there was some kind of trouble.'

'Between her and Ged?'

'Could be. She wouldn't say.'

'You think he's hurt her?'

She knew it! Her instincts were right about that smug bastard.

Ollie sighs. 'What she said is that it was important that we didn't tell anyone we'd been to dinner there last night.'

'Why?'

'I've no idea. She was just wound up. She gets like that. And she made me promise.'

'I've already told my mum.'

'Well, who's your mum likely to tell?'

'Everyone she meets, probably.'

'Can you ask her not to? Kristin said it was really important.'

'Ollie, it doesn't make sense. And if Ged's threatening her—'

'She never said that. She just begged me to promise. And I did.'

'Well, okay. I'll call Mum, but I can't guarantee that she hasn't already been bragging to everyone at this bloody seminar she's attending.'

Ollie pulls her close and kisses her forehead. 'Do what you can? I feel I'm finally connecting with Kristin again. I don't want to upset her.'

Sophie scans him. He's tense with anxiety. She strokes his forehead.

'Okay,' she says. 'I'll do my best.'

13

_____

Boden walks across the stable yard towards the security office. There's a pungent smell of hay and horses. She sees a small, stocky bloke with a close shaved head and a dark suit, coming out of the office towards her. She presumes this is Raoul Kemp. He has his phone to his ear and a scowl on his face.

'Yeah. Don't worry. I will.' As soon as he sees her, he scowls even more and hangs up.

It's clear their arrival has been announced.

Boden has instructed the two DCs to spread out and look around.

'Mr Kemp?' she says, pulling out her warrant card. 'I'm DS Boden.'

'Yeah, I've been expecting you. I left a message with the officer at the gate for you to come straight here.'

Boden smiles. 'Your boss giving you grief, is he? Because we went up to the house.'

He gives her surly look. 'Don't know what you mean.' Then he appears to rein himself in.

Sighing, he says, 'Listen, Sergeant, it's a difficult situation, y'know. These bloody protesters, it's not the first time they've targeted Sir Gerald. And frankly, in the past, the police have done sweet FA. He gets pissed off.'

'Who wouldn't?' says Boden. 'So what happened?'

'You want to come in the office? I'll make you a coffee.'

'Thanks.'

The security office is more of a suite, comprising several large rooms off a main reception area. It's clean but spartan, a couple of black leatherette IKEA sofas, and through an open doorway, Boden can see a bank of monitors covering all of one wall. An expensive set-up.

Another man appears. Same suit, same haircut, but much younger.

'Can you get the sergeant a coffee,' says Raoul. 'How do you take it?'

'Black, no sugar,' says Boden. Raoul Kemp has morphed from sullen to unctuous in the space of less than two minutes. He looks like a worried man. But worried about what?

He invites her to sit, and she takes one sofa. He perches on the edge of the other, opposite her.

Leaning forward, he steeples his fingers; a small paunch strains over the waistband of his black polyester trousers.

'So here it is,' he says. 'And I'm going to be honest with you.'

'Good,' says Boden. She adjusts her body worn video to make sure he's in shot. 'Mind if I record this?'

He grins. 'That's a bit high-tech. No little notebook? I had to write it all down, back when I was in the job.'

She wondered if he was going to mention that. En route, she'd had Prisha do some checking. He was ex army, then briefly in uniform, in Manchester, but lasted less than a year.

The other security guard returns and hands Boden a mug of coffee. It's instant, with granules still floating on the top. She sets it down on the table next to her phone and smiles.

Kemp puffs out his cheeks. 'Right, well, eleven thirty last night, the perimeter fence was breached. It's steel mesh. They used bolt cutters. A dozen of them. As I already said, not the first time. So we know the drill. They string up a banner, sometimes daub things with slogans, video it for social media. Two of my boys were on shift. Brandon, here.' He nods toward the other guard. 'And Kobe.'

'You weren't here?' says Boden.

'I was. I've got a flat at the back of the stables. Soon as the alarm went off, I was straight down here. Cause, y'know, it could be someone after the horses.'

'Which are worth a lot of money?'

'Indeed. But I knew what it was about as soon as I saw them. Before, there were only two or three of them. Tend to be crusties and student types. This time, as I say, I counted a dozen. Some big lads among them. A more extreme faction, I'd say. The real headbangers. They outnumbered us.'

'I'm surprised you don't have dogs,' says Boden.

'Nah, they'd spook the horses. Well, one thing led to another, and it got out of hand. Brandon got punched in the mouth. I tell you Sarge, we feared for our safety. Kobe picked up a baseball bat—'

'A baseball bat? From where?'

'Sometimes we have a game, y'know.' Kemp is pacing himself, speaking slowly, keeping an even tone. 'Kobe swung it, accidentally hit this girl. Then they all panicked and legged it. We called an ambulance. And of course, you lot.'

Boden nods. 'You've got quite a sophisticated set up here, lots of cameras. I presume you've got CCTV of all this?'

Kemp clears his throat. 'Well, some of it.'

'Some of it?'

'Not all of it. Software glitch. They're a bit too bloody complicated these systems. We've been waiting for the engineer to come out and do an update.'

'Where's Kobe now?'

'He's gone home. Obviously I called Sir Gerald.'

'Who was where?'

'Oh, he was in London. Came back this morning. He was upset. Sacked Kobe on the spot. Sent him packing.'

'You have an address where we can find him?'

'Of course.'

Kemp smiles. He seems relieved, like a nervous interviewee who's got to the end of a difficult pitch.

Mackie appears in the doorway. Kemp shoots him a hostile glance.

'My colleague, DC Mackie,' Boden says.

'You got some lovely horses here,' says Mackie.

Kemp nods. He's still tense, but not as jittery as Brandon, who shifts from foot to foot.

Boden stands up and goes over to him. 'Were you badly injured, Brandon?'

Brandon takes an involuntary step backwards. He doesn't look more than twenty; ginger hair, the skin on his face red and blotchy from acne.

He reddens even more with the scrutiny. 'Well, y'know, yeah, it hurt I suppose. But I'm all right now.'

Boden can't make out any visible bruising, but it's hard to tell because of the acne.

'Good,' she says. She turns to Mackie. 'Scott, we're looking for a baseball bat. Also, can you arrange for digital forensics to come down and collect footage from the CCTV system.' She swivels back to Kemp. 'If that's okay with you?'

His jaw is set, his foot tapping, but he nods. 'Of course.'

14

Back in the office, Sophie eats a late lunch of sushi at her desk. They're expanding their product range, and this is a recent addition. It comes in two sizes and is flavoursome and filling.

As she savours it, she considers the culinary wizardry of her business partner, Claire. In many ways, Ollie is a male version of Claire, not hugely confident or showy, but determined. Claire has always surprised her, coming up with unexpected solutions to problems. Hidden depths. That's what her mother says about Claire. It's a pity she can't see that in Ollie.

Her three phone calls to Deirdre have gone straight to voicemail. She's also tried a text. But she knows her mother; Deirdre regards it as bad manners to always be checking your phone. So chances are she's already blabbed to other seminar attendees over coffee or lunch. Sophie can imagine it; Deirdre's a born snob and loves to boast about her connections. *My daughter just had dinner with her new brother-in-law, Sir Gerald.*

Sophie has a mountain of things to do, emails to send,

calls to make, but the question of Ged Sullivan keeps niggling at her. What's going on? What's he done to upset Kristin?

As she eats, she types his name into the search bar on her laptop and trawls.

The jet-setting billionaire, the grammar school boy made good, Sophie can see how his lifestyle and wheeler-dealing has made him a pin-up boy for conservatives of her parents' generation. He looks young for his age, collects beautiful wives and racehorses; and is often pictured rubbing shoulders with royalty at various race meetings.

But Sophie doesn't dig far before a trending news item pops up. An incident took place at his estate near Newmarket last night.

The facts are in dispute; it depends which serpentine thread you follow. But some time after she and Ollie left for their helicopter ride back to London, there was a break in at the Sullivans.

Climate activists, or a gang of climate extremists, depending on who you read, have targeted him because of the continual toxic waste dumping carried out by the company of which he's CEO. This is just the tip of the current iceberg. Ged has his fans, galvanised by a slick PR campaign, and his detractors. He's a fossil fuel guzzling monster and climate denier, or an enlightened technocrat with a plan for the future, depending on whose version you favour.

Sophie opts for a mainstream news outlet for a summary of the supposed facts. Climate protestors broke in, they clashed with security personnel, a young female protester was badly injured. Sir Gerald, was not at home at the time.

He's lying!

He's made a public statement, expressing his concern for the protester, who is in hospital in a critical condition.

Now it makes sense. She and Ollie are being asked to

assist in some kind of cover-up. Unless Ged left the estate immediately after them, he was at home. They'd just had dinner together. Why doesn't he want to admit he was there?

She phones Ollie. He doesn't pick up. He must be with a client.

She feels both irritated and intrigued. If she had a number for Kristin, she'd call and ask what the hell's going on.

In the absence of that, she's frustrated. She returns to her trawling; a video pops up. It's dark and grainy, some kind of body cam attached to the chest? The person wearing it is running. Clumsily. Desperately. The soundtrack is poor. Muffled shouts. The person pitches forward. Now they're on the ground. A confusing melee of limbs. A long narrow object swings towards the camera. Impact seems inevitable. But the frame freezes. A small caption appears underneath: *Sir Gerald Sullivan attacks Cary Rutherford, 18-year-old student and climate change activist, with a baseball bat.*

Sophie stares at the screen. She's filled with horror. Could this be true? Or is it just some manufactured propaganda to discredit Ged? It's impossible to tell anyone's identity from the video. She doesn't like him. He's pompous and egotistical. But she ate dinner at his house. Could he have gone out less than an hour later and done something like this? She has an eerie feeling he could.

15

DS Boden gazes out of the window, as they drive north from Newmarket through the flat Fen country towards Ely. She finds this landscape curious; level and desolate like an open prairie, but also rich farmland. It feels as if these things should be at odds. The horizon stretches away; the sky is vast and banked with grey clouds.

She thinks about Raoul Kemp and his nervousness. People often appear apprehensive when dealing with the police, but that doesn't make them liars. Yet her gut is telling her that Kemp is a man on the edge. Is he clinging on to his job? Does his employer blame him for what occurred? Kobe Jackson, who they're en route to question, is the culprit. But is Kemp being held responsible by Ged Sullivan?

Or could the real story be more complicated?

She turns her head to address Chakravorty in the back seat.

'What do you make of it, Prish?'

The DC is watching and re-watching a video on her iPad. It's being shared all over social media.

'I've told the analysts to take a look,' says Chakravorty.

'They can enhance it. But basically there's no evidence from this that the body cam is on our protester. Could be anyone. Anywhere. Also, you can't assume that this is an attack. You don't see the moment of impact.'

Mackie is at the wheel. 'I think if this mob had some concrete evidence that it was Ged Sullivan who whacked the protester, then they'd be showing it.'

Boden sighs. 'Maybe they are trying to smear him. It's an obvious thing for them to do. But then you have to factor in his wife.'

'She is so hot,' says Mackie.

'You are so lame,' says Prisha.

'What? Now it's sexist to appreciate a beautiful woman?'

'Okay,' says Boden. 'But what do we get from her manner and attitude?'

'Upset about the protester, so he hadn't told her,' says Prisha.

'Also,' says Boden, 'upset about the break-in. And in a way that suggests she was there in the house when it happened.'

'She was there, he wasn't,' says Mackie.

'That's not what he told us,' says Boden. 'He said they were in London.'

They wind their way through the narrow lanes of Ely, overshadowed by the magnificent cathedral.

'Ship of the Fens, that's what they call it,' says Mackie, peering up at it.

'You took the tour, then?' says Prisha.

'I'm not a total moron,' says Mackie. 'I took my nan round. Medieval Gothic, although it was originally

Romanesque, and the first church on the site was Anglo-Saxon.'

Prisha raises her eyebrows. 'Next you'll be reading Beowulf.'

'Who?'

Boden smiles. Their banter has become the backdrop to her working life. It's clear to her they fancy each other, but neither wants to be first to admit it. She doesn't have any friends in Cambridge; she hasn't been there long enough. And she still misses London. But these are her workmates. The three of them rub along, and that's good enough for now.

The address that Kemp gave them leads to a tiny Victorian terraced house in a back street. The road is choked with parked cars, but Mackie finds a slot and they get out.

A young woman opens the door. She's in her middle twenties, with large dark eyes, hair neatly braided. A small girl, about four years old, peers out at the police from behind her.

Boden shows her warrant card and says 'Is Kobe at home?'

The woman seems unsurprised. She nods and the three officers follow her inside. The front door opens into the sitting room.

Kobe Jackson sits on the sofa cradling a baby. It's only a few months old. He looks up, giving Boden a blank look.

'I'm DS Boden. We're here because of an incident that took place last night at Sir Gerald Sullivan's estate. I understand you work there?' she says.

He nods. Mixed race, in his middle twenties too, large, six four or five, and well-built. He looks like a typical bouncer.

But he doesn't feel dangerous; just a father cuddling his baby. Still, she has Mackie and Chakravorty behind her to back her up.

She takes the section 8 PACE from her bag and holds it up. 'This is a warrant to search these premises, which we're going to do now. Okay?'

He sighs. 'Yeah, do what you gotta do.'

Boden nods to the DCs. They fan out. There was no sign of the baseball bat at the stables. If they find it here, and it's got the protestor's blood or DNA on it, that's game over for Kobe.

But why would a man his size hit a girl with a bat? He wouldn't need a bat. He could've easily immobilised her. Did he lose his temper?

Boden looks around. The place is small and compact; one main room downstairs with a kitchen area at the back. Neat and clean, just a few toys on the floor. Photos and knick-knacks dotted about. A cosy family home.

'Been here long?' she says.

'Two months,' he says. 'Just after this little one came, and I got the security job.'

'You came here because you got a job with Sir Gerald Sullivan?'

'Yeah, we wanted to get out of London.' He glances at the little girl, who is being given a drink of orange juice by her mother. 'We thought, get in the country, get some cleaner air, to help Jasmine with her asthma.'

Boden glances at the child and her mother. The four of them seem the perfect family group.

'You worked in security before?' she says.

'Yeah, in London. Done all sorts. Club doors. Pubs. Shopping malls. Personal protection. You name it.'

'You must be used to dealing with difficult people then?'

He gives her a vague smile. 'Yeah.' The baby sucks his little finger.

Boden can hear Mackie and Chakravorty moving around upstairs.

She watches the Jacksons. The wife remains in the kitchen with the little girl. He's on the sofa with the baby. They're both sad and resigned. Boden knows she should just arrest him, caution him and take him in. But she's hesitating. Why?

He seems to read her mind. 'You taking me in then?'

'Yes.'

He stands up and hands the baby to his wife. On his feet, he is huge. Did he really just lose it? It feels unlikely to Boden.

'But first I'm going to caution you,' she says. 'You do not have to say anything but it may harm your defence if you do not mention when questioned something which you later rely on in court. Anything you do say may be given in evidence. Okay? You'll have a chance to speak to a solicitor before we question you.'

He shrugs and his gaze slips away over Boden's shoulder. 'No need for that,' he says. 'I admit it.'

'You admit what, Kobe?'

'Things got heavy. I hit her.'

'Why?'

Again he shrugs. 'I dunno. Sometimes stuff happens.'

He glances at his wife. She looks back at him. But there's no recrimination.

Boden scans them; he's admitting it but not explaining it.

She feels her phone vibrate in her pocket. She takes it out. The DCI.

'Excuse me,' she says. 'I need to take this.'

Mackie comes down the stairs shaking his head.

She moves past him, and steps out of the front door into the street. It's lined with wheelie bins.

She answers her phone. 'Yes, boss.'

'Where are you?' says Hepburn.

'In Ely. Questioning the possible prime suspect. He's admitted it.'

'Right. Well, you should know that the protester, her name's Cary Rutherford, just died on the operating table. We'll need the results of the post mortem. But the word from the hospital is that she had skull fractures in several places, suggesting she was hit more than once.'

Boden sighs. 'Okay, boss, thanks. We'll bring him in.'

16

It's after six, when Sophie Latham finally escapes from the office. She's spent half the afternoon in a spin. There was a technical meltdown at the coffee roastery. By the time she found out, their Shoreditch branch was running out of coffee. She screamed at a few people, made a slew of frantic calls and in the end sourced an alternative supply.

She walks home through Spitalfields and through the backstreets of Whitechapel down to Wapping. It takes half an hour and helps her come down from the adrenaline high. Her father once told her she was addicted to crises. She denied it of course, but in her heart she knows he's right. She loves that pressure, the edgy sense of risk, then the buzz when disaster is averted.

The flat they're renting is in a splendid warehouse conversion overlooking the River Thames. Bare brick and long chunky beams right across the ceiling. She knows she'll miss it when they move to the new house. But it only has one bedroom; great for her when she was single. Now they need more space and a garden; a place that'll be a home for years to come. A family home.

As she lets herself in, the aroma of cooking assails her. Something hot and spicy. She feels a rush of love. She's coming home to her husband, and he's cooking for her. Did she ever think she'd say that? Four months ago, turning the key in that lock evoked a very different set of feelings. This man has transformed her life, this lovely man. How did she ever get this lucky?

She walks into the large open plan sitting room. In the early evening darkness, lights are glinting on the river. At high tide, this dark artery flows by only meters below their balcony. The sharp smell of it, the chill from the water rising up. It always reminds her what a great city London is. She'll miss this view.

Ollie is in the kitchen area, his back to her, as he stirs something on the hob.

'Hey,' she says. 'Smells delicious.'

He turns and beams at her. Shorts, a vest that reveals his amazing torso, and an apron. She still gets butterflies when she looks at him.

'I was wondering where you'd got to,' he says. He has that dreamy look in his eyes; she's noticed it before. He's far away, in a world of his own. She wishes she could go inside his head. See the world as he sees it.

She laughs. 'Ol, if you ever checked your phone, you'd know.'

He's such a space cadet.

He shrugs. 'Sorry. The gym was mad this afternoon. Then I was in a hurry to get to Waitrose.'

'So you haven't looked on the net?'

'No.' He opens the fridge. 'Is white okay?'

She goes over to him, flings her arms round his broad back. 'You are hopeless,' she says. 'I sent you four texts with links to all this stuff about Ged.'

'Ged?' He gives her a blank look.

'Your brother-in-law? Who doesn't want us to tell anyone we went to dinner there last night?'

'Oh yeah. I hope you're hungry. I'm doing a prawn linguine.'

She shakes her head and kisses him.

'Want me to make a salad?'

'No need,' he says. 'I'm on it.' He's pouring her a glass of wine. 'So tell me, what's this stuff about Ged?'

He really doesn't know?

She accepts the wine and perches on a bar stool at the kitchen counter.

'Okay, well it seems soon after we left their place last night, a bunch of climate protestors broke into the estate.' She frowns. 'You sure Kristin didn't say anything about this?'

'It was a quick call. She was upset. Just said please don't tell anyone you were here.'

Sophie sips her wine. 'Anyway, there was some kind of fight. One protester, a girl, was badly hurt. And there's a video on the net which claims to show Ged attacking her.'

'No kidding? Shit!'

'He's saying he wasn't even there.'

'Does this video look like him?'

'You can't tell.'

'But it could be?'

Sophie shrugs. 'It explains why Kristin's asking us to keep quiet.'

'You think he did this?'

Sophie sighs. 'I don't know. Why's he saying he wasn't there? Could just be he wants to avoid hassle with the police?'

Ollie frowns. He's very still. He picks up a spatula and

stirs the linguine. But she can sense the tension in him, the rising anger.

He turns back towards her; his face is tight, his jaw clenched. There's a tremor in his voice. 'I can believe he did it. He's a thug. Gets her pregnant when he knows the risk to her. Now this. How did she end up married to this scumbag?'

Sophie has a short fuse herself. But this escalation from composure to fury is rapid. Nought to sixty in the blink of an eye. It's the first time she's seen him get mad like this. She's taken aback.

'It's terrible, I agree,' she says. 'If he did it.'

She looks at him. Tears well in his eyes. 'I don't know what to do, Soph. What can I do? I just want to rip him limb from limb. Is that bad? Ever since she was little, I've tried to protect her. And I've failed. I've completely failed. It's my fault.'

Sophie senses something is surfacing; the tip of an iceberg. But she always suspected her new husband came with some emotional baggage.

She gets off the stool and walks round the kitchen island to him.

'Oh Ollie, sweetheart! Come here.'

As she loops her arms around him, he leans down towards her, lays his forehead on her shoulder and cries.

She strokes his hair. 'Hey, it's okay. It's natural to want to protect your sister. But it's not your fault.'

17

Deirdre Latham wipes her hands on a tea towel. The dishwasher is loaded. She turns it on. Her trip to London means that dinner was late for them. But she's still on a high from her day.

Roger appears in the kitchen doorway. 'Want to see a bit of news?' he says. 'I recorded it so you wouldn't miss it.'

'Why not?' she says.

The Six O'Clock News from the BBC is part of their daily ritual. It's accompanied by a glass of wine or a G and T. They eat dinner afterwards and chat over the events of the day. Rituals keep a marriage afloat; she read that years ago in Cosmopolitan, back when she had time for women's magazines. Now she's always got council papers to read. Being a local councillor may only be politics on a small stage, but she takes her responsibilities seriously.

She hates always being online, getting news alerts on your phone, being bombarded with information you neither want nor need. A phone is a phone; texts are useful. But other than that, an update on the news once a day is quite enough for anyone's stress levels.

She follows her husband into the sitting room. He's already settled in his armchair recliner; it's good for his back. Since retiring, he's developed quite a paunch. The doctor has prescribed him statins and told him to lose weight. But he does like his food. He plays a lot of golf, but she suspects they spend as much time in the bar as on the fairway.

He smiles at her, points the handset at the TV and clicks.

She sits on the sofa. It's Parker Knoll, traditional, which suits the room, and it wasn't cheap. She glances around; the cleaner came in this morning while she was in London. They use an agency and they're good, but it's as well to keep an eye on things. And Deirdre prides herself on having a sharp eye.

Fiona Bruce pops up on the screen. She likes Fiona. Fiona has such class. Proof that a woman can be hugely successful, but still charming and feminine. She's never less than impeccably groomed. Sophie could take a leaf out of Fiona's book.

As Fiona runs through the headlines, the usual mix of atrocities in places no one's heard of; too many refugees trying to cross the Channel in inflatable dinghies; Deirdre feels sorry for them, particularly the children. But really, someone needs to tell them not to come. The UK is a small island. She and Sophie have argued about this endlessly. We're the fifth largest economy in the world. That's always her daughter's line, but it doesn't make the place any bigger.

Roger seems to read her mind. 'How was your meeting with Sophie?' he says.

'Fine,' says Deirdre. 'We had breakfast at a nice place near King's Cross.'

'Excellent,' he says. He's waiting for her to say more.

She sighs and adds, 'She apologised.'

'I thought she would.'

'Only because you told her to.'

He chuckles. 'You two,' he says. 'If you knew how alike you are. It's why you argue.'

'Don't say that, Roger. You have indulged that girl her whole life. Treated her like some kind of princess—'

'She is a princess. And you're my Queen.'

She can't help smiling. 'Oh, you are soft!'

She's about to reach over and pat his hand when her attention is caught by the image on the screen. Fiona has disappeared to be replaced by Ged Sullivan.

'My goodness, we were just talking about him,' she says. 'Turn it up. Apparently, Sophie and Ollie had dinner with them last night.'

'In London?' says Roger.

'No, they went to his place in Newmarket. In a helicopter.'

On screen, a montage of images of Ged and his wife — this must be Kristin, Ollie's sister, and she is beautiful — is accompanied by the reporter's voice-over.

Climate change protesters broke into the estate near Newmarket last night, when Sir Gerald and Lady Sullivan were not at home. In the ensuing confrontation with security personnel, Cary Rutherford, an eighteen-year-old protester, was seriously injured and subsequently died in hospital. Police have arrested a twenty-five-year-old man.

Ged Sullivan appears in front of a forest of microphones. He shakes his head and says, 'Obviously, the death of a young woman in these circumstances overshadows everything else. It's terrible. My wife and I want to extend our sincere condolences to her family. I was in London when this tragedy occurred. But my staff and I have been offering the police our full co-operation. However, I do think that the group to which she belonged must take some responsibility for what happened. Violent protests and illegal actions can soon get out of hand and lead to tragic consequences. Thank you.'

As he turns away, a cacophony of questions follows. The reporter faces the camera, microphone in hand. 'Police have yet to confirm that the man arrested is a security guard employed by Sir Gerald.'

Deirdre turns to her husband. 'My goodness. What a terrible thing to happen.'

'It certainly is,' says Roger.

She frowns. 'But it doesn't make sense. Sophie said they had dinner there last night. How could they have done that if the Sullivans were in London?'

'Perhaps you misunderstood her, and she said it was the day before yesterday?'

'Roger, I did not misunderstand her. It was last night. That's what she said. Why would she tell me that if it wasn't true?'

Her husband rubs his chin. 'Maybe it is true.'

'Where's my phone?' Deirdre gets up. 'I'm going to look a complete fool. I was telling people over lunch Sophie went to dinner with the Sullivans last night. And they sent a helicopter to collect her.'

'And Ollie,' says Roger, drily.

'Yes. Him too. I explained that Kristin Kelly is Sophie's new sister-in-law. Have you seen my phone?'

Roger laces his fingers across his belly. 'Darling, you may want to hang fire and think about this, before you go ranting to our daughter on the phone.'

'I'm not going to rant. I'm just going to ask her why she lied about it.'

'That's my point. What if Sophie is not the one who's lying?'

'That doesn't make sense. You just heard what they said

on the news. The Sullivans weren't at home. They were in London.'

'It's very convenient, isn't it? A girl is killed, but they weren't there.'

Deirdre frowns. 'You think they're saying that because they're worried about bad publicity?'

'I don't know what I'm saying. But something's amiss.'

18

DS Jo Boden sits at her desk, arms folded, staring at her computer screen. It's been a long day, she'll have racked up the overtime, but she isn't thinking about that. She's watching Kobe Jackson.

On her screen she can see him. He's in the interview room; he also has his arms folded, but he's staring into space.

When he heard that Cary Rutherford was dead and he was looking at a murder charge, a strange inertia came over him. Boden read it as resignation. This could be because he was facing the terrible consequences of his angry outburst, a momentary loss of control in which he battered his victim round the head a number of times. Or is it something else?

Boden is uneasy. She has too many questions she can't answer.

Kobe's confession was short and lacking in detail. He admits he used a bat, but can't say where it came from. It was just *around*. He can't explain why the situation got out of hand, or what the protestors were doing. He thought they were trying to daub slogans on the buildings. But no paint materials or spray cans have been recovered by the police. And no sign of the bat.

Chakravorty puts her phone down, gets up from her desk and walks over towards Boden. She has a wad of paper in her hand.

'What have you got, Prish?' says Boden.

Chakravorty puts the documents in front of Boden. 'Printouts of his bank statements and credit card bills. The cards are maxed out; he's drowning in debt.'

'Okay.'

'I've been through all his outgoings and, apart from rent, there's one big item that stands out. Five grand a month to a private company that runs care homes. I followed it up. Just talked to one of their places in Essex. It's a specialist centre in dementia care, and Kobe's mother is a resident. She's in her sixties and has early onset dementia.'

Boden absorbs this. 'He's got a new baby, a small child with asthma and a wife, plus a mother in private residential care. No wonder he's in debt.'

Prisha points across the room at Mackie. 'Scott's still on the phone to his previous employers. But he's talked to three already, and they're saying more or less the same thing. Kobe's reliable, experienced, cool-headed. Good at diffusing tricky situations.'

'Okay,' says Boden, standing up. 'I'm taking this to the boss.'

Chakravorty smiles. 'You'll be popular.'

'Tell me about it.'

Boden makes her way down the corridor to DCI Hepburn's office. He looks up and beams at her. 'All squared away, Jo? Good day's work.'

'I'm worried, boss.'

'About what?'

'The confession is thin. The CCTV that should've been available to show what happened is not. This is supposedly because of some computer glitch.'

'Which happens.'

'True. But Kobe Jackson is all wrong for this. He could've almost picked Cary Rutherford up with one hand. And there's no sign of this bat. We've done a thorough search.'

The DCI leans back in his chair. 'I hope you're not being influenced by propaganda material circulating on the net. If Cary Rutherford's mates have got any evidence about what happened, then why have none of them come forward to speak to us?'

'They were breaking the law. And they don't trust us.'

'They ran away and left her.' Hepburn's tone is irate. 'Now they're using her death to score political points.'

'I know. But Jackson acted out of character, plus he has serious financial problems.'

'And you reckon he's being paid to take the rap? That's a life sentence he's facing, Jo. Okay, to start with, when it was just GBH, I could buy that. But now the girl's dead, don't you think he might reconsider?'

'That's possible. But I just want to dot the Is and cross the Ts.'

'Meaning what?'

'I want to talk to Sir Gerald Sullivan again. And his wife. I think, with a little pressure, she might open up.'

The DCI sighs. 'And where's that going to get us? No. The CPS are satisfied. It's a solid case.'

Boden knows that's always top of his list. What does the Crown Prosecution Service think?

'Yeah, but that's because he'll plead guilty. And in mitigation, he'll say it was a moment of madness and he was really stressed.'

'And that could be true. Hasn't he got a new baby and a young child?'

'Yeah.'

'Well, I can tell you, from personal experience, that means no sleep. You're looking for a reason he lost his rag. Trust me, that'll do it.'

Boden sighs. 'I know the media are all over this because—'

Hepburn raises his palm. 'Jo, let me stop you right there. If I thought for one moment that Ged Sullivan had paid off his security guard to cover his or someone else's crime, then I wouldn't hesitate. I don't care how much bloody money he's got. But he wasn't even there.' He wags his finger at her. 'Don't go looking for something that isn't there because of some fake news on the net.'

He staring right at her. She can feel the power of that flinty, unremitting gaze.

'Are we on the same page with this?' he says.

She inhales and nods. 'Yes, sir.'

19

Kristin sits at the table and fiddles with the napkin; it's folded in the shape of a fan. The restaurant is high end but old-fashioned, with white tablecloths and snobby waiters; not the kind of place she likes. She's surprised that Sophie has chosen it, and she's annoyed that her new sister-in-law is late.

She hates having to sit alone at a table, people staring at her. Even now, after all these years, it feels as if they're questioning her right to be there. She attracts curious glances wherever she goes, the price of being tall and black and striking. She sees their eyes scanning her, creeping over her body and judging her. It gives her goosebumps.

On set, it's different. It's all totally professional. She's a cog in the wheel. Everyone's just doing their job. They paint her face, dress her, but it's all about creating an image. It's not personal. She never feels exposed, unlike in real life.

As she flicks back her hair, she gives the maitre d' a hostile glare. What's he got to be so snooty about? Her husband could buy him and this whole stupid place; it would be small change to him.

She sighs. Checks the time on her phone.

It's been an absolute shitshow. The break-in, followed by the police. She feels like a criminal and she's done nothing. The last thing she wants or needs right now is to have lunch and be nice to this stupid woman. But Ged was insistent. It's necessary.

He's been in a foul mood, and on the phone continually. To his lawyers and the PR people. He shouted at them. But he's changed his tone towards her.

Needs her onside. And he knows it.

She did what he asked and called her brother. But Ged decided it wasn't enough.

'Darling,' he said. 'You can do this. It's a lunch. We just need to keep your brother and his new wife onside. We can't have them blabbing to the media, can we?'

He was right of course. She has no choice.

Why the hell does Sophie want to have lunch with her, anyway? Does she think they're about to become friends?

She sees Sophie hustling towards her across the restaurant; breathless, flushed, wreathed in smiles. She's by-passed the maitre d' and he swoops to intercept her.

He's such a horrible little toad.

But Kristin smiles to herself. That'll teach her.

After some conversation and explanation, he escorts Sophie to the table.

'I am so sorry!' she exclaims. 'It's been ridiculous this morning. Took me ages to get a cab; traffic was crazy.'

She leans over. She smells of Jo Malone and sweat, mostly sweat. Her cheek is damp; it brushes Kristin's ear as she goes for an air kiss.

Kristin smiles. 'It's fine,' she says. 'I've been entertaining myself watching the wildlife.'

Sophie is sitting down on the chair held out for her by the slimy little maitre d'.

'Oh,' she says. 'I thought you'd like it here. Because it's posh. And Ollie says when you go to ordinary places, you get hassled a lot, and targeted by the paps.'

'He's no idea what he's talking about.'

'We can always bail, if you'd prefer?'

Sophie's trying to be nice and understanding, which is even more annoying. And she doesn't seem phased by any of this. The maitre d' is judging her, but she doesn't seem to either notice or care.

How does she do it?

'We're here now,' Kristin replies, with what she hopes is a chilly smile.

A waiter appears and hands them menus. He then spends an age reciting the specials.

Kristin hands the menu straight back. 'Grilled sea bass, green salad. No dressing.'

Sophie shrugs. 'Yeah, sea bass sounds good. I'll have that too.'

The waiter dips his head. 'Can I send the sommelier over?'

Sophie gives her a quizzical look.

Kristin shakes her head. 'Not for me.'

'Of course, I'm sorry,' says Sophie. 'The baby.'

Yeah, the bloody baby.

The waiter retreats. The two women are left facing one another. Kristin picks up the stupid napkin and unfurls it. Sophie is watching her. It's so awkward.

Sophie's phone chirrups. 'Sorry,' she says. 'I should've switched this off.'

'Answer it.'

'No, it's not important.' Sophie takes a deep breath. 'I'm so glad we could do this.'

'Why?'

The directness of the question seems to flummox her, which is good. Attack is the best form of defence, that's what Ged says. And Kristin tries to follow his advice when she can. As a result, she's gained a reputation, especially with the media, for being a bitch. Better that than a pushover.

But Sophie tilts her head to one side and smiles. What the hell has she got to smile about? With that pointy, boney nose? Ged's right about one thing, a drunken Saturday night shag.

'You must've been a bit surprised when Ollie announced he was getting married,' says Sophie.

If only she knew.

Kristin shrugs.

'My family certainly were,' says Sophie. 'But when you know you've found the right person, you know. And I'm thirty-nine. The old biological clock is ticking. I want kids. And if they end up looking more like Ollie than me, well, that's got to be a bonus, hasn't it?' She has a jaunty, lopsided grin, which is weird.

'I hate being pregnant,' says Kristin.

'Yeah,' says Sophie, with a chuckle, 'I'm not looking forward to that bit. And not labour and popping the little bugger out. But the end product has got to be worth it, hasn't it?' She hesitates then adds, 'Ollie says you've had a few problems before.'

Ollie says! The question hangs in the air. Nosey bitch.

Kristin decides to ignore it.

'So how did you two meet?' she says.

'He was my personal trainer.'

'My personal trainer's a muscle-bound dyke with a face like the back of a bus.'

Sophie laughs. 'I expect Ged's glad about that.'

They lapse into silence. A waiter comes and fills their glasses with mineral water.

Sophie picks hers up and takes a sip.

'Listen, Kristin,' she says. 'This is awkward. You don't know me. I'm just some random stranger your brother's hooked up with. I expect you've met plenty of people in your life, who've tried to use you. It can't be easy, being a super-model, a famous face that everyone recognises. You've always got to be on your guard. I get that.'

Does she? Kristin doubts it.

Sophie goes on. 'My agenda's simple. I love your brother. That brings me into your life. And I'm thinking, okay, we may or may not have things in common. But it's worth exploring the possibility that we could become friends. I'm sure you've got loads of friends already. But if you've got room for one more, we might have a laugh together. And finally, I should say, this restaurant was a terrible choice. The maitre d's got a bug up his arse, and I can tell you, before we even get it, that the food will be crap.'

The last part makes Kristin smile.

'You're really gobby, aren't you?' she says.

Sophie raises her glass. 'Yep. Not known for my subtlety either.'

'Since I got famous, I don't have many girlfriends. Girls I knew before are all jealous bitches. Think it should've been them, not me.'

Sophie smiles; she smiles a lot. 'Yeah, well, I've got no illusions. No one's ever going to put me on the front cover of Vogue, are they? And that's fine.'

Kristin meets her gaze. She has a very open way of looking at you. It's probably a con. But then, what's in this for her? Ged looked her up, says she has a very successful business. So it's not the money.

It's just strange, her being married to him. It makes no sense. Or perhaps it does. Kristin can't be sure.

She sighs. 'Y'know, it's complicated, me and my brother. Family stuff.'

'Tell me about it,' says Sophie. 'I've got a brother called Nick. We've been fighting like cat and dog since we were little kids. He is such a pain. He just doesn't get me at all. Never has. But I say, let's keep the men out of this.'

Kristin nods in agreement. There is something about Sophie, hard to say what. She's easy to be with. She wonders if they could become friends. After all, isn't this what Ged told her to do?

Their meal arrives. Two waiters set the plates down in front of them, removing domed covers with a flourish.

Sophie stares at her plate and frowns. Then she raises her index finger imperiously.

Just like Ged.

The waiter bends forward towards her. 'Is there a problem, madam?'

'Yes,' says Sophie loudly. 'There is.' Other diners are looking round at her. 'I thought I ordered sea bass.'

'Yes,' whispers the waiter. The maitre d' is heading their way with an anxious expression.

'Well,' says Sophie. 'This looks to me more like a shrivelled up kipper.' She prods it with a knife. 'I mean, look at it. Like an old bit of shoe leather.'

Kristin grins. *This is unexpected.*

Sophie soon has the executive chef out of the kitchen, a bevy of waiters and the maitre d', all dancing round her and listening to her complaints. She baits the chef, asking him where he trained. Wondering why they only have one Michelin star.

It's the most fun Kristin's had in ages. Sophie has such cheeky confidence. Everyone in the restaurant is staring at them. Some are amused, some aren't. But Sophie doesn't care. She's enjoying herself. Kristin would love to learn that trick. To never care what people think.

Could Sophie teach her?

If they became friends, it looks like it could be a laugh. The only women Kristin spends time with are other models who are so competitive, or people that work for them. Staff. It would be good to have a mate, if Ged didn't mind. And this was his idea.

20

Sophie Latham escorts Kristin into the Shoreditch branch of *Sophie and Claire's Place.* Heads turn. It's amazing to watch the effect she has. But then she is over six feet tall, strikingly beautiful, and recognisable from enormous billboards and posters on the tube; her face is all over London, and not just her face.

Spending only a short amount of time with Kristin Kelly, it's easy for Sophie to understand why she has such a spiky carapace. Her gift is also her curse. The Uber driver who ferried them here from Fitzrovia asked for an autograph; for his girlfriend, he said. And although Kristin looked daggers at him, she did it, scrawling a large K on the back of a petrol receipt. Sophie felt defensive on her behalf.

Why do people think that if they recognise you, they know you? That they can make demands. You wouldn't accost a random stranger and ask if you can take a selfie with them. Yet this happens to Kristin all the time. This explains why she prefers to travel by helicopter.

Sophie was surprised that when she offered to show

Kristin where she worked, Kristin agreed. It suggested the plan was working.

She's doing this for Ollie. She has to find a way of making friends with her sister-in-law, and winning her trust. It didn't help that Ollie pointed her in the wrong direction in terms of restaurant choice. He doesn't know his sister as well as he thinks.

Fortunately, Sophie turned that to her advantage. She made Kristin laugh with her performance, ripping the piss out of the stuffy maitre d' and the unfortunate chef. They left the restaurant giggling like a couple of teenagers, and a bond was forged.

Sophie gets the impression that under Kristin's haughty exterior, there's a scared little girl. She pulses with anxiety. Often her hands are clasped, fingers interlaced; or she twists her many rings. She's a jangling bag of nerves. Sophie wants to reach out and reassure her. But she knows she must be careful, so as not to frighten her off.

In Shoreditch, Sophie is on home turf. They sweep through the coffee shop. It's busy. A slew of regulars, tapping away on their laptops; for many, this is their office, their study area, the place they hang out with mates.

As they sail past the counter, the manager stares at them and does a double-take.

Sophie smiles at him. 'Cal, could you bring a couple of espressos up to the office?'

'Of... course,' he stutters.

In her peripheral vision, Sophie counts at least three people videoing them on their phones.

Kristin has her chin tilted upwards; she's focusing on the rear wall of the shop. It's the cool catwalk stare, as if she's telling herself that she needs to stroll from A to B, pivot, and stroll back. She seems oblivious to the fact that half the people in the shop are watching her.

The upstairs office is an open plan space. Its best feature is the enormous windows overlooking the street. They were constructed to bring light into the Victorian workroom, where a dozen girls used to sit at their benches sewing.

Now there are three long tables and an area at the far end with sofas. This is divided off by shelving and an array of plants.

Sophie employs four office staff to handle admin and marketing. She also has a couple of buyers to source ingredients, but they're out on the road. It's a tight operation.

Her assistant, Leanne, jumps up, iPad in hand, then freezes when she sees Kristin following Sophie into the room.

'Hey, Leanne,' says Sophie, 'Cal's making us a couple of espressos. Can you go down and check on them?'

'Sure.'

Leanne is a smart kid, only eighteen, but Sophie promoted her from the shop. Leanne is adept at reading Sophie's mind and anticipating her needs. The three other employees are craning round in their seats and gawping. But within moments, Leanne hustles them out of the room.

Kristin wanders across to the windows.

'This is cool,' she says. 'Such lovely big windows.'

'It's because it used to be a sweatshop,' says Sophie. 'The girls needed light to sew and the boss didn't want to spend money on more candles than he had to.'

Kristin gives her a wistful smile. 'You know a lot of stuff.'

Sophie shrugs. 'Too much education.'

'I wish I'd had more.' She seems so melancholy. Maybe it's the eyes. They carry such a look of tragedy.

That bastard she's married to has a lot to answer for.

'I'm looking for bigger premises,' says Sophie, keeping it light. 'We're expanding and I need to hire more bodies.'

'Ged says you've done well. He checked your company out. He's impressed.'

'That's a compliment I'll take.'

Sophie waits. Kristin is about to say more, but hesitates.

Finally, she says, 'I wanted to say thank you. Y'know, for this thing the other night. Thanks for not saying anything.'

'It's okay.'

Kristin frowns. 'It's not. I hate lies. I always have.'

She's avoiding Sophie's eye and stroking the leaves of a large rubber plant that stands in the corner near the window. Her long fingers, with their elaborately painted nails, tremble.

She must be embarrassed because her husband has made her lie for him. Ged Sullivan is a piece of work! No doubt about that. But Sophie doesn't want to upset her.

'Well,' she says. 'Sometimes stuff can get complicated. Happens to all of us.'

Kristin has turned away. Her shoulders are hunched, head tipped forward, as if she wants to make herself smaller.

She sighs. 'It's just that Ged has all these stupid people attacking him all the time. They blame him for things that aren't his fault. He's just a businessman.'

'People think they can say all sorts on the net that they wouldn't dare say to your face.'

Kristin turns towards her. Tears brim in her eyes.

'He's not a bad man,' she says. 'He takes care of me.'

That's the biggest lie of all.

He's got her pregnant at risk to her health, even her life. His vast fortune creates a shield, giving her some measure of privacy. But it comes at a price. And Ollie's right. Kristin could earn enough to create her own safe bubble.

'And you want to protect him too, I get that,' says Sophie. 'He's your husband.'

Kristin is scanning her. She's looking for something, but what?

'Do you think that's wrong?' she says.

'Not necessarily.'

'But it could be, couldn't it?'

Sophie knows it's a risk. But those amber eyes are staring straight at her, pleading with her.

Ask the question.

'Kristin,' she says. 'Did he attack this girl?'

Her head dips right down. She turns away. Sophie thinks she's blown it.

Then Kristin whispers, 'I don't know.'

'Have you asked him?'

'No. I can't. I don't want to upset him.'

Course she doesn't. She's petrified of him. That's clear. And it makes Sophie's blood boil.

21

'I think she's scared of him,' Sophie says. She's in the bathroom, cleaning her teeth.

Ollie steps out of the shower and grabs a towel. She can see him over her shoulder in the mirror. She takes full advantage of that.

He rubs his hair dry. Then she sees the scowl on his face.

'Now do you believe me?' he says. 'I already told you that.'

'Of course I believe you.'

He glares at her. 'It's easy for you. She's not your sister.'

'Oh, that's a low blow,' says Sophie. 'Particularly when I've spent half my day on Project Kristin.'

He huffs. Fastens the towel round his waist. He has the look of a sullen boy, which makes her smile.

He fidgets with the towel. A small puddle has formed round his bare feet. His toes are long and perfect. It's easy to see the physical similarities between him and Kristin, even though they're half-siblings.

After a moment, he sighs and says, 'Yeah, okay, you're right. I'm being a dick. I'm sorry.'

She laughs and tugs at the towel. 'You will be.'

He smiles but retreats. He's still wound up.

Sophie follows him into the bedroom. He dumps the towel and gets into bed. He picks up his headphones.

The strange process of living with someone and getting to know their habits fascinates her. Ollie likes to listen to music in bed. But it's not proper music; it's slow and eerie, some kind of therapy music. He says listening to binaural beats calms him and helps him sleep. She also knows that it's a signal. When the headphones go on, he withdraws into himself. He shuts her out. And no sex.

She perches on the edge of the bed. 'What if I told you I've got a plan?' she says.

He's fiddling with the jack plug on the headphones, inserting it in his phone. 'What plan?'

'It's what we talked about before. I have to find a way to take Kristin to see my gynaecologist.'

Ollie frowns. 'Ged would never allow it.'

'Why does he have to know?'

'You don't get it. He watches her like a hawk. I bet he's got a spy app on her phone.'

Sophie scans him. 'Has she told you that, or are you guessing?'

He doesn't answer. When he's upset, he becomes sulky. Ollie, the tough big brother, has lost his role as his sister's protector to her rich, older husband? Is this what it's all about? Male pride? Does Ollie feel diminished? Rejected? Is that why he hates Ged so much?

Ged's arrogant and obnoxious. He's also lying in order to distance himself from a serious crime. But it's an assumption that Kristin wants to escape from him and can't. She's not a prisoner. She came to lunch. They spent the afternoon together; she didn't call Ged or say she needed to get home. She travels alone and works.

Sophie knows she has to tread carefully. She's still learning her new husband's moods, and dismissing his fears could stoke his resentment. The last thing she wants is for him to do something rash. She senses he's capable of it.

'Listen,' she says. 'I need to go for a check up.' She grins. 'After all, I'm hoping to get pregnant soon myself. So I'll ask Kristin to go with me. My gynaecologist is great; she's expensive enough. I guarantee Kristin will like her.'

'And how long's all that going to take?' says Ollie. 'She needs an abortion now.'

There's a harsh petulance in his tone.

'Well, maybe, or maybe not,' she says.

'I've told you. Having a kid is too big a risk for her.'

'And if that's true, having a second opinion from a top consultant is something Ged will have to listen to. Isn't it?'

She takes his hand, traces a heart on his palm. His face softens.

'I know you're only trying to help,' he says. 'I expect you think it's odd that I'm so upset about this. But, y'know, stuff has happened to Kristin…'

His chin trembles. She waits. Will he open up and say more? His gaze veers off to the window. He's retreated inside his own head.

So she says, 'Ollie, I get it. You don't have to justify your feelings to me. You just want to rescue her. But let's not do anything stupid, eh? You can't go round there and thump him. However much you want to.'

He gives her a ghostly smile. 'I'm not an idiot, Soph. I know how powerful he is. Men like him get to hurt women, and they get away with it. But someone like me, I'm just a personal trainer. A nobody. If I so much as threaten him, I'll be nicked by the police and thrown in jail. You think I don't realise how impotent I am?'

Tears well in his eyes. He's in pain. And she can't stand that.

She kisses his hand. 'Which is why we have to be smart. Okay? I'm with you on this. If Kristin needs rescuing, then we'll do it together.'

He draws her into his arms. 'I'm so lucky I've found you.'

'And you're not a nobody. You're amazing.'

He kisses her and rolls her over onto the bed next to him. She can feel his desire. He tugs at her bra. Soon they're making love. Her heart sings. And in that moment, nothing else matters. Just being with Ollie.

22

DS Jo Boden has the morning off; so she's driving up to Ely on her own time. It's better that she's doing this alone. She doesn't want to get either of the DCs into trouble. The boss only told her not to go back and question Sir Gerald and Lady Sullivan, so she's not disobeying him. She arrested Kobe. It's a follow up. But he'll be hacked off, no question.

Wives can be pivotal in a case; they're the keepers of secrets. If they can be persuaded to open up, it can change everything. Teresa Jackson and Kristin, Lady Sullivan, may have nothing in common. But to Boden they're both wives who seem uncomfortable with the probable lies they're being asked to tell. Ideally, she wants to question them both. But if she can't get to one, it's worth trying the other.

Boden finds a parking slot round the corner from the Jacksons' small terraced house. It's still early. A bin lorry is making slow progress down the street and blocking it. Children are heading for school.

It seems unlikely that Kobe Jackson will get bail; the case is too high profile. And when Teresa opens her front door, it's just her and the children. The look of panic on her face tells Boden what she needs to know.

'DS Boden, remember me,' she holds up her warrant card. 'Can we have a word?'

'I need to take Jasmine to nursery. And we're late already.' The tone is desperate.

Boden smiles. 'This won't take long.'

Teresa is at a loss; she doesn't know how to refuse. She dips her head to conceal her frustration and holds the door open for Boden to enter.

Jasmine is still in her pyjamas and playing on the floor with some toys. No nursery for her today. Teresa gives Boden a guilty look, but the cop says nothing.

'You want a coffee or something?'

Boden scans her: a decent young woman with an impossible dilemma. She decides to accept the hospitality being offered and slow things down. The longer she's there, the more Teresa will feel the pressure.

'Thank you,' she says. 'Just black, no sugar.'

The baby is in its basket and burbling. Boden is clueless when it comes to tiny infants. Is it a boy or girl? She can't tell.

Teresa puts the kettle on. 'Is instant okay?' she says.

'Fine,' says Boden. 'So what's your baby's name?'

'LeBron.'

'After the basketball player?' She dredges that from somewhere in the recesses of her brain. Famous sportsman? LeBron James?

Teresa nods and smiles. 'Kobe's a big basketball fan. He used to play loads when we lived in London.'

'He's tall enough. What part of London?'

'Lewisham. But we were on the South Circular. And the traffic pollution was terrible. And Jassy got asthma.'

'It is bad for kids. I used to work in London. My mum lives in Greenwich.'

Teresa nods. She spoons granules into a mug.

Boden watches her. 'You like it here?'

'It's okay. Bit different. But Jassy's doing much better. Hasn't had an attack since we got here.'

Boden thinks of the wind that blows across the flat Fenlands. That's going to clear the toxic crap away if anything will.

'That's good,' she says. 'But new places can be hard.'

'I've met a few other mums with kids at the school. They're friendly enough. Jassy's had some playdates.'

Boden nods.

They're both staring at the kettle, waiting for the water to boil.

'I have to ask you this Teresa, has Kobe ever been violent towards you? You or the children?'

Teresa huffs, gives a vehement shake of the head. 'He may be big. And he looks tough. But he wouldn't swat a fly. That's why he's so good at security.'

Boden smiles. 'Yeah. That's what I'm thinking. So what's going on here, Teresa?'

The kettle clicks off; Teresa busies herself pouring boiling water on the coffee. She knows she's said too much. Keeping her back to Boden, she's trying to reset.

'I don't know,' she says. 'I guess he lost his temper.' Her tone has changed. Guarded. Fake. She's not a good liar. She gives the coffee a vigorous stir.

Boden accepts the mug.

'You believe that?'

'It's what he says. That's why he's confessed.' Teresa's facing her now, and she has a mulish expression. She's hoping to front this out.

Boden sips her coffee. 'Well,' she says. 'Cary Rutherford, that's the girl he killed, she had multiple skull fractures consistent with a pretty savage attack with something like a baseball bat.'

Teresa swallows hard.

After Kobe's arrest a forensic team went through the entire house and found nothing.

'Does Kobe like baseball too?' says Boden. 'Or cricket?'

Teresa shakes her head. She's trying not to cry. She strides across the room, picks up her baby son and cuddles him.

'C'mon, Teresa,' says Boden. 'We've been through all your finances. We've seen how much debt you're in. We know about Kobe's mother.'

Teresa clutches the baby. He cries. She's crying too. 'What the hell d'you want me to say?'

'Just the truth. Where was he the night before last?'

'At work.'

'You sure?'

'Yes!'

'How old's Jasmine?'

'Four.'

'If Kobe's convicted of murder, he'll get a life sentence. It was a brutal killing, so he could serve fifteen or sixteen years. Jasmine will be twenty before he gets out. LeBron'll be a teenager. Don't you think they need their father?'

Teresa wipes away tears and snot with the back of her hand.

'What do you expect me to do?' she shouts.

'I can't put words in your mouth,' says Boden. 'That would be wrong. But here's what I think, and I'm only guessing because we've got no evidence. Kobe is trying to protect his family — you, the children, his mum. But maybe you need to protect him. You need to talk to him. Get him to consider what he's doing. You're the only person he'll listen to.'

23

Sophie takes a cab to Hackney. She's in the back seat, checking emails, when her phone buzzes. An incoming call from her mother. She sighs. Deirdre Latham has left her four messages; and she can guess what it's about.

She glances out of the window. The cab is crawling in sluggish traffic along the Mile End Road. It's raining, a thin drizzle, but enough to make everyone fractious.

Sophie takes a deep breath and accepts the call. She can't avoid it any longer. She may as well get it over with.

'Hey, Mum.'

'Didn't you get my messages?'

'Yeah, sorry. Things have been manic. I've had a few problems to sort out.'

'Well,' says Deirdre, 'I just wanted to clarify something. You told me you and Ollie went to dinner at the Sullivans on Tuesday, didn't you? Your father thinks I might've got it wrong.'

'No, you haven't.'

'So, it was definitely Tuesday? A week ago?'

Sophie sighs; she doesn't see why she should lie to her

own mother at Ged Sullivan's behest. 'Yes, it was. And I know what you're going to say next, because I'm assuming you've seen the news. Ged is saying he was in London that evening.'

'Why would he do that if it's not true?'

'I've no idea.'

'Well, don't you think it's rather odd? Is he so busy that he mixes up what he did when? That happens to me sometimes if I'm stressed. And we're a similar age.'

'I doubt it's that.'

She knows she has to bite the bullet and do this.

Another deep breath.

'Listen, Mum, he's got a lot of PR people advising him, and, I don't know, maybe they reckon, with this poor girl getting killed, it's best to keep a low profile and say he wasn't around. What happened was between his security people and these climate protestors.'

Why is she making excuses for him? She knows the answer. There's no point in telling her mother he's a scumbag. Deirdre wouldn't believe her. She'd say, don't be ridiculous, the Queen has knighted him, so that makes him beyond reproach.

'I feel sorry for the girl and her poor family,' says Deirdre. 'But these people go too far with their protests.'

Climate emergency. More extreme weather. The arguments flit through Sophie's brain. But she bats them away. The last thing she wants on this grey morning, sitting in a traffic jam, is a row with her mother.

'That's probably Ged's view,' she says drily.

'Have you spoken to him?'

'No, Ollie's talked to Kristin. And if you could not mention to anyone that we were there, I know both Ged and Kristin would be really grateful.'

She's spoken the magic words.

'Of course,' says Deirdre. 'I've been in politics long enough. I understand the need for discretion in certain circumstances. Reassure them that they can rely on us. I only mentioned it to a couple of my fellow councillors over lunch. But they're so doddery, they won't remember what day I said. And, anyway—'

'Thanks, Mum. I knew you'd understand. Got to go. I've got a meeting.'

'Okay, darling,' says Deirdre breezily. 'Love you!'

'You too,' says Sophie, and hangs up. She has a hollow feeling in the pit of her stomach. None of this feels right. Lies and more lies. But her priority has to be keeping Kristin onside in order to protect Ollie.

He was quiet this morning. Said little over breakfast. Brooding, she suspects. He had an early client at the gym. He must be busy, because he hasn't called, although she's sent him a couple of texts.

What she told her mother is true. She has got a packed schedule, but she's decided to fit in a visit to the house. If she sorts out this nonsense with the builders over the RSJ's that will take some pressure off him.

The cab turns into what will soon be their new street. The bones of these old Victorian properties remain elegant. Many have already been turned back from multiple occupancy into lovely homes. They pass several skips, evidence of the changes going on. The shabbiness, the rubbish, and the rows of bins are disappearing to be replaced by BMWs and four-by-fours.

As they pull up kerbside, Sophie gazes up at the huge London plane tree that's right outside their house. Its leaves are turning to russet and gold. This magnificent tree is one of the things that sold her on the place. It could be a hundred and fifty years old; a symbol of solidity and certainty, of endurance in a changing world.

Living in a street like this, walking her kids to school, having barbecues and playdates in a sizeable back garden, has been her secret dream for years. And now the pieces of the jigsaw are slotting into place.

Perfect.

She walks up the front path. A flat bed truck is parked in the rough driveway that runs down the side of the house. From the pile of scaffolding poles on the back, she concludes it belongs to the scaffolding firm that the builders are employing. But why are they here? You don't take down the scaffolding in the middle of an extensive refurbishment. Yet that appears to be what they're doing. Two blokes are balancing on boards, high up the side of the house, and dismantling the structure.

'Excuse me!' Sophie calls. 'What are you doing?'

'Speak to the gaffer, love,' one of them replies. 'He's inside.'

Sophie runs up the steps to the front door, which stands ajar. Inside, she can hear voices. She follows the sound down the cavernous hallway to the back of the house.

Standing with his back to her, she recognises Craig, the builder. He's chortling at something the other bloke has just said.

'Morning,' she says.

Craig spins round to face her.

'What's going on?' she adds. 'The scaffolding appears to be coming down. Why?'

'Because we're off the job,' says Craig. 'I thought your husband would've told you.'

'He told me you were waiting for the RSJs. So he's called a temporary halt until they arrive.'

Craig is glaring at her; he's not happy. He shakes his head and puts his hands on his hips. 'The RSJs are in my yard. We've been sacked.'

Sophie frowns. 'There must be some misunderstanding.'

'No. Your old man was pretty blunt. I'm just here to pick up our tools and materials.'

Sophie stares at him in disbelief.

'I'm sorry, Craig. Someone's got their wires crossed here. Ollie hasn't sacked you.'

The builder folds his arms and sighs. He's large, a shaved head and the physique of a body builder. 'Look, Sophie. I've worked for you before. Have I ever tried to rip you off?'

Craig's firm had the contract to refurbish two of the coffee shops.

'No,' she says. 'You did a great job.'

'Came in on time, on budget?'

'Yes,' she replies.

'You need to tell that to your old man. And, out of respect to you, and the fact we've always had a good relationship, I'm not going to say any more. Although I am going to speak to my lawyer about what we're owed on the contract. And you'll be hearing from him.'

Sophie is reeling. What the hell has happened here?

'Craig, I'm sorry. You're going to have to say more. Because none of this makes any sense to me. When did this happen?'

He sighs, glances at his companion. 'Wednesday morning. He was here when we arrived. Accused us of all sorts. Called me a cowboy. Added a few expletives. Said he wanted us off the site immediately. So we left.'

It was the morning she came round; after she'd had brunch with her mother. This is nonsense. It doesn't tally at all with Ollie's account.

'He was just upset about the RSJs.'

'He didn't give a monkey's about the RSJ's. I had them in the back of my truck. We were about to unload them. He told me to take them away. And that he wouldn't be paying for them.'

'I need to talk to him about this.'

'Yeah, you should.'

She takes out her phone, clicks on Ollie's number. It goes straight to voicemail.

'He's busy. He must be with a client.'

The two men exchange knowing looks. Stupid woman is what they're thinking. It riles Sophie, but she bites her tongue. Ollie will have had his reasons, even if he didn't explain them to her.

'Okay,' she says, 'I'm going to sort this out.'

Craig nods. His jaw is set, and he has a bullish expression on his face.

'I wish you'd just come clean with me,' he says.

'I don't know what you mean.'

'If you've changed your minds, and this place is not for you, and you want to sell it on, and make yourselves a tidy profit, you could've said so, instead of accusing me of being a thief and worse.'

'Hang on, we have no intention of selling it on. It's only half finished. We want to live here.'

'I'm not daft, Sophie. I've worked as a builder round here my whole life. I know all the estate agents.'

'What do you mean?'

'Your old man had one of them come in to value this house last week, as it stands now. The agent's a mate of mine. He told me. The market's gone up. Even as a half done shell, with planning permission, you'll make a mint. My mate has got a list of clients who'll take it on at the drop of a hat. And pay top whack.'

Sophie can't believe what she's hearing. Why would Ollie do such a thing? How can any of this be true? It makes no sense.

24

DS Boden gets to the office mid-morning. She wanders in. It remains to be seen if her visit to Teresa Jackson will have any impact. Maybe she's got it all wrong and Kobe did lose it. That's the version Hepburn's going with. As far as he's concerned, it's done and dusted.

Prisha greets her. 'Thought you were off this morning.'

'Yeah, supposed to be.'

'You look miserable. What's up?'

Boden doesn't know how to explain her restlessness and irritation to the young DC. So she shrugs.

At times the system depresses her; following procedures and protocols, the way it all has to be done. She understands the reasons. But then there's instinct. And that niggling feeling that won't leave you alone. Hepburn would say following a hunch and not the evidence leads to bad decisions. Personal biases come into play.

Does she suspect Ged Sullivan because he's rich and over-entitled? Is that her bias? How would he persuade a man like Kobe Jackson to go to prison for his crime? What sort of pay-off would be enough? A serious criminal involved in organised crime might do such a thing. But Sullivan's a wealthy businessman. Is it reasonable to suspect him?

She's pondering this when Mackie breezes in. He's carrying a coffee and a half-eaten ham baguette.

'Morning, Jo,' he says, plonking down at his desk.

She gives him a nod. Mackie seems to eat twice as much as anyone she knows. And he devours his food in gulps, like a hungry dog. It's disturbing to watch.

'Interesting thing,' he mumbles, mouth full of bread and ham. 'Just been talking to some guys—'

'Am I supposed to understand what you're saying?' says Boden.

He chomps and swallows. 'Sorry,' he says. 'My mum reckons I eat too fast.'

'She's got a point.'

Boden catches Prisha's eye and they exchange smiles.

He wipes his mouth with the back of his hand. 'I've been talking to these guys I know in uniform. They've been called out to the farm next to the Sullivan place a couple of times. Woman that lives there, she's a farmer, is pissed off about the helicopters.'

'The helicopters?' says Boden.

'Yeah, the Sullivans have got a helipad, or whatever it's called. It's on the edge of their property and these helicopters come and go at all hours, and they often hover over this farmhouse before they land. The farmer, she's so hacked off, she keeps a log of all the comings and goings and the times. She's complaining to the council, wants to take legal action.'

'A log,' says Boden, and her eyes light up. 'I think we should go and see this farmer.'

25

_____

Sophie is in a complete funk. Since going over to Hackney to the new house, her day has gone from bad to worse. In order to stop Craig, the builder, from taking the scaffolding down, she made an immediate transfer into his bank account to cover the cost of the scaffolding sub-contractors.

Ollie is not answering his phone.

Still not answering his phone!

Back in the office, she continues to fume. Leanne and the other office staff are cowering at their desks.

Be patient. He's with a client.

But Sophie isn't patient. She decides to go to the gym to see him.

If he's with a client, she'll wait. She has no intention of embarrassing him. But this is ridiculous. They have to talk. He has to explain himself.

The gym is a brisk, ten-minute walk away, in a narrow lane in the City, close to Moorgate tube. The location and the high membership fee mean most of the clientele work in financial services. City traders, insurance brokers, and a range of ages. The young and fit, hoping to stay that way, but also those with medical conditions and under doctors' orders to lose weight. Ollie specialises in helping such clients; it's how they met. She was trying to lose weight.

Sophie doesn't recognise the receptionist. Since the wedding she hasn't been there as often as she would've liked. Ollie suffered a good deal of friendly teasing from his colleagues when he married a client. They've never discussed it, but she senses he prefers her not to use the place. They still train here together on occasion, but it feels awkward.

She glances at the receptionist's name tag and smiles. 'Hey, Bonnie,' she says. 'I'm looking for Ollie. Is he with a client?'

The receptionist looks her up and down, forcing a smile. 'Are you wanting to book some training with him?'

'I'm his wife.'

'Oh,' says Bonnie, as if that's a dubious concept. 'I'll check his schedule.'

She clicks on her computer screen. 'He's on his lunch break. Next client at two.'

'Could you call him and get him to come down?' She knows that her tone is brusque.

'Can't you call him?' Bonnie's smile becomes wider and more fake.

Sophie sighs and shrugs. 'My battery's dead, that's why I thought I'd pop in.'

Bonnie wrinkles her stubby nose and picks up the phone on the desk.

Sophie would like to strangle her. Her vacuous smile, her mane of white blonde hair, her attitude. Sophie knows she must rein in her irritation. It takes the best part of five minutes for her husband to appear.

He gives her a sunny smile. 'I'm just having my lunch,' he says.

Sophie is aware of Bonnie's beady eyes watching them.

'Can we go for a walk?' she says.

He glances out of the electronic doors and grimaces. 'Looks quite grey and wet out there. Why don't you come up to the cafe?'

Sophie nods. She doesn't trust herself to speak.

She allows him to usher her through the security barrier and up a wide flight of stairs to the cafe.

It's sizeable, with floor to ceiling picture windows overlooking the pool. He guides them to a corner table and checks his watch.

'I've got about ten minutes,' he says. 'You look a bit upset.'

A bit upset!

'Why haven't you been answering your phone?' she says.

He sighs. 'I can't when I'm working. You know what Malcolm's like.' Malcolm is the manager and Ollie's boss. 'He has a fit if he sees any of the staff on their phones.'

'I went to the house this morning. And I bumped into Craig.'

Ollie raises his eyebrows and inhales. 'Oh, I see.'

'They're taking down the scaffolding. What the hell is going on?'

He rubs his chin. 'Yeah, I've been meaning to talk to you—'

'When?' She's trying to keep the annoyance out of her voice, but she can't. Are they about to have their first real row?

He looks at her and huffs. 'Well, I've been distracted. This stuff with Kristin. It's upsetting.'

He's not wheedling his way out of this.

'Is it true you've sacked the builders?' she says.

He's tutting.

The nerve!

'Sophie, don't go off on one.'

'Don't fucking patronise me, Ollie. When I came round the other day, you'd just done it, hadn't you? Why didn't you say something instead of feeding me a load of guff about RSJs?'

He puffs out his cheeks. 'Cause I knew you'd be like this. I needed us to be in the right situation for me to explain properly.'

And that wasn't?

She glances round the cafe. She notices a couple of the other trainers, two girls, sitting at a nearby table; they're watching them and whispering. This is why he brought her up here, to shut her down. She considers standing up and making a scene. It would serve him right.

Then she says in a quiet voice. 'Okay, I'm listening, I'm calm. Let's hear it.'

He sighs and folds his arms. 'I think you've got a very naïve view of Craig.'

'In what way?' She matches his tone of voice. She can be cool and offhand too.

'Well,' he says. 'I've worked on building sites. And I've had plenty of bosses like him.'

'You've never mentioned that before.'

'I did all sorts when I was young. Had to. I've told you that. Mostly I had labouring jobs. It's not exactly something I put on my CV. Craig's the kind of builder who's great with the clients. Particularly women. Big and butch, knows how to be reassuring. But I've spent time in the house, looked at the work they've done. They've been cutting corners all over. The electric cabling they've put in is cheap crap.'

'How do you know?'

'When I was a teenager, I started an electrical apprenticeship. Never finished it. But I learnt enough. My early twenties I worked on loads of sites. I was making a list of all the stuff they've done that's wrong. I was going to show it to you. But then Craig got wind, and we ended up having words.'

'He says you got an agent in last week to value the place.'

Last week!

Back then he was acting like a wimp, making out he needed her help to even make a decision.

'Yeah, I did,' he says. 'And I was going to tell you that, too. Soph, he's conning you. Trying to land us with a substandard house. We need to cut our losses and sell it on. We should be able to cover the cost of the contract and still come out ahead. I was just trying to be the kind of husband you wanted, and take care of things.'

Sophie realises she has tears running down her cheeks. 'I wanted that house. With the tree outside.'

He reaches out and grabs her hand. 'I know. But we'll find somewhere better. I'll project manage it myself. And what's wrong with the flat? You love living beside the river. We don't need to move right away.'

'What if we have a baby?'

'It'll be fine. How much space does a baby take up?'

'Why didn't you talk to me about this?'

He sighs. 'You're always busy. I was trying to take some of the burden. I know you earn all the money, and you paid for the house. But I'm not having some scabby builder rip us off.'

'You sure that's what he's doing?'

He bristles. 'You want to go round there after work? I'll go through my list and show you.' The tone is tetchy.

'Don't get upset, Ol. Please.'

'I'm not upset. Bottom line is, either you trust me, or you don't.'

What a stupid mess! Jumping to conclusions.

'Of course, I trust you,' she says.

He stands up, kisses the top of her head. 'Right,' he says. 'Now I've got to go and drag an obese commodities trader round the gym. He wants to lose twenty kilos by his son's bar mitzvah.'

She watches him walk away. There's a jauntiness to his step.

Her thoughts are in turmoil. Why has he never told her he's worked on building sites? Was he ashamed to tell her he was once a labourer? He left school at sixteen with no qualifications, and he's touchy about that.

Sophie made an offer on the place in Hackney soon after they got together. Okay, it was impulsive. But she was in love. She knew what she wanted and saw no reason to hang about. Then, when they got into the process of talking to the architect, hiring the builder, why did he never mention he'd worked in the building trade? He kept quiet and just agreed with everything she wanted. Why?

The money intimidated him?

This is all her fault.

But if he thought Craig was dodgy, why didn't he say? Is it really about the money? One minute he can't seem to make a decision on his own. Now it turns out he's gone behind her back.

It's miscommunication.

She feels foolish. The other two trainers are still glancing at her and giggling.

She gets up, raises her chin, and gives them a regal smile as she walks past them.

26

DS Boden knows she should get the nod from the DCI. But he was out of the office at a meeting. And, anyway, she's just tying up loose ends. This is what she tells herself. She doesn't need his permission for that.

Mackie drives. She prefers to drive herself, but he'd sit in the front seat and fidget. He's a ball of restless energy and his chunky limbs never seem to fit well into a small space. Still, she's become used to him. He's not the most imaginative detective, but sometimes he comes up with gems like this.

The farm is down a narrow, rutted track, which opens out into a concrete yard with a red, brick-built farmhouse and a range of outbuildings. It's a working farm; a jumble of rusting machinery in a patch of weeds, two brown hens scurrying and flapping out of the path of their car, and chained to a kennel, a Border Collie, which jumps up and barks.

Boden is struck by the contrast between this place and the Sullivan estate next door. Once farms like this would have dominated the area. It's rich arable land. But the money horse racing brings gazumps all that.

They park next to an old Land Rover and get out.

Mackie raps on the front door with his knuckles; there's no bell. A woman opens the door. She's in her fifties, grey hair pulled back in a bun, and a defensive frown on her face, as if she's expecting trouble.

They show their IDs.

No sooner are they across the threshold, the woman starts talking.

'I'm so pleased someone's finally taking this seriously,' she says. 'These damned helicopters come and go at all hours. They make a hell of a noise. And it's not as if they couldn't have put the landing place on the other side of their property away from us. I raised that with them. Got told that Sir Gerald doesn't want the helicopters landing too near the stables and spooking his horses. He doesn't care if our sleep is disturbed, if the noise makes our lives miserable. All he cares about are his bloody horses.'

She pauses for breath, pushes back a stray lock of hair. She looks worn and frazzled.

'I understand you're planning to take some legal action, Mrs Webber,' says Boden.

'Much good it'll do me. I've talked to my solicitor. But he doesn't hold out much hope.'

'But you've complained?'

'Oh, I've complained loads. Their response was, if we don't like it, Sullivan will buy us out. He'll just buy this whole farm, rather than shift where he lands his bloody helicopter.'

'You don't want to sell?' says Mackie.

'No, I don't,' says Mrs Webber. Her face reddens and she clenches her fist. 'I won't be driven from my home. We're not tenants. My family have owned this land, farmed this land since the end of the First World War. For over a hundred years, it's been handed down. My son is nineteen, he wants to take it over. Why should he be denied his birthright?' She's seething. The words tumble out. 'There're plenty of racing stables round here. I know a couple of trainers personally. They provide a lot of jobs, they're part of the rural community, we've always lived side by side. When the races are on, the toffs come, then they go away again. But then this bugger arrives next door! Behaves like a Lord. Builds that bloody monstrosity. Who knows how he ever got planning permission? Bought it, I guess. Well, he's not buying me.' She shakes her head angrily.

'Have you ever talked to him about any of this?' says Boden.

Mrs Webber gives a hollow laugh. 'You're joking! He won't talk to the likes of us. Sends his lawyer round. Or his head of security, a creepy bloke. A weasel. Although I did talk to the wife once.'

'Lady Sullivan?'

'Yeah, quite often she walks round the perimeter of their property, just wanders along on her own. She always looks sad to me. Sometimes, she sits under the trees and reads a book. I was out doing some hedging one time, and she came along on the other side of the fence. So I said hello. She seemed friendly enough. Very nervy. I gather she's some kind of model.'

'You know about the trouble the other night?' says Boden.

Mrs Webber nods. 'Oh yes. Last couple of days I've had press and telly and all sorts knocking on the door asking if they can set up their cameras on our land. I gave them short shrift.'

Boden can imagine that.

'I'll be honest with you, Mrs Webber,' she says. 'I don't think there's much chance we can help you. Nuisance is a civil matter. But we're hoping you can help us. One of the protestors that broke in, a girl, was killed. We're investigating that. And we understand you keep a detailed log of when the helicopters come and go.'

Mrs Webber's frown dissolves. 'I do,' she says. She tilts her chin upwards, and there's a triumphant glint in her eye. 'I saw Sullivan on the TV news, saying he was in London that night. Well, I can tell you for a fact he's lying.'

'How d'you know that?'

'I saw him. He was here. And they had some visitors. It's in the log.'

'How did you see them?' says Boden.

'There's a good view from our front bedroom window. You can see the path from their terrace down to the landing spot. They've planted a row of Leylandii, grow like weeds those bloody things, but they're still quite small. They had some people over that night, youngish couple, came in the helicopter. But he was on his terrace, seeing them off again at about half ten. Then a bit later, I heard shouting, some kind of commotion, so I looked out.'

'What time do you think that was?'

'After midnight. He came out onto the terrace again. Went down the steps and round the corner to the path that leads to the stables.'

'How did you know it was him?' says Boden. 'It was dark.'

'They've got security lights around the house. Y'know, with motion sensors. Anything moves and that place lights up like a football stadium. You can see everything from upstairs. Come and look.'

Boden smiles. 'Thank you, Mrs Webber. We will.'

27

Sophie has spent a sleepless night wondering what the hell is going on.

When she got home from work, Ollie greeted her with another home cooked meal. It was simple enough, a small, juicy fillet steak and a side-salad.

She half expected him to come out with the revelation he once worked as a chef. But he chatted about his client, the obese commodities trader, and followed this with an anecdote about an encounter in the lift with one of their neighbours and her yappy dog.

His mood seemed buoyant. He was attentive, making sure her wine glass was filled. As a result, she drank more than she intended. He didn't mention the house, or the sacking of the builders. She began to realise that, from his point of view, the matter had been dealt with. They'd discussed it. It was over.

But nothing was resolved. She'd paid Craig a shedload of money to keep the scaffolding up. They needed to get the architect back in to give her opinion. Then, okay, they could hire another builder. It was absurd to sell it. She wants that house. Normally, she'd just go ahead and do these things. But then he'd feel undermined. She needed to be patient and give him space to change his mind. And Sophie is not a patient woman.

She went to bed desolate. Unusual for her. He stayed up playing a game on his PlayStation, told her he had too much energy to sleep yet. When he came to bed, she pretended to be asleep. He stroked her naked back.

No way she was having sex!

She was still wound up. If he couldn't see how upset she was about the house, then she was damned if she was going to pretend that everything was back to normal. He soon fell asleep.

When she woke up in the morning, it was later than usual. She discovered he'd gone to work, leaving a note in the kitchen.

Thought I'd leave you snoring, sleepyhead. Have a great day Xxx

She took two paracetamol and headed for the office. Leanne brought her a large coffee and one of Claire's newest creations, a riff on the classic Danish pastry. Even that failed to cheer her up.

Her irritation continued to fester. All new marriages go through this process, she reasoned. Their first major disagreement. It's what's meant by: the honeymoon is over. But she never dreamt this would happen to them. And so soon.

What an idiot.

How can she adore this man and be so pissed with him at the same time? She tried calling Claire. The line was busy. She even thought about calling her mother, but stopped herself in time.

Why was Ollie so blind to her unhappiness? He wasn't

some emotionally illiterate bloke who dealt with conflict by pretending it didn't exist. Or was he?

Don't be silly. This is Ollie.

In the end, the only way she could silence the nagging doubts was to work. And she had more than enough to do.

It's late morning, and she's finishing an email to the recruitment agency about new staff. Getting good people has become a major problem. Her phone buzzes. She's hoping it's Ollie wanting to apologise. She's surprised to see the call is from Kristin.

'Hey,' says her new sister-in-law, 'Wondered if you fancy going shopping with me?'

This is unexpected.

'Shopping, yeah,' says Sophie. 'Great.'

'Ged says I need to get some maternity stuff. I have this personal stylist. But she's such a moron. Insists I look great in everything. I'd value an honest opinion.'

'Yeah, okay,' says Sophie. What do you say to a woman who does look great in everything? 'I can do that. When were you thinking?'

'Now.'

'Now?'

'Yeah, I'm in Bond Street. Maybe we could get coffee or lunch? But you're probably too busy.'

She is busy trying to solve the recruitment nightmare. But she doesn't want to say no. She suspects that an overture like this from Kristin won't come again if she does.

'No, it's fine,' says Sophie. 'I'd love to. There are some advantages to being your own boss, y'know. If I want to go shopping, I can go shopping.'

'Great!' says Kristin. She sounds excited.

Sophie is calculating. How quickly can she get to Bond Street? A cab will be ridiculous; she'll have to take the tube. A brisk walk to Liverpool Street, then she can get on the Central Line.

'Okay, let's do it! I'll text you as soon as I get to Bond Street, and you can tell me where you are. I reckon I'll be about half an hour.'

'Cool,' says Kristin. 'You sure this is okay? I don't want to put you out.' Now she sounds timid, almost embarrassed to be asking. Is she this isolated and friendless? Is this what marriage to Ged has done to her?

'It'll be fun,' says Sophie.

It'll be a nightmare.

She hangs up. Ollie had better be grateful. She's doing this for him.

The tube is rammed; when she reaches Bond Street, it's raining and she forgot to bring a brolly. She's teed off, and her headache has got worse.

She finds Kristin tucked away in the back of a Starbucks just off St Christopher's Place. Given the number of upmarket alternatives in the vicinity, this seems an odd choice.

Kristin is wearing a headscarf and Jackie O sunglasses. Sophie does a double take. Sunglasses inside on a rainy day? Her comic disguise is far more likely to draw attention to her. Perhaps she's being ironic?

Perhaps not.

As Sophie approaches the table, Kristin stands up to greet her, knocks the table and spills her drink. She seems ridiculously nervous.

They hug awkwardly.

Sophie looks at the drink. A Caramel Brownie Cream Frappuccino, if she's not mistaken. She knows the menus of all her rivals.

Kristin giggles. She's dressed like a middle-aged diva, but she seems more like a teen. 'I know,' she says. 'It's disgusting. And this is my second. I feel guilty. But I figure if I'm turning into a beached whale, I may as well pig out.'

'Foolish not to,' says Sophie. She's read somewhere that loads of models have eating disorders, and this may be true of Kristin.

The more time Sophie spends with her sister-in-law, the harder it's becoming to read her. Is she as naïve as she appears? Sophie gets the impression there's much more to her. She's pretty smart, but keeps it under wraps. Why?

So as not to upset her controlling husband?

Sophie gets herself a fruit tea and persuades a reluctant counter assistant to come and wipe up the spilled frappuccino on their table.

Once they're settled with their drinks, there's an uncomfortable silence. Sophie decides not to break it. What does this woman want from her? To shop for maternity outfits? She doubts it. That's an excuse. She waits.

They exchange smiles.

'I guess it's sort of confused me, meeting you,' says Kristin. 'You're not my brother's type.'

'Really? What have his other girlfriends been like?'

'I've never met any of them. But, don't be offended, you're obviously very clever. And Ged agrees.'

'You saying Ollie doesn't go for clever women?'

'I wouldn't have thought so.'

They lapse into silence again.

'We all change as we grow up,' says Sophie. 'My brother's wife wasn't what we expected; she's got a PhD and runs marathons. Nick used to whine every time we went out for a walk together. I can't imagine what she sees in him, but people change.'

Kristin nods. She takes off her sunglasses. Her eyes are dark and moist. She's trembling.

'I just never thought he'd get married,' she says. 'It's an odd thing for him to do.'

Why would she think that?

'Y'know, he cares about you a lot,' says Sophie. 'And he worries about you. Marrying me in no way detracts from that.'

Kristin shifts in her chair and her shoulders hunch even more. Her gaze darts off into the distance. 'He doesn't need to worry,' she says. 'Ged takes care of me.'

'I'm sure. His wealth can provide you with the privacy you need, away from being hassled by the paps.'

'Sometimes I feel like I'm in a bubble. But yes, you're right, Ged stops me from getting hassled. He protects me.'

'Are you happy?' says Sophie. She's careful not to say *with him.*

Kristin considers this. She takes a slug of her disgusting drink. 'I dunno. Happy? What does it even mean? You just have to get through, don't you?'

'Just getting through? Is that good enough for you?'

'Are you happy with my brother?'

Sophie wants to say: not at the moment, because he's being a complete knob. But they don't know each other well enough for those sorts of confidences. Not yet.

She says, 'Yeah, I am happy. Being married has its ups and downs, but I think I've picked a good one. How about you?'

Kristin's lips are pursed. She inhales. 'What about when you have sex? What if he wanted you to do weird stuff?'

The tension is zinging off Kristin. Her fingers are laced; she's gripping them so tightly that her knuckles are white.

Now they're getting to the crux of it; Ged has twisted sexual tastes. Is this surprising?

'You mean like S and M?' says Sophie.

'Yeah, sort of.'

'You're talking about playing games?'

Kristin nods.

'Is it just a game?' says Sophie. 'Or does he hurt you?'

Kristin's head is dipped. She twists and tugs at the rings on her fingers. Her voice drops to a whisper. 'He likes to hurt me. That's what turns him on. And he wears a mask, so he can pretend it's not him.'

She raises her head and stares right at Sophie. Her eyes are full of raw pain. 'Is it like that for you?' she says.

Sophie shakes her head.

Kristin frowns. 'You sure?' The tears brim over her dark lashes and roll down her cheeks.

Sophie leans forwards and squeezes her hand. 'Kristin, you don't have to do stuff you don't want to do. Your husband shouldn't hurt you. That's wrong.'

Kristin buries her face in her hands. Her body rocks. Sophie moves closer, puts an arm round her.

'Hey,' she says. 'It's okay. It needn't be like this. You don't have to let him hurt you. I promise you. You don't. And we're going to help you. Me and Ollie. I promise you that too.'

28

At the beginning of the morning shift, Boden reported Mrs Webber's accusations to the DCI. He was at his desk, with sleeves rolled up and a harassed air. As he listened, he sighed and folded his arms. Boden knew he wasn't happy, but he was calculating the odds. If he ignored this and did nothing, would it come back to bite him?

'How credible is this witness?' he said.

'She's got a grudge against Sullivan. Put her in the witness box under cross-examination and that will come out. So, yeah, it'll be easy for a smart brief to discredit her. Do I think she's lying? No. Although I can't rule it out. From the upstairs window of her house there is a clear line of sight to the terrace of the Sullivan house.'

DCI Hepburn stroked his chin. 'Even if he is lying about where he was that night, doesn't mean he did anything?'

'True. But then why lie about it? I just want to put the accusation to him. He's covering something up.'

Boden knew she was being bullish. But rich blokes like Sullivan get away with far too much. She wanted to rattle his cage. And she wanted to see the wife's reaction.

The DCI shook his head. 'We're jumping ahead of ourselves here. I'm sorry, Jo, but I want corroboration he was there. Proof he's lying. Then we'll ask him why he was lying.'

'How about we ask to see Sullivan's phone?'

Hepburn gives her a baleful look. 'This Mrs Webber says he had visitors that night. Find them.'

It was a predictable response from the boss. And he was right. Although tracking down his visitors would be a tedious task.

Staring at a computer screen all day and charming information out of people on the phone is Boden's least favourite job. But she has Mackie and Chakravorty plus some back office help.

Mrs Webber was happy to lend them her log. It's written in a neat, rounded hand in a spiral-bound notebook. There are pages of it. Boden has one of the analysts photograph them all and create an evidence file on the system.

Unfortunately, Mrs Webber's view is that a helicopter is a helicopter. She doesn't distinguish between those owned by Ged Sullivan's company, with the navy and gold livery, and others that may have been privately hired on a one-off basis.

The list of companies providing private hire is quite long. Eighteen in London, and there's no guarantee that's where the Sullivans' visitors came from.

Chakravorty is staring at the list on her screen. 'What if they came from Birmingham?' she says.

'What if they'd flown in from the States, landed at Schiphol, and hired a helicopter in Amsterdam?' says Mackie.

'Let's not overcomplicate this,' says Boden. 'Looking at

the time frame, these people most likely came to dinner. Scotty, you start with air traffic control. Clearances to fly into the Newmarket area. Not sure how their system works, but they'll explain it.'

He nods. 'Ever been up in a chopper?' he says. 'I had to escort a suspect in the air ambulance once. It's amazing.'

'Tell that to Mrs Webber,' says Chakravorty with a grin.

It takes them an hour to establish that four private helicopter charter companies had permission to enter the air space at the relevant time. They drilled this down to one company, operating from the Battersea Heliport. A phone call to their operations manager produced a reluctant admission that Kristin Kelly is an occasional client.

'So, can you tell me if she made a booking on Tuesday evening of last week, to transport two of her friends to Newmarket and back?' says Boden.

'I'm afraid that's confidential information,' says the Sloaney woman on the other end of the phone.

'You don't want to co-operate with us on this matter?' says Boden.

'I'd love to, officer. But my hands are tied. We have a number of clients, who are High Net Worth Individuals, and privacy is a big issue with them.'

Boden sighs. Charm only gets you so far.

'Well,' she says, 'my issue is that this is a murder investigation. I can get the necessary warrants to come to your offices, seize all your computers and other files. I don't want to do that. You certainly don't want the disruption and adverse publicity that will cause. So, you can decide to help us with our enquiries now and give me the information, and we'll avoid all that. And your High Net Worth Individuals need never know.'

There's silence on the other end of the line.

Then a surly, 'I need to speak to my boss.'

'Good idea,' says Boden, 'I'll hold.'

Chakravorty is chuckling. 'Have we got grounds for a warrant?' she says.

'I doubt it,' says Boden. 'But her attitude was annoying me.'

A few minutes later, the woman comes back on the line. 'Kristin made a booking for that evening.'

Kristin! She makes it sound like they're buddies.

'Have you got the names of the passengers?'

A moment of hesitation. A hand fumbles over the receiver. She's consulting again.

She comes back on the line. 'Ollie Harmon and his wife. Our premium car service collected them.'

'Have you got an address?'

She hesitates. 'I think so. Do you want that?'

'Yes,' says Boden. 'I do. And thank you for being so helpful.'

29

The shock of Kristin's admission has been reverberating through Sophie's head for most of the afternoon. On the one hand, the idea of a man like Sir Gerald Sullivan inflicting sadistic sexual practices on his wife is not that surprising. Such lurid stories crop up in the media; rich, controlling men using their power to indulge their sick proclivities.

What bothers Sophie is that this is a woman she knows. The torment in her sister-in-law's eyes is etched in her mind.

They sat in the back of Starbucks for ages and Kristin cried. Sophie tried to comfort her. But her soothing words and promises of help seemed to bounce off Kristin. She remained sealed in her own misery. And totally inaccessible.

Then, without warning, she stood up and said she had to go. She dried her eyes and thanked Sophie for coming. Her manner was distant and formal, as if this was the end of a business meeting or an interview.

Sophie watched her stride out of the coffee shop and disappear. She couldn't fathom what had happened. Kristin had confided in her, and she seemed to be asking for help.

But then what? She changed her mind? Was it panic? She lost her nerve?

Did revealing that her husband abused her to Sophie mean now she had to leave him and she couldn't cope with the idea of doing that? He abused her in the privacy of their own home, but he protected her from the world. Was that the contradiction keeping Kristin in her cage?

Sophie wondered if she'd pushed too hard, making promises of help to leave him. Faced with the reality of what that might mean, had Kristin taken fright? If she had, that was understandable.

On the way back to the office, Sophie texted: *hey Kristin, if I pushed too hard, I'm sorry. I can't imagine what it's like to be in your shoes. But we're here for you. Call me any time.*

She walked into the office to find mayhem. The espresso machine at their smallest branch in Liverpool Street Station had broken down. A nozzle had become blocked and the manager's attempts to clear it had created a bigger disaster. The machine was an Appia, a traditional espresso machine made in Italy. Leanne was on the phone, trying to find a technician to come in and fix it. She had the shop's manager on the other line, telling her they already had a queue of exasperated commuters.

Sophie phoned the main UK distributors for Nuova Simonelli and cajoled them into sending someone urgently. She went over to the shop herself and placated customers in the queue by giving out vouchers to come back the next day and get a free coffee.

Sophie puts the key into the front door of her flat with some relief. She sent Ollie a text earlier, explaining what was going on. He didn't reply, but she didn't read anything into that.

She's concluded that harassing him for his non-response to texts is pointless. In view of their recent disagreement over the house, she needs to build bridges. Hearing about the horrors of Kristin's marriage has made her appreciate the husband she's got.

She walks into the flat, pulling her jacket off as she goes. 'Bloody hell, Ol, you will not believe the day I've—'

Her complaint is left hanging and she freezes. Her husband is perched on the edge of one sofa. Two complete strangers are sitting on the other sofa.

All three stand up when they see her. Sophie knows at once who they are.

But the woman steps forward. 'Sorry to startle you, Mrs Harmon. I'm Detective Sergeant Boden and this is my colleague Detective Constable Mackie.'

'Actually, it's Ms Latham. Sophie Latham. We're married, but I've kept my name.'

The woman nods and smiles. 'Sorry. Ms Latham.'

Sophie can't help glancing at Ollie. He's nervous. Why does a visit from the damned police make people nervous? And they're cunning bastards; they know this and they play on it.

The woman, the sergeant, looks smug.

Sophie grasps the nettle. 'I'm the one who should apologise,' she says. 'Difficult day. I've got a busted espresso machine and I've had to wrangle a bunch of crotchety commuters denied their caffeine fix.'

'Sounds complicated,' says the sergeant with a relaxed smile.

'So how can I help you?' says Sophie.

The other officer, the DC, who's rather large and intimidating, places his phone on the coffee table. 'All right with you if we record this?' he says, as he clicks it on.

Not much choice.

Sophie nods. 'Yes, of course.'

The sergeant smiles again. 'An incident took place last week,' she says, 'on Tuesday evening, at the estate of Sir Gerald Sullivan outside Newmarket. You may have seen reference to it on the news or online.'

Sophie glances at Ollie again; she can't help herself, it's involuntary. What has he said? Has he denied they were there?

She frowns, as if trying to recall. 'Yes. Weren't some climate change protestors involved?'

'Sadly, one of them was killed.'

'Yeah,' says Sophie. 'I saw that. It's dreadful. I've been on a few marches myself, about the climate emergency. Nothing illegal though.'

The cop is watching her. She has a penetrating gaze. They probably go on a course to learn how to do this.

'And you were there earlier in the evening, I believe?'

'In Newmarket?' Her pulse is racing.

Like a rat in a trap.

'A few miles outside. At Sir Gerald's estate.'

Ollie jumps in. 'I've already told the officers that Kristin invited us to dinner. She wanted to meet you.'

Sophie beams. She feels a rush of relief. 'Yes, I'm sure Ollie's told you we recently got married. But his sister and brother-in-law didn't make it to the wedding. So I was eager to meet them.'

He's decided not to lie. And why should they? After what Kristin's just told her, there's no way she's covering for that bastard.

But Ollie is looking at her, trying to catch her eye.

'It's a pity Ged was called away at the last minute,' he says. 'Sophie was dying to meet him, too. But he had some important deal going through. Had to be in London. But Kristin didn't want to cancel. So we went anyway.'

What!

'You had dinner, just the three of you?' says the sergeant. And she's staring straight at Sophie.

Sophie takes a breath and nods. 'Yeah, the three of us.'

What the hell else can she say?

The cop nods. 'Okay,' she says. 'Thank you.'

Sophie watches the DC. He picks up his phone from the table and clicks it off. She's lied to the police, blatantly lied, and they've recorded it. A wave of guilt and shame is washing over her. She wonders if it shows.

She wants to scream, but forces herself to smile.

'I hope that's helpful,' she says.

30

Sophie escorts the police officers to the door. Have they bought Ollie's story? It's impossible to tell. The sergeant hands her a card with a phone number.

'This is where you can reach me,' she says. 'Any time.'

'Okay, thanks,' says Sophie. 'But we've told you everything we know.'

She's just compounded the lie. The knot in her stomach is tightening; she may well throw up. She has to get them out of the flat. But the cop seems inclined to linger.

'That's my mobile,' she says. 'But we're based in Cambridge.'

Sophie can feel the piercing gaze drilling into her. Are they like dogs? Can they smell fear?

The blood thumps in her ears. 'I love Cambridge,' she says. 'My brother went to uni there. Took us punting on the river, it was great.'

The cop nods and smiles. 'I've never been punting. Keep meaning to.'

Just go!

It's agonising, but finally Sophie shepherds them out and

closes the door behind them. She bolts for the bathroom and vomits down the toilet.

Hot. Shivery. Another wave of nausea sweeps over her, but this time she retches. There's a hand on her back; she feels Ollie stroking her hair.

'Babe, you all right?' he says. His voice is soothing.

She grabs a handful of toilet tissue and wipes her mouth.

'No, I'm not! What the fuck, Ollie?'

He nods. 'Sorry, I couldn't warn you. But I reckon they bought it, don't you?'

'No, I don't. You see her look when she handed me her bloody card? Like she was saying, this is for when you decide to tell us the truth.'

'You're reading too much into it. They always give out their cards.'

'How do you know? How many times have you been questioned by the police?'

He sighs. 'Listen, Kristin called me this afternoon. This is what she asked me to say.'

'How did she even know they were coming?'

'The helicopter people phoned her.'

Ollie puts his hands under her arms and lifts her to her feet.

She clutches his arm. 'Jesus wept, Ol. Why are we lying for this bastard?'

'Kristin asked me. I couldn't say no.'

'Yes, you could. Anyway, I saw her earlier today.'

He frowns. 'Oh. She never said.'

Sophie shakes her head. 'I need some water.'

Ollie follows her into the kitchen. He goes to the cupboard.

'I'll get it for you. Sit down.'

She slumps on a stool and, elbows on the counter, props her head in her hands. Bile stings her throat.

This is ridiculous. What happens when they're found out?

'She phoned me up out of the blue,' she says. 'Asked if I wanted to go shopping. But we didn't go shopping. We sat in a bloody cafe, and she gave me chapter and verse on how her husband likes a bit of S and M. He wears a mask so he can pretend it's not him. Then he proceeds to hurt her.'

Ollie freezes. He's holding the glass under the tap. The water spills over and splashes onto his hand. He turns off the tap, picks up the tea towel, and wipes up the spilled water. He puts the glass of water down in front of her. But his gaze is diamond hard.

That was a mistake. Blurting it out like that.

She watches him.

He takes a deep breath. She wants to reach out; apologise. She can see how shocked he is.

'She actually told you that?' he says. There's a chill in his voice.

Sophie sighs. 'Yes. Sorry. I didn't mean it to come out like that. But it's obvious the shopping thing was an excuse. She wanted to tell me. It wasn't a random conversation. She'd planned it.'

He clenches his fist. 'I'm going to kill that bastard.'

'No, Ollie, you're not. But we are going to help her escape him.'

He shakes his head. 'She's never going to be safe until he's dead.'

'Or in jail. Come on, use your brains. I know you're angry but—'

He's been standing stock still; now his fury explodes. 'You think we can rat him out to the cops and they'll nick him and he'll go to jail for this dead protester? What planet are you living on? He's already got one of his security blokes to confess. It's not like we saw him do it. We don't know what happened. All we know is, he was around.'

'Calm down, Ol. We can still—'

He turns and glares at her. His lips twist into a sneer. 'Don't tell me to calm down. Look at you; just an over-privileged fool. You got no idea how the world works. You tell one little lie to the police and it sends you into such a spin you puke your guts up. You're pathetic. How did I end up married to an idiot like you?'

He strides towards the door, snatches his leather jacket from the peg, and he's gone. The door slams behind him.

Sophie realises she's shaking. To steady herself, she reaches out and picks up the glass. She takes a sip of water. The tears come.

Such hatred in his eyes!

She can't believe he spoke to her like that.

31

Boden is sitting in the car outside a Chinese takeaway in Wapping. She's listening to the recording Mackie made on his phone.

The driver's door opens, and he gets in with a large carrier bag.

'That is one fancy takeaway,' he says. 'Hope you're hungry.'

Boden is about to reply when she sees Ollie Harmon come striding round the corner. He's walking fast, shoulders hunched, hands shoved deep in the pockets of his jacket. He has a thunderous look on his face.

'Well, well, look at this,' says Boden.

Harmon passes by on the other side of the road. He doesn't notice them.

Mackie unpacks his carrier and place cartons on the dashboard.

'He set up the lie. She's pissed. They had a row about it?' he says. 'Do you like sweet and sour pork?'

'I think's that's the size of it,' says Boden. 'But Hepburn's still going to want his corroboration. If their story is the sister was there, but Sullivan wasn't, then all we've got is Mrs Webber, who'd like to see Sullivan go down.'

'We could go back and harass Ms Latham?'

'I'm not sure that would get us very far right now,' says Boden. But seeing Harmon storming off clarifies one thing. Sophie Latham is worth tackling again, and on her own. She's confident and self-possessed, but she didn't like being forced to back up her husband's lie.

'What do you want to do then?' says Mackie.

'Eat our dinner. Cause it smells great. Then a change of tack. We're in London, we may as well make the most of it.'

Mackie grins. 'Aww, Sarge. You're taking me clubbing!'

'In your dreams, Mackie. No, I reckon we should check out Cary Rutherford's mates.'

'I thought some detectives from the Met interviewed them.'

'They did. And I've read the reports. All they say is we know nothing, we saw nothing, and we weren't even there. I don't buy that. Someone took Cary's body cam and put the footage up on the net.'

Mackie is cramming several dumplings into his mouth. 'Could just be fake? Not her at all.' he mumbles.

Boden watches juice run down his chin.

'You need a bib,' she says.

Her phone buzzes. It's Chakravorty.

'Hey, Prish. What's up?'

'The boss wanted you to know that Kobe Jackson has withdrawn his confession, and his wife has made a statement saying he was at home with her,' says Chakravorty.

'Okay,' says Boden. 'Has he explained why he made a false confession, if he wasn't even there?'

'Nope. He's being tight-lipped about that. And he's got lawyered up, so he may be worried about being accused of perverting the course of justice. But he's miraculously found his phone, which he was alleging he'd lost. His lawyer says it will prove he was home all evening.'

Boden doesn't know how pleased to be. It proves she was right all along; it's also likely to result in the DCI being seriously pissed off.

'How's Hepburn taking it?' she asks.

'He said to tell you he's hoping for a good result from your trip.'

'That's what he actually said?'

Chakravorty hesitates. 'Well, no. What he said was tell Boden to pull her bloody finger out.'

Boden smiles to herself. This is the closest she'll get to a vote of confidence from the boss.

32

It's dark outside. Sophie stands on the balcony, staring down at the river. Black and murky, it rushes by. There's a biting breeze. Lights wink at her from the far bank. Other lives running in parallel to hers. Other marriages. She wonders if her mother was right all along; she's acted like a lovesick fool.

Ollie is a complicated man, she knows that. He's seen tough times, and didn't grow up with loving parents. He's always been evasive about the details, but Sophie has read between the lines. His relationship with his sister, and the belief he must take care of her, seems to be the lifeline that's kept him afloat.

He's angry with Ged, not her. But she's the one who's there, so she gets it in the neck. Telling him like that was stupid. Too much of a shock. She was angry, so she blurted it out. Of course he reacted.

It's not his fault. Don't be aggrieved.

She's got a short fuse. That's always been her problem. She's like her mother; Deirdre flies off the handle, but her dad is so laid back. He calms everyone down.

She goes back inside, wondering if she should call him and apologise. The fact he's out there, wandering the streets, and hurting, upsets her. He was in a bind; Kristin asked him to lie. They had no chance to discuss it. What else was he going to do?

She picks up the glass of water from the counter and takes another sip. He's right; she is pathetic. So she lied to police? But for good reason. To protect Kristin. If Ged Sullivan is a violent man, their refusal to go along with this new story could have serious repercussions for her.

She hears the front door open, and her heart lifts. He's come back.

He walks into the kitchen, head dipped, and plonks two paper carrier bags on the counter.

'I got us an Indian,' he says. 'From that new place you said you wanted to try.'

She has a lump in her throat. 'Ollie,' she says. 'I—'

He raises his index finger. 'No, me first. Please. I can't believe I did that.' He shakes his head; he has tears in his eyes. 'I am a total shit. An absolute prick. I don't know what came over me. Just blind rage. But when you told me about Kristin…' The tears are rolling down his cheeks. He wipes them with the back of his hand.

'It's my fault,' she says. 'I should never have told you like that.'

'I lashed out. And that's unforgivable. What I said to you, is not even what I think. It's not true, any of it.'

'I know.'

'All you've tried to do is help me, and I treat you like that. I'm so sorry. You must wonder who you've married. What kind of vicious brute I am. But give me another chance, it will never happen again. I promise you that.'

She walks round the counter to him and takes his hand.

'Ollie, you'll get angry with me again,' she says. 'And I'll get angry with you. But we have to learn to manage our disagreements better. To dial it down. And that takes years. But we've got years, and we can learn together.'

He draws her into his arms and kisses her on the forehead. 'I don't deserve you,' he says.

She hugs him close.

'Yes, you do. You care about your sister. You've tried to protect her, her whole life. That tells me all I need to know about the kind of man you are.'

33

Boden and Mackie checked into a budget hotel on the edge of the Docklands. Autumn was Boden's favourite season in London; it gave her a sense that the city was returning to the people it belonged to. Londoners like her.

She spent the evening walking beside the river. It was chilly. But seeing the lights dancing on the water made her sad. She wondered if she'd ever get a job in the Met again.

A quick discussion on the phone with the DCI had clarified where he saw the inquiry going.

The PR company representing Ged Sullivan had put out a press release saying that on the night Cary Rutherford died, he was attending a private dinner in London. At that dinner, an important government contract was discussed, and the implication was at least one Cabinet minister was present.

'He's telling us, and the world, he's got a heavy duty alibi,' said Hepburn. 'But you know what, Jo, first Jackson, now this. I'm getting suspicious.'

Boden smiled to herself. The boss didn't want to admit it; it wasn't just about the evidence. Like all good detectives, he had finely tuned antennae, and Sullivan's behaviour was making them twitch.

'I think it's worth seeing if any of Cary's mates will talk to us,' she said.

'Agreed. Good plan.'

'We'll get on that in the morning.'

She returned to her solitary walk. She was doing her job, giving the boss what he wanted. But would any of it help her find her way home? To the city she loved. One day.

When she was alive, Cary Rutherford shared a Victorian terraced house in Leytonstone, in East London with four others. It's on a busy main road. A heavy multi-coloured piece of fabric obscures the bay window at the front, and there's a handwritten placard propped up in the middle. It reads: *The climate is changing. Why aren't we?*

Mackie lifts the rusty door knocker and gives the door a hammering. Boden notices a twitch in the cloth covering the window. Nothing happens. Mackie tries again. The entire frame reverberates with the force.

The front door opens a crack on a chain.

A small, reedy female voice says, 'We're not talking to the media.'

'Fair enough,' says Boden, holding up her warrant card. 'But if you want to know what happened to Cary, you should talk to us.'

'Maybe I already know.'

'Then we should discuss that,' says Boden.

The door shuts, then it opens with the chain off. A girl stands in the hallway; she's slight, in an oversized jumper; her dark, curly hair is tangled and straggly. Her eyes are blood-shot from crying.

'I'm Jo Boden, and the first thing I want to say is how sorry I am for your loss. It's terrible to lose a friend like that.'

The girl stares at her. Her chin quivers. She's seventeen or eighteen, a similar age to Cary. She gives a curt nod and allows them in.

The narrow hallway is a clutter of bicycles. It's hard to squeeze past. She leads them through to the back of the house and into the long, narrow kitchen. It's light and airy. The window sill behind the sink is crammed with plants.

A man sits at the table with a mug of tea and a laptop, which he closes. He's an adult, in his late twenties, head shaved, and a full beard. He peers at them through round granny glasses.

Boden introduces herself and Mackie, shows him her ID.

He inspects her warrant card. 'Y'know,' he says, 'you can buy ones just like this on the dark net.'

'Doesn't surprise me,' says Boden. 'If you want to check our credentials, you can call the main switchboard at Cambridgeshire Police and ask for DCI Hepburn.'

'As I told your mates in the Met, we've got nothing to say.' His gaze is hard and uncompromising.

The girl hovers in the background. She doesn't speak.

'If you're worried about getting arrested for—'

'Worried?' He chuckles, takes off his glasses, and rubs his eyes. 'I've done jail time already. And I'll probably do more. Because, in case you haven't noticed, the planet is burning, and flooding, the polar icecaps are melting, and a million species are threatened with extinction.'

'I have noticed,' says Boden. 'I also think that if Cary lost her life in pursuit of her beliefs, we should bring the culprit or culprits to justice.'

'Justice?' he says. 'And what would that look like, officer?'

'An arrest, a charge, a trial, the presentation of evidence to twelve ordinary citizens, a conviction and a sentence.'

'And you think that a man like Ged Sullivan can't buy his way out of that? Hasn't he already got his security guard to confess?'

'Charges against Kobe Jackson have been dropped.'

The man raises his eyebrows. 'Wow! And what's that supposed to prove?'

'What's your name, sir?' says Boden.

'Luke Cameron. And I've already made a statement. I've got nothing to add.'

Boden sighs. 'And I've read all the statements, but here's what I'm thinking, Luke. Cary didn't go on that protest alone. She wore a body cam; that footage is already out there. But whoever else was there that night, I'm thinking they wore body cams too. If their video footage shows what happened and a jury sees it, I think they'll find the right person guilty. Money won't come into it.'

Cameron chuckles. 'You remind me of me, five years ago.'

'You must be older than you look then,' says Boden.

'In spirit, yeah, I am. I feel like an old man sometimes. Y'know, I trained as a lawyer. Shirt and tie, nice haircut, no beard. I thought we could make the system to work. Reason would triumph.'

Boden scans him. He has a flinty stare; he's thin and round-shouldered. But a cold fury pulses off him. Were he and Cary involved? Is his anger fuelled by grief? He's unlikely to tell them.

'But even if your lot could persuade the CPS to charge Ged Sullivan,' he says, 'there'd be so much horse trading and motions back and forth, you'd be lucky to get the footage anywhere near a jury. Chances are some judge, who's mates with a mate of whoever, would rule it inadmissible. If they don't rule it out, a shedload of experts'll be called to discredit it and say it's fake. By then Sullivan's media lackeys'll be crowing from the rooftops about what a wonderful chap he is. If, by some miracle, he gets convicted, they'll appeal it. He'll be out on some procedural technicality. That's how the legal system works.'

'So you're saying video footage of what happened to Cary does exist?' says Boden.

'I'm saying he'd walk. Ninety-nine point nine per cent certain.'

'That's possible. But what are you going to do with this footage?'

'If it exists, and I admit nothing, it'll be put out there at the right time. Millions will see it, not just twelve random halfwits.'

'When will the right time be?'

'I can't tell you that. But I'll tell you this. I went to the mortuary to identify Cary's body, to save her mum from having to do it. It was hard to recognise her. And there will be justice for her murder, I promise you that. But it won't be in a court of law.'

He stares straight at Boden. It could all be a bluff. But there's a stillness about him that's disturbing. His self-belief is absolute.

'Where will it be then?' says Boden.

'You'll know when the rest of the world knows,' he replies.

'I understand how upset you are,' she says, 'but I must warn you against planning any acts of violence or retaliation.'

Cameron smiles. 'Retaliation? You understand nothing, sergeant, that's the problem. The violence is already happening all around us. The destruction is going on every day, and we're all complicit. I'm just one soldier in a war that we're losing.'

He's implacable. Boden stares straight at him. 'You meet violence with violence. Is that ever an answer?' she says. 'But, what do I know? I'm just a stupid cop, who gets to pick up the pieces.'

She glances at Mackie. He shakes his head and they walk out.

34

Sophie took the morning off. She and Ollie spent most of it in bed. Their first make-up sex, and he wanted to please her. She's midway through her menstrual cycle; if she got pregnant now as a result, it would be brilliant. The pain of the row, and of her own stupidity, would be erased. She's learning though, learning how to understand his moods and reactions. In the future, they'll both do better.

As she breezes into the cafe, she's still on a high; until she sees the two cops occupying a window table, and her heart sinks.

How did they track her down? Not that hard. Type her name into a search bar and it's all there.

Be upfront but charming. What choice does she have?

She walks over to their table. The sergeant looks up from her laptop and smiles.

'My guess is this is not a coincidence,' says Sophie.

The sergeant shrugs. 'My colleague is a country boy. He's never been to Shoreditch before. I'm showing him the sights.'

The DC grins. 'Yeah,' he says. 'Tower of London, Madame Tussauds, that's all I've done.'

'Anyone would think we're a million miles from Cambridge,' says Sophie. But the comment seems to wash over them.

'So, what can I do for you?' she adds. 'Would you like another drink?'

'We're trying to fill in some background,' says the sergeant.

Sophie pulls up a chair and sits down. 'Happy to help,' she says.

'Tell me about Kristin,' says the cop.

Sophie is taken aback. The sergeant seems to home in with unerring accuracy.

That morning, as they ate croissants in bed, she and Ollie had discussed the situation and agreed that they couldn't risk exposing Kristin to her husband's wrath.

'Truth is,' says Sophie. 'I don't know her that well. We only just met.'

'You didn't meet before the wedding? During your engagement to her brother?'

'It all happened quite quickly; there wasn't time.'

'A whirlwind romance?' says the sergeant. 'That's lovely.' Is her tone sarcastic? Sophie glances at the DC. He's demolished one of Claire's famous muffins in two bites.

'Can I get you another one of those?' she says. 'Have you tried the double chocolate chip?'

He grins. But the sergeant answers. 'I'm sure he wouldn't say no.'

Sophie waves at the manager.

The whole palaver provides a distraction and gives her a few precious moments to think. Is there a way to deal with this without repeating the lie? It's worth a try.

A counter assistant delivers a fresh muffin.

Sophie turns to the sergeant. 'Look,' she says. 'Can we speak in confidence?'

'Depends what you're going to say.' Typical cop reply.

'Okay, I hardly know Kristin. But I can tell you this. She's frightened of her husband.'

Sophie waits for a response. The cop says nothing.

So she ploughs on, 'What I'm saying is, he's a lot older than her, he's very wealthy, she's like the trophy wife. But he controls her.'

'Give me some examples.'

'I'm not sure I can. She lives in a bubble with him. It protects her from the paps, and all the scrutiny she gets because of her modelling career. But it comes at a price, if you get what I'm saying.'

'Are you saying he abuses her?'

'Depends what you mean? He's into S and M, and I'm pretty sure she's not a willing participant.'

'Your husband told you this?'

'No. She told me. Ollie and I are very concerned about her safety. We're trying to persuade her to leave him. But I'm sure, as a police officer, you're very well aware of the dangers inherent in that. And he's a powerful man.'

The sergeant nods. She's pondering. Then she says, 'Have you seen evidence of his temper? Or any injuries Kristin's sustained?'

'No. But she's scared. And also quite ashamed.'

'Abuse victims often are,' says the cop.

This is hitting the mark.

'We're only trying to take care of Kristin. But it's tricky.'

The cop nods. 'You think if Sir Gerald found out that you'd spoken to us about what happened that night, he would take it out on her?'

'It's possible,' says Sophie. 'But the truth is, I've no idea if Ged had anything to do with what happened to that poor protester. We'd already left. And if I'd seen something, or knew for a fact he was involved, believe me, I'd tell you. But I don't know.'

The sergeant smiles. 'Okay. Thank you for your candour, Ms Latham.'

'Sophie, please.' She sighs. 'You think I wouldn't like to see him go to jail? It'd solve a lot of problems.'

The sergeant is scanning her.

'I can see it might.'

She seems quite an ordinary woman, a few years younger than Sophie. No ring. Single? With someone? She's just doing her job. And she knows what it means to be young and female.

Sophie wonders how she copes with some of the people she has to deal with. Murderers, drug dealers, violent criminals. Having a sidekick the size of a rugby prop forward to back her up must help.

She watches them pack up their stuff.

'You've got my card,' says the cop. 'If you ever want to speak again.'

'Yes, I have,' says Sophie. 'Thank you.'

She watches them leave with some relief.

Sorted.

Her phones buzzes. A text from Ollie. Things are looking up.

She reads it: *Kristin and Ged have invited us for the weekend. What d'you think? Should we go?*

35

Kristin wanders round the house. They have a regular staff of four, plus a chef, who travels between this and their London base, as required.

It's taken her a long time to get used to having a parade of strangers, basically servants, in and out of their home. She hates the lack of privacy. As a concession to this, Ged has arranged for them to live in accommodation near the stables and away from the main house. They can be summoned if needed, but Kristin doesn't feel she's being spied upon all the time. Before she was married, a cleaner she had in her London flat photographed pages of her private diary and sold them to a gossip mag.

It turned into a media feeding frenzy for several months. Everyone she knew or had hung out with was targeted and offered money to dish the dirt. Later, she discovered one of the tabloids had hacked her phone. All her private calls, the rants to her agent, the rows with her then boyfriend, a well-known musician, were monitored. Embarrassing things turned up in the press. She accused friends of betraying her. When the truth emerged, most of the people she cared about found it hard to forgive her. She ended up isolated and paranoid.

She casts her eye over the guest suite. It looks immaculate. She's followed her husband's instructions and invited her brother and his new wife for the weekend. This is the last thing she wants, after her stupid meeting with Sophie.

Why did she do it? Completely mad!

Now she feels exposed. Her nerves are in shreds.

She told Ged she didn't want them to come. But he insisted.

'We need to keep them onside,' he said. 'Okay, it's not ideal. I just need you to be charming, put them at their ease.'

Kristin didn't argue with him. Once his mind's made up, he's hard to shift. It's easier to go along with what he wants.

Returning to the ground floor, she's jittery and in need of a distraction. She searches for her laptop. Too much stuff in too many places. Hard to keep track.

They've recently bought a penthouse apartment in London, overlooking Hyde Park, and she's persuaded Ged to let her create an art collection for it. His taste is conservative, and all that interests him is the asset value of anything he purchases. He relies on experts to advise him.

But Kristin wants to surprise him. Maybe impress him. She's been studying, doing online courses in art history. School was a washout for her, although she always liked to read. In between sessions on long, boring photoshoots, she devoured any books that came her way. She got teased for it, and called a nerd. Models are airheads, everyone knows that.

Ged assumes she spends her time reading romances.

Your little books. That's what he calls them. But if she knows enough to stop him getting stiffed on some overpriced, over-hyped painting, he may change his tune.

She wishes she could remember where she left her laptop.

As she passes the study door, she overhears Ged. He's on the phone, and he sounds pissed.

'I don't fucking care! This is your mess. You need to sort it out. You told me he'd be co-operative. Now he's reneged on the deal. If he talks to the police—'

Ged is on his feet, back towards her. She hides round the corner of the door and watches him.

'Yeah, well, you said this would work,' he says.

Why is he still so rattled?

When she first met him, what impressed her the most was how chilled he was. Nothing ever phased him. He'd glide into a room like a wily fox. He always knew how to get people to do exactly what he wanted. Get them onside was a favourite saying of his. Ged was the expert at this.

Early on, he took her on a date to Las Vegas. She'd never been to a casino before. She watched him play poker. Then he'd given her a tray of one hundred dollar chips and showed her how to play roulette. She lost them all, but it was fun. And he was the perfect gentleman; she had her own suite. He didn't hassle her for sex, not like some of the rich men she'd been paid to hang out with. She decided he was what she was looking for, a man who could protect her.

He hangs up the phone and notices her in the doorway.

'Everything's ready,' she says. 'And I've agreed the menus with Andreas. So we're all set.'

He walks towards her and takes both her hands. 'Good girl,' he says. 'I know it's irritating, and spending time with him is not what you'd choose. But I appreciate you agreeing to this.'

She pouts.

Where was the choice?

'And anyway,' he adds. 'You don't want to fall out with your brother. It looks bad.'

She tilts her head, plays coy. He likes that. 'Yeah. But I knew he'd be funny about the baby.'

Ged puts on the big daddy face and pats her hand.

'I've told you,' he says. 'It's all going to be fine. You're a healthy young woman. What happened to your mother will not happen to you. You think I'd risk losing you? You're the centre of my world, Krissy. We're going to have a lovely son, and our lives will be perfect.'

If only.

She smiles. 'Just promise,' she says. 'Don't leave me alone with them.'

He kisses her hand. 'Darling, I won't. Now I've got a couple more calls to make.'

She frowns. 'Is it going to be okay? This other stuff?'

'Of course it is.'

'You should've never gone down there that night.'

'I had to. They were trying to let the horses out. They could've done untold damage. But I've told you, I've done nothing wrong. It's all propaganda.'

'I know. But surely Raoul could've—'

'Raoul's an idiot. Once this is over, I'm getting rid of him.'

'What if the police come asking more questions?'

He shakes his head. He's getting impatient with her. 'Krissy, trust me. I've got it covered. They won't.'

36

Sophie and Ollie drive up to Newmarket. This is Sophie's idea. If there's any unpleasantness with Ged, she wants to make an independent getaway. No waiting around for a bloody helicopter. One of the security guards tells them where to park, and they follow the path through manicured gardens to the house.

Ollie carries their two holdalls, although the man offers to do it for them. Her husband is tense. They've had a discussion about how to approach this. Ollie wants her to distract Ged so he can talk to Kristin alone. He seems to have some crazy hope Kristin will agree to leave with them, and they'll all drive off into the sunset.

In his dreams. It'll never work.

A small, plump woman, presumably the housekeeper, opens the front door. She escorts them up the sweeping glass staircase to the first floor and shows them to their room. It's massive, and reminds Sophie of an expensive hotel suite but with the addition of several Old Master paintings, the genuine article, not a copy or a print. There's a large vase of fresh flowers and an array of expensive toiletries in the bathroom.

'Sir Gerald and Lady Sullivan will meet you for drinks in the Drawing Room at seven,' says the housekeeper; her accent is soft and Spanish. Then she dips her head and backs out of the door.

The situation is bizarre. Sophie's ventured into the world of the super-rich before, and it's her second visit to the Sullivans. But this time they're being treated to the full pantomime. She would've expected Kristin, at least, to welcome them in person. No sign of her though. Is this retreat into formality designed to put them in their place? Ged is reminding them of his status and power. It has the opposite effect on Sophie. Any attempt to bully has always made her more feisty.

'How can an ultra modern concrete bunker like this have a Drawing Room?' she says. 'Makes it sound like it's Downton bloody Abbey.'

Ollie dumps the holdalls on the bed and sighs.

'I should've brought a DJ,' he says.

Sophie laughs. 'Don't be daft. Not that I think you wouldn't look great. Very James Bond. Have you even got a DJ?'

He smiles. 'No.' It's the most relaxed she's seen him since they left London.

She walks over and kisses him. 'Don't worry. It'll be fine. Just don't let him wind you up.'

'It'll be fine because I've got you,' he says, and kisses her back.

Sophie times it to perfection. They walk into the Drawing Room, a glass cube with floor to ceiling windows cantilevered onto the back of the house, at five past seven. It's like a fish tank. Kristin and Ged are sitting in separate wing chairs. They both get up.

Kristin is wearing an ivory silk sack of a dress; as usual,

she looks amazing. She heads straight for Sophie, leans over and kisses her on both cheeks. 'So lovely you could join us,' she whispers. She's heavily made-up; but her mascara is smudged.

Ged and Ollie shake hands. Ollie manages to smile.

Ged's biceps are straining against a tight denim shirt. Its open neck exposes a triangle of grey chest hair. Why is it men of a certain age think they look good in denim? They don't.

He moves in on Sophie. 'What a lovely dress,' he says. 'And now we're related, if you'll permit me?' He leans forward and gives her a small peck on the cheek. He seems to regard himself as attractive to women, but Sophie gets more of a pervy old uncle vibe. Easy to imagine him wearing his full-face mask.

Creepy.

The ritual of greeting over, Ged offers drinks, which are dispensed, as before, by a boy in a blue butcher's apron. There's a sparkly, granite topped bar with a mirror behind it at the back of the room. It looks like something that's been parachuted in from a nightclub.

'You have some really interesting design concepts in this house,' says Sophie. She has to warm up the conversation somehow.

Ged stands, legs apart, with a smug, master-of-all-he-surveys expression.

'Yes,' he says. 'Kristin likes a mixture of styles. The bar is vintage. To remind us of our trip to Vegas.'

Sophie turns to Kristin. 'Mixing styles is quite a trick,' she says.

Kristin says nothing. Just smiles. She's clutching her glass of mineral water like a talisman and avoiding eye contact.

Poor woman must be bricking it.

They sit down and the conversation continues in the same

vein for the next ten minutes with Ged explaining aspects of the house in terms of what Kristin likes or has chosen.

But Kristin is fidgety; she gets up. 'I'm going to see if Andreas is ready for us,' she says.

'Darling, there's no need,' says Ged. 'He'll let us know.'

'I think he's being slow,' says Kristin. 'I'm sure we're all hungry.'

She hurries out of the room.

Ged shrugs. 'Kristin's very particular about the food. She and Andreas get on well. I try not to interfere. More drinks?'

Sophie scans their host. He's working hard to be genial, but he's not as relaxed as before. He flicks his fingernail against the back of his thumb as he downs his second large Scotch.

Andreas has prepared a seven course tasting menu, which is served in the barn of a dining room, where they ate on their first visit. He comes in to introduce each beautifully constructed plate. There's a different wine to complement each course.

Sophie appreciates the food, though she suspects she's the only one who does. Ged eats on autopilot, while talking. He rolls through various topics of conversation, all boring. Sophie gets the impression he's used to doing this. Kristin picks at her food and sips her mineral water. Ollie scoffs each course, his eyes darting back and forth to his sister, who continues to avoid his gaze.

Sophie finds it curious that they're so uncomfortable with each other. But perhaps it's not that surprising. Ollie is trying to force her to confront the reality of her marriage to this awful man. She must be scared that after her conversation with Sophie, he'll say something to expose her.

By the time they get to the last dessert course, a chocolate pudding with lavender sorbet, Sophie is fed up with the sound of Ged's voice. It feels like it's going to be a long weekend.

She's tried to keep a strict curb on her own drinking, but it's difficult. The wines are delicious.

Ged orders port to be served with the cheese. He's looking flushed. He instructs the boy to put the decanter on the table, then dismisses him. This is the opportunity Sophie's been waiting for.

Ged is droning on about the difficulties of sourcing a decent port, and how he was put on to his current supplier by the sommelier at his favourite Michelin-starred London restaurant. Kristin is examining her nails. They match the ivory of her dress and are set with tiny stars.

Sophie glances at her husband, then she says, 'So, shall we talk about why you've really invited us this weekend? I don't think it's just to sample your very fine port.'

Ged blinks at her over his glass. 'Not sure I get your drift,' he says, giving her a smile mellowed by booze.

'Here's my drift,' says Sophie. 'The police came to see us. They're very interested in where you were on the night that protester got killed. And you need us to pretend you weren't here, because you're saying you were in London. So you're asking us to lie.'

'Is that a problem?' says Ged with a shrug.

'I'm not sure,' says Sophie. 'Depends on why you need us to say that.'

Ged sighs, drains his glass, and tops it up. 'My dear Sophie, you have to understand that a man in my position is an easy target for these idiots. I'm a businessman; I have no control over climate change. That's the concern of governments. But they think they can break into my property and protest, as they call it, by frightening my horses.'

'That's the opposite of the spiel you gave us before,' says Sophie. 'You said it's industry and the billionaires who are going to save us.'

He puffs out his cheeks. 'Did I? I don't recall.'

He pontificates so much, how would he?

'Come on, Ged,' she says. 'You know what I'm asking. How did this girl get killed?'

'I don't know.' He stares straight back at her. Poker-faced. But sweat is beading on his upper lip and forehead.

He's lying.

He's good at it. But not that good.

'Why don't you just tell the police that?' she says.

He smiles. 'You're a smart girl in many ways, but don't you think you're being naive? It's not just about the police. Bad PR hits my share price.'

He's trying to patronise her into submission, which is annoying.

Sophie shrugs. 'I'm pushing forty. So I think girlhood is behind me. I'm just looking for a straight answer.'

Ged chuckles and dips his head. 'Apologies. I'm not politically correct. But I have a daughter who's practically your age. I still think of her as a girl.'

And a wife even younger. What do you think of her as?

Sophie says nothing. But she's not letting him off the hook. She waits.

Kristin comes to his rescue. 'Sophie, it wasn't his fault. He had nothing to do with what happened to that poor girl.'

Does she believe that?

Ged's lip curls into a smile as his wife backs him up.

Sophie says, 'I'm not saying he did. But you are asking us to lie to the police. Surely that entitles us to know what we're covering up?'

Ollie is watching her. Sophie can sense the tension in him.

But he's holding aloof, keeping himself in check, which is good.

Ged takes another drink; he's losing patience.

Short fuse.

Ball's in his court.

He sighs. 'I've got a stable of thoroughbred racehorses out there. They're worth a great deal of money. And I'm fond of them. They were being threatened. Also, we didn't know how many of these thugs there were. It was like an invasion. Kristin was frightened.'

'I get that' says Sophie. 'But a bunch of climate protestors? This girl was a student, not a thug. And they're unlikely to harm animals. Part of their aim is to save animals.'

'They didn't care. They ran amok and spooked the horses.'

'Even so. A horse is a horse, spooked or otherwise. It doesn't justify the death of a young woman.'

Ged stares at her. His gaze is hard and unrelenting. Tension ripples through his jaw. Sophie can feel how much he's hating this. He doesn't like to be challenged.

'Good God, woman!' he says. 'I'm not saying it does. I'm not saying that at all. The point is, the girl put herself in that situation. They were the lawbreakers.'

'And you have every right to defend your property. I agree.'

This catches him off-guard. He wasn't expecting sympathy. He scans her. Takes another slug of his drink.

She enjoys a joust, especially when she's winning.

Nudge him.

'I can imagine how it was,' she says. 'Dark. Confusing. You didn't know what was happening. Perhaps the climate protestors were out to provoke you.'

He looks at her. 'Yes, they were.'

Blame them. It's obvious this would be his line.

She says nothing. Leaves a silence for him to fill.

He's trying to figure out how much to trust them.

He inhales. 'There was a fight. And somehow this girl received a blow to the head. Maybe she got in the way. I don't know. It was an accident. I arrived after the event. But I made sure an ambulance was called. Is that what you want to know?'

'Then you scarpered before the police showed up?'

He laughs. 'Yes, all right, I scarpered. I left it to my head of security. I didn't want any misunderstanding of the situation.'

He wipes the sweat from his forehead with his palm. Kristin is watching him with an anxious frown.

'Was it really one of your security guards who hit her? On the net they're saying it was you.' says Sophie.

Wham! He wasn't expecting that.

His eyes register shock and a flicker of uncertainty.

But then his expression changes. Hardens. A stillness descends on him.

Taking his time, he pours himself another drink, before turning his steely gaze on Sophie.

'I told you,' he says, 'it was an unfortunate situation that got out of hand. The stupid girl put herself in harm's way. And maybe you're right, she did it deliberately to provoke me so these idiots could use it to smear me.'

No denial this time.

He's changed tack. But there's no mistaking the tone in his voice. Quiet and menacing. It sends a chill down Sophie's spine.

It takes a moment for her to realise what's happening. The gloves have come off. He's issuing a veiled threat.

Telling her this is what can happen to people who cross him.

If she wasn't sure before, she is now.

He did it.

This is the real Ged Sullivan. A man who controls and abuses his wife. And who beat a teenage girl to death for upsetting his horses.

She's sitting across the dinner table from a monster.

37

Sophie wakes in the early hours from a troubled sleep. Moonlight is leeching through the blinds and dancing across the super-kingsize bed. Ollie is fast asleep beside her. She suspects, from his snores, that he's drunk too much. She certainly has.

Once Ged had made his point, he steered the dinner conversation back to innocuous subjects. Sophie played her part. But she couldn't suppress her alarm. Ged didn't care if she and Ollie thought he was capable of extreme violence. He'd stopped denying it. In fact, he's as good as admitted it, and is using it as a threat to bully them.

Ollie's fears for Kristin are real.

Wide awake, with her thoughts racing, Sophie gets out of bed, and wanders in and out of the bathroom. They must help Kristin escape from Ged.

But how?

Kristin's behaviour makes sense. She asked Sophie to meet her and told her about the abuse. This was a cry for help. But she lost her nerve. And who can blame her? It shows how frightened she is of her husband.

There's no doubt about the power Ged wields. He's persuaded an unnamed Cabinet Minister to back his story that he was in London. Faced with that, simply telling the police that this is a lie is unlikely to be enough.

As she paces the room, Ollie stirs in his sleep. She doesn't want to disturb him. He's been carrying the burden of this alone for far too long. In the half-light, she can just make out the contours of his face; his eyelids flicker, and a rush of love for this man surges through her.

How did she get this lucky?

To support him, she needs to come up with a plan. She's antsy and her brain is nattering. She needs to move.

Opening the door, she tiptoes out into the hallway.

The thing that sickens her the most is the way Ged tried to turn it around and blame the dead girl, claiming she put herself in harm's way.

Her fault. She deserved it. It's the age-old excuse.

The house is silent and still; the raw concrete walls give it a sombre feel, like a mausoleum. Sophie makes her way downstairs, bare feet on the cold glass treads, and into the cavernous atrium.

The moon is full; its light floods in through the tall windows. The art alone must be worth millions. There's an eclectic mix. In its chilly beam, she recognises a couple of Rothkos. Then some nineteenth century pastoral landscapes, and a watercolour that might be a Turner.

As she rounds a corner, she sees a glimmer of light down a narrow corridor behind the stairs. This must be the kitchen; the domain of the chef and the staff. They're still at it, cleaning up.

Ged treats them like servants and ignores them. More fool him. They see and hear everything and would know what's going on. But can she get them to talk to her?

She walks down the corridor towards the light. The kitchen is spacious and high-tech, a T shaped central cooking island, surrounded by steel cabinets. And perched on a stool at the central counter is Ged, eating a bowl of frosted cornflakes.

He looks up at her. His expression remains neutral.

Shit! Be cool. Don't panic.

'Oh, sorry,' she says. 'I couldn't sleep.'

He nods, mouth stuffed with cereal. He swallows it and says, 'Fancy food's all very well, but it doesn't soak up the booze.'

'Yeah, you need a sugar and carbs hit for that.' She sounds calm enough, but she's unnerved. Another encounter with Ged is the last thing she needs.

'Want some?' he says.

She shakes her head and wanders round, trying to look interested in the Miele ovens and the eight burner hob.

'Nice kitchen,' she says.

She's intruded on him, but he doesn't seem to care. Of course he doesn't. He's already put her in her place. Neutralised the threat.

He finishes his bowl and pushes it away. She wonders if he'll leave it, or put it in the sink. He leaves it.

Folding his arms, he looks her up and down. He's sobered up and scans her with the shrewd, calculating look he had when they first met.

Now what?

A queasy fear seeps upward from her gut.

Keep the conversation light and get out.

He frowns. 'You know what I can't figure,' he says. 'How did you get suckered by a low-rent operator like him?'

'Excuse me?'

'I get it on one level. You've never been much of a

looker, but you're smart. And the old clock's ticking. Along comes Mickey with his muscles and his bullshit, and you fall for it.'

Sophie freezes; she feels as if he's slapped her.

WTF!

'What are you talking about?' she says.

He chuckles. 'Okay, we all make mistakes. I've made a few of my own. The issue is always how you respond. Don't you agree?'

He gets off his stool, bare, muscular forearms still folded, and moves towards her. There's a malicious glint in his eye. He's wearing a T-shirt and pyjama bottoms; a big man, lean and fit for his age. He reeks of booze and stale sweat. And he exudes menace.

Get out! Now!

The problem is he's between her and the door. This is payback for challenging him. What happened at dinner was a taster. Now he's got her on her own. He wants to scare her. That's what turns him on.

But she juts her chin and says, 'Are you talking about my husband?'

Don't let him see the fear.

He stops right in front of her, towering over her by several inches.

He tips back his head and laughs. 'You silly bitch, you don't even know his real name, do you?'

'His name's Oliver Harmon.'

'He must've picked that one out of a women's magazine. His name's Mick Kelly.'

'You're lying.'

He leans towards her and sneers. 'C'mon. You think Kristin doesn't know her brother's name? The guy's a con man.'

It's a lie. Another lie. He wants to frighten her. He's succeeding.

There's a rushing in her ears. The sour stench of alcohol on his breath is nauseating. And he's just standing there, this monster, inches from her face. Threatening her, accusing Ollie. How dare he?

'You're such a liar,' she says. 'And I know you abuse your wife. But you don't scare me.'

He laughs. 'What? Who told you that? Mickey?'

'She told me.'

He tilts his head and frowns. 'She never said that.' He laughs again. 'You poor, dumb bitch, you still don't get it, do you? He's using you. This is what he does. Plays dogs like you for money.'

Inside her, from nowhere the anger erupts, wiping out the fear. Hot, molten fury cascades through her.

Lying bastard!

She's consumed by blinding rage. Her right arm swings back and she whacks him round the face with all her might. Her palm stings with the impact. The blow knocks his head sideways.

It feels great!

For a second.

He turns back to face her, eyes livid with wrath.

He fingers his cheek. It must smart.

'You vicious little slag,' he says. 'You need teaching a lesson.'

She tries to dodge sideways, but he's boxed her in against the worktop.

It happens fast. His arm goes back as he clenches his fist.

Here comes the punch!

This is what he did to the protester. Punched her so hard he fractured her skull.

Not this time. No way!

She's pumping with adrenaline. Instinct kicks in. She glances around for a weapon.

The knife block!

On the counter behind her. A fancy set of Japanese chefs' knives.

She flings her arm across and grabs at it. Pulls. No chance to see what's in her hand. Any knife will do.

Hurt him first.

It's her only chance. She snaps her head sideways to duck the blow and thrusts the knife forward at him.

38

Sophie lets go of the knife. The blade is embedded in Ged's stomach up to the hilt. His face is inches from hers, eyes wide with shock. He exhales a low and guttural grunt and staggers backwards, both hands clutching at the knife.

Her heart pounds.

Shit! Shit! Shit!

From nowhere, like a bullet train, the horror of what she's done hurtles through her brain.

He gave her no choice! It was self-defence!

He lurches and drops to his knees. A dribble of blood oozes from his mouth. His eyes are full of pain and incomprehension. She reaches out to his shoulder and steadies him.

'Oh my God!' she says.

No! NO!

What has she done?

'Get someone!' he gasps.

She's left her phone upstairs. She glances around. Are any of the staff about? Or is it just them? It's late.

She lost it. Lost it completely.

How? HOW?

He was going to hit her. He clenched his fist. She's certain of that.

Now a tsunami of fear and regret engulfs her. How could she have done this terrible thing? He was definitely going to hit her. Get an ambulance. Wake someone up.

She sees his phone on the kitchen counter, and picking it up, she dials 999.

Her panic is rising to a crescendo. A figure appears in the doorway. Ollie? It's Ollie!

Ged is on his knees close to her feet, one hand on the floor to support himself. The other clutching the knife.

On the phone, there's a voice. 'Emergency. Which service do you require?'

Her husband rushes across the room towards her.

'Ambulance,' she says. 'It's a stabbing. We need help urgently. The address? Oh my god, Ol, what's the address?'

Ollie grabs the phone. Thank god he's here.

'Tell them the address,' she says.

But he clicks the phone off and tosses it on the counter.

What!

He grasps her by the shoulders. 'It's okay,' he says. 'Calm down. Breathe. I'm here now.'

'We've got to get help,' she cries. 'I don't know how it happened. He was going to hit me! It was self defence, I swear!'

He shakes her. 'Hey, stop this! Now!'

'I had no choice.' Tears roll down her cheeks. Everything's spiralling out of control.

'I know,' he says. 'It'll be okay.'

How can it be okay? HOW?

She's reeling.

Ged grasps the edge of the kitchen counter, and, with

supreme effort, pulls himself to his feet, and reaches for his phone.

But Ollie snatches it first. He shoves Ged in the chest.

Ged collapses to his knees. 'Get help!' he gasps. 'I need an ambulance.'

Ollie towers over him. For half a second, the two men stare at one another. And Ollie smiles.

He raises his bare foot and kicks Ged over.

Ged groans in pain as he rolls sideways.

What! What's he doing!

'Ollie?' she cries. 'He could die.'

He looks straight at her. 'Listen to me,' he says. 'You want to spend the next twenty years of your life in jail?'

'It was self-defence.'

'Says who? You?'

He turns away, eyes darting round the room, searching for something.

'But… he tried to hit me.'

He did, didn't he?

Ollie doesn't reply. He pulls a meat mallet from the steel pot of cooking utensils next to the hob and smashes Ged's phone.

Panic ricochets through her as she watches in disbelief. She tries to speak, but no sound will come.

Ollie moves quickly. He leans over Ged and wrenches the knife out of his gut. It's a long narrow blade. A boning knife with a sharp tip designed to cut meat.

Ged groans. 'Please help me,' he whispers. He's drifting towards unconsciousness.

But Ollie twists Ged's head sideways and calmly slashes his throat.

He's gone crazy!

There's a spurt of arterial blood from the jugular, and Ollie jumps back to avoid it.

Ged splutters. His eyes glaze over. Blood pulses from his neck.

Blood everywhere!

She stares at him in terror and dismay.

The pulsating gush of blood slows to a crimson rivulet.

One second, two seconds, three seconds, and he's gone.

Everything's spinning.

Sophie's knees buckle and she sinks to the floor. She can't comprehend what she's seen. The puddling blood soaks her pyjamas.

With cool calculation, her husband slit a man's throat. He did it with precision, as if butchering an animal. He expected it would be messy, and he stepped out of the way.

So much blood!

She feels sick.

Ollie seizes her arm and hauls her to her feet.

'Come on, get it together,' he says.

She stares at him. Then at Ged's corpse.

He was alive. Just now.

'You killed him!' she gasps.

'I had to,' he says with a matter-of-fact sigh. 'We couldn't just hang around and wait to see if he croaked.'

She's light-headed. Time has slowed to a crawl. She can't seem to move.

'Sophie,' he says. 'I need you to move. Wash your hands.'

'I can't…'

'You can.'

He tears a piece of kitchen paper from the roll on the counter and lays the knife on it. It's as if she's watching this from far away. Her head is spinning. It must all be a terrible dream. She feels his hand. He takes her by the shoulders.

'Listen.' He shakes her. 'You've had a terrible experience,' he says. 'You're in shock. Listen to me and do what you're told. I'm going to take care of you. Okay?'

She nods.

Why is she nodding?

He goes to the sink, turns on the tap and washes his hands.

She's still frozen.

'C'mon, Soph,' he says. 'Come and wash your hands.'

She walks over to the sink like a zombie and lets him guide her hands under the stream of water. It's hot. She watches the water.

'Rub them together,' he says.

She obeys. She can't think.

He gets a hand towel from the rail at the end of the counter. Wipes his hands, passes it to her. He's glancing around him. There's a roll of clingfilm on a wall dispenser. He rips a piece off, folds the kitchen paper round the knife and wraps it in clingfilm. He picks up Ged's smashed phone and wraps that in clingfilm too.

Why is he doing this?

Her thoughts wander. She can't focus.

He frowns. He seems to be searching for something else.

There's a white board attached to one of the steel cabinets, and a black marker pen hanging from it.

He walks over to it, picks up the pen, uncaps it, and ponders for a moment.

Then he scrawls on the board.

dear krissy

really sorry to see you and ged having problems

feels like we're in the way

dont wanna make it any worse

decided to go back to London

call me

Ol x,

What does he even think he's doing? Constructing an alibi?

He turns to her. 'Okay,' he says. 'Bring the towel. We need to pack and leave, as fast as we can.'

'This won't work,' she says.

'Trust me, it will.'

'It's mad. I can't do this.' She's paralysed.

He comes over, takes her hand and drags her. 'Sophie, you can. It's simple. You made a mistake. But now, you do what's necessary to survive. We all do.'

He's smiling at her. But his eyes are hard and chilly.

Kristin!

'What about Kristin?' she says.

'Kristin chose him. But I choose you. You're my wife. And I'm going to protect you. Now, let's go.'

He's pulling her towards the door. An overwhelming despair is engulfing her. But he's right.

Isn't he?

She had to stab Ged. She did it to survive. It is that simple.

He is right.

39

Kristin is still in bed when she hears the scream. A piercing wail full of shock and horror.

She hasn't been awake for long. She's checking her phone. Ged is up before her. He works out in the basement gym for at least half an hour before breakfast; he's always very disciplined.

She gets out of bed, hurries to the door and opens it. The master suite is at the top of the stairs and opens into the triple height atrium. As she steps forward onto the landing, Martina, the housekeeper, comes rushing out of the kitchen. She sinks to her knees in the middle of the hallway, head in hands, sobbing.

Kristin stares down at her. She has a weird sensation in her stomach.

'Martina?' she calls.

The woman looks up at her. She's mumbling something in Spanish and crossing herself.

An icy chill cascades through Kristin's body. Something bad has happened. And she knew it would. But Ged insisted on inviting him.

She runs downstairs.

As she passes Martina, she says, 'Call security! Do it now!'

She runs into the kitchen. A sharp metallic smell hits her. Then she sees him lying on the floor. He's on his back, a dark congealed puddle of blood around him. The stench is sickening.

'Ged!' she shrieks. She dashes towards him and flings herself down on the floor beside him.

There a large open gash in the side of his neck. His face is grey. She reaches out to touch it. His skin is cold.

'No!' she howls. 'Please God no!'

She throws herself on to his chest and hugs him tight.

'Ged!'

The blood soaks her nightdress. She can feel the stickiness on her face and in her hair.

He doesn't move. He's so cold.

'C'mon, babe,' she pleads. 'You're tough. I know you're tough. Come back to me.'

She clings to his chest, begging him and praying. Repeating his name, over and over. He doesn't move.

She holds him, rocks him, strokes his hair. She's keening, like the women you see on the TV news, powerless and deranged with grief.

Then there's a hand on her arm, pulling her gently.

'Kristin, let go. Let me look.' It's Raoul. He's leaning over her.

Raoul's an idiot. I'm getting rid of him.

'All the blood,' she says. 'He's lost so much blood.'

'Let me see.'

She lays Ged down. Other hands help her to her feet. Andreas. Martina. Other guards whose names she can't remember.

Raoul kneels beside her husband. He was once in the army. He'll know what to do.

'Help him, please,' she begs.

Raoul turns and looks up at her. 'Kristin, he's dead.'

'No, he can't be! Help him.'

'He's gone. There's nothing anyone can do. I'm sorry.'

No! This can't be!

She's going down. Andreas guides her to a stool. She slumps on to it.

A dark shroud descends upon her. She can't breathe. She's choking. Choking on her own tears. The surrounding voices are a fading babble. She can't make out the words. She's dizzy and falling. A chasm is opening up, sucking her down.

Blackness. Nothing.

40

Sophie sits on the shingle bank, clutching her knees and staring at the horizon. Leaden clouds hang low over the vast expanse of the roiling North Sea. The wind is sharp and blowing in her face; it smells of rain. She's shivering but doesn't want to move. Ollie has put his jacket around her.

They left the Sullivan estate about four am and drove east. Dawn was hardly discernible; the darkness dissolved to be replaced by a washed-out greyness. Ollie was driving. He headed for the coast. They didn't discuss it.

She holidayed in Aldeburgh as a child with her parents. Windy and wet is her only memory of it.

There are fishing boats on the deserted beach. Waves crash on the pebbles, followed by the swooshing suck of the backwash. She finds the elemental power of the sea calming. There's a heavy swell and a storm brewing; not a good day to go fishing.

In the aftermath of panic, her mind is limp and drifting, but she can feel the pull of those North Sea rollers. It would be one solution; she could load her pockets with stones and walk into the sea. She wonders what it would be like to drown. Would it be terrifying? The coward's way out.

Every few minutes, she gets a flashback to what happened. There's no chronological order, just random fragments tossed up, like the flotsam on the tideline. What she can't erase is the look on Ged's face. That keeps coming back.

Shock. Panic.

Her hand had barely let go of the knife when she saw the raw terror in his eyes. And she was the cause. Then it hit her. She did this. She did this horrific, violent thing to another human being. How could she? This is not who she is.

But it was self-defence, wasn't it?

Ollie is walking towards her across the beach. He's carrying a cardboard holder with two cups of coffee. She watches him approach. He's her husband; he acted on instinct. His first thought was to protect her. Isn't it what any man, any decent man, would do for a wife he loves? She created the situation, not him. It was her madness. He stepped into it. Even if he over-reacted, she's still to blame.

But it was self-defence. She had no choice.

He smiles at her. 'The cafe doesn't open until eight,' he says. 'But I persuaded them to do me a takeaway.'

How is he so calm?

He sits down beside her and hands her a coffee. She takes it, but her hand shakes so much she can't remove the top. He does it for her.

'Thanks,' she whispers.

He sips his coffee and stares out to sea.

Then he says, 'So what happened? What kicked it off with Ged?'

She has to answer. He's owed an explanation.

She looks at him, searching his face. 'He said your real name is Mick Kelly. And you're a con man.'

He looks away. 'Oh,' he says.

Her thoughts are writhing and slipping. She can't hold on to anything.

'Well, is it true?' she says.

'Which part?' He's smiling, but there's a wary look in his eye.

Which part?

She wants to scream. To stand facing the cold North Sea and howl with despair.

'Any of it,' she says.

He tilts his head and fixes his gaze on the far horizon. 'Well,' he says. 'It's partly true. But my real name is Michael Byrne. Same as my father.'

Michael Byrne?

She can't speak. She stares at her coffee. The surface vibrates from her trembling hand. If she tries to drink, she'll spill it.

He heaves a sigh. 'Listen,' he says. 'I couldn't tell you.'

Why?

'I don't understand.' The words come out of her mouth, but it sounds as if another person is speaking. Not her.

His shoulders are hunched. He finishes his drink and tosses the dregs.

Sophie watches the coffee spray across the pebbles. In the space of a few short hours, her life has come unmoored. She's adrift.

Who is he?

'Okay,' he says. 'Here goes.' There's no mistaking the tetchiness in his tone.

'I was born in South Armagh in 1987. My father was a soldier in the South Armagh Brigade.'

What's he talking about?

'He fought for his country and his people, like any soldier. That's how he saw it. But he was in the IRA; it's why I never talk about the past in any detail.'

Not the hippy drug dealers with a cute dog rolling round the countryside in an old ambulance, then?

He's scanning her. 'You probably think I lied to you before.'

He did.

But she's too shell-shocked to care. Compared to what they're facing now, it's nothing.

'I needed a story to tell myself and other people. Okay, it was a fantasy. A comforting fantasy. But I've always wanted to come clean with you. It just never seemed the right time.'

He gazes at her. And there's such earnestness in those eyes.

'You have to believe me, Soph.'

She looks away. There's chaos in her head. She can't trust anything.

Can't trust herself, that's clear.

'We came to England in 1990, when I was three. My dad was part of a team tasked with acquiring and smuggling weapons back home. He brought me and my mother as cover and we took the name Kelly. That's when I became Mickey Kelly.'

Ged wasn't lying? She lost her temper and slapped him for telling her the truth!

The horror of this reverberates through her.

But Ollie is ploughing on. 'My dad worked on building sites,' he says. 'And now and then, he took trips abroad. To the States. To Libya. To buy weapons.'

Sophie can hear the words, but they wash over her. She

can't process this. Inside, she's howling. Caught in a mael-strom of dread.

Focus! Just focus on this.

Ollie has a wistful look. 'The problem was,' he says, 'they needed money to finance the operation. They were smuggling guns anyway, so they smuggled drugs too. They got involved with drug gangs in Liverpool and Manchester. That's how they raised the cash.'

His face. So sad.

This is the face she loves so much. She can't help it.

'When I was five, we were living in Manchester,' he says. 'My father went on one of his trips, and he never came back. We never saw him again. Years later, my mother heard from a distant cousin that some UDA thugs who knew him caught him in Belfast when he came to report to his commanding officer. They tortured him and shot him dead. His body was never found.'

She drops her cup of coffee on the shingle as she reaches for his hand.

He turns towards her with tears in his eyes. 'I was fifteen when we found out. It sent me off the rails a bit.'

'Oh, Ol,' she whispers.

We don't get to choose our parents. This is not his fault.

'My dad did business with a gangster called Lloyd. When he didn't come back, Lloyd moved in on my mother. He was Kristin's father.'

Ollie wipes his face with the back of his hand. 'The reason I never told you before is I thought you wouldn't marry me. A personal trainer is one thing. But the son of a terrorist? I can imagine what your mother would say.' There's a bitterness in his tone.

Sophie has been trying not to think about her parents. She pushes any thought of them aside.

Focus.

But it takes all her strength to hang on to his words.

'Lloyd was a piece of work,' he says. 'A total bastard. He expected me to earn my keep. I became a drug runner for him when I was ten. He bought me a fancy BMX bike, and I made deliveries.'

She looks at him. It's heartbreaking.

This is what's made him who he is.

He turns to look straight at her. The wind ruffles his hair. This man has just done a terrible thing to protect her.

If that's not love.

There's a hardness behind those eyes, but now she understands why.

'I'm so sorry,' she mutters. 'I never meant…'

He squeezes her hand. 'Hey, all I need is for you to understand. Mickey Kelly was a young tearaway, because he had no choice. But I'm not that boy anymore. I'm Ollie, your husband. And that's who I want to be. I'd do anything for you, Sophie. Anything at all. You must know that now.'

She does.

They gaze at each other.

She must be crying, because he leans forward and brushes the tears from her cheek with the tips of his fingers.

41

Jo Boden was still in London when she got the boss's call. She was intending to have Sunday lunch with her mother in Greenwich.

'Ged Sullivan's dead. Throat slashed. Found this morning,' said Hepburn, in a matter-of-fact tone.

Her immediate thought was Luke Cameron. His talk about justice contained a veiled threat. Plus the obsessive nature of the man. But she'd reported it to the DCI. Sent him the recording that Mackie made of their encounter with Cameron.

Hepburn said he'd contact Counter Terrorism and the security services, to see if Cameron was on their radar. It remains to be seen if he did that. If he didn't, and this was Cameron, there'd be a whole heap of trouble.

Would he land her in it, to save his own skin?

She ponders the question as she drives to Newmarket. In her experience of the DCI, he's always been a straight shooter. But the murder of a man like Sullivan, particularly in view of what went before with the climate protestors, is going to be big news. The media, politicians, everyone will have a view of what should or shouldn't have been done. The police will be under intense pressure. And if Alistair Hepburn sees his brilliant career heading down the pan, it may well tempt him to look for a scapegoat.

Boden shows her ID to the police officer on the gate, and drives into the Sullivan estate. There are already two local TV crews parked up in their vans. News is spreading fast. It won't be long before the place is besieged. She has the cynical thought that Mrs Webber, at the adjacent farm, may well succumb to temptation too and rent out pitches on her land to the media pack at whatever exorbitant fee she cares to charge. And who can blame her?

Boden gets out of her car. The stable yard has been cordoned off. Sullivan's own security is nowhere to be seen. It's all police. Squad cars, uniforms, two forensic trucks. A mobile incident room has just arrived on the back of a low-loader. Hepburn has brought in a new DI from the other team based in Hertfordshire, and she's been told to report to him.

He's standing at the centre of a group of officers and issuing instructions. This gives Boden the chance to observe him before he sees her.

'… and get someone who knows what they're doing to move these horses,' he says. 'This whole place is to be treated as a crime scene.' He's tall, bordering on the lanky, sharp suit, trendy haircut. And he's around the same age as her. He's probably also got a degree in something silly and spent about five minutes in uniform before becoming a detective. She doesn't like him already. *Who says the police aren't institutionally sexist?*

She walks up to the group. 'Morning, sir,' she says. 'DS Boden.'

He grins. 'Just the person I've been waiting for,' he

replies. He holds out his hand to shake. 'Tom Roscoe. Glad to meet you, Jo.'

His hand is long and slim, like the rest of him. It's hard not to be charmed, and this is undoubtedly his intention.

He beckons for her to follow, and starts off, with a long loping stride, towards the house. 'Right, well, I'm playing catch up here. And I'll be relying on you a lot.'

'Did the DCI mention Luke Cameron?'

He shakes his head. 'Nope, but then we had a very brief conversation on the phone. He wanted me to get over here asap. He said you'd bring me up to speed.'

Boden's heart sinks. She's going to have to tread carefully.

'Who is he?' says Roscoe.

'We just interviewed him in connection with the death of Cary Rutherford, the climate protester. He blamed Ged Sullivan and made some veiled threats, all of which I reported to DCI Hepburn.'

Roscoe gives her a knowing glance. 'I'm sure you did. We'll get to that. First, there's something I want to show you.'

He leads her towards the house. Outside they get suited up in protective gear, provided by one of the forensic team.

Boden follows him inside and towards the kitchen. The central area of the room is cordoned off. The corpse has been removed, but it's clear from the blood on the floor that this is where Sullivan died.

They skirt round the edge of the room to a whiteboard attached to the door of one of the tall steel cabinets. There's some writing on the board. Roscoe points to it and says, 'What do you make of this? The chef knows nothing about it.'

It appears to be a note, written in black marker pen, in a

childish, cramped hand. The lines slant. No capitals. No punctuation.

Boden reads it.

dear krissy

really sorry to see you and ged having problems

feels like we're in the way

dont wanna make it any worse

decided to go back to London

call me

Ol x

Roscoe folds his arms. She can feel him scanning her.

'Well,' she says. 'I think Krissy is the victim's wife, Lady Sullivan. Ol is her brother, Oliver Harmon. He and his wife were here for dinner the same evening that Cary Rutherford was later killed.'

The DI nods. 'According to the housekeeper, they were here last night too. Came for the weekend. But they've left. What do you make of that?'

'Harmon got married recently to Sophie Latham. Sullivan insisted he was in London on the night the protestors broke in. The story is Harmon and Latham came to have dinner just with Lady Sullivan. But we wondered if this was true. Questioned them together. Then we tried Sophie on her own. That was interesting. Her story is that Lady Sullivan was scared of her husband, was being abused by him, and that the brother-and sister-in-law were worried about her and wanted her to leave him.'

'You think the brother wrote the note?'

'That would be my assumption.'

Roscoe smiles. 'Okay, could we be looking at a scenario like this? They come for the weekend. Things get awkward because Sullivan and his wife are *having problems,* as the note says. So brother and wife leave. Sullivan sees the note.

Gets angry. He and Lady Sullivan row about it. She thinks he's going to hurt her. Goes for the knife.'

Boden shrugs. 'It's possible, I suppose. But very speculative.'

He nods, strokes his chin. 'You've met her before?'

'Briefly.'

'Okay. I don't want to freak her out. Let's see if she'll talk to you.'

42

When Kristin came to, she was lying on the sofa in the Drawing Room. She looked at her hands; they were covered in dried blood. It had formed a crust under her nails and round the edge of the little decorative stars. Then she remembered why.

She got up and walked out onto the terrace. The stone slabs were icy on her bare feet, but the shock of it helped her focus. She had to get out of that place. Now. Escape.

There were voices in the room behind her. Ignoring them, she ran. Down the steps and into the garden. She was fleeing. Because Ged couldn't protect her. She'd touched his face. It was so cold. How could he leave her like this? Abandon her. She had to hide. But where?

The grass was wet with dew. She ran over the short, springy turf. She knew from her morning walks round the perimeter that there were no gaps in the fence. How would she get out? The gates? She couldn't risk that.

Beyond the neat lawns and the flowerbeds, the ground was rougher. Ged had planted an orchard of fruit trees. He'd done this for her as a birthday present. She told him once that she loved the idea of picking an apple fresh from a tree.

They were short and round, more like big bushes, but laden with fruit. She looked at them and a terrible sense of despair swept over her. He was gone. There was no way out; it was pointless to run. She sat down under one of the sweet little trees and stroked its gnarled bark.

She was lightheaded; her thoughts meandered. Places she'd been with Ged. How she felt walking into a room with him beside her. It was like being surrounded by a force field that other people couldn't penetrate. Somehow, he created it around them. But all that was lost. She was lost. Then she saw Raoul walking towards her with two police officers. She hated Raoul.

Kristin sits in a wing chair which has been moved from the Drawing Room out onto the terrace. The house is a crime scene and is taped off. She feels disconnected from her body. Her mind is drifting.

They brought her back and wrapped her in a blanket. She didn't resist. Andreas brought her some hot tea. She didn't drink it.

A woman walks towards her. She comes and squats down beside Kristin's chair. 'I don't know if you remember me,' she says. 'DS Jo Boden. I came here before.'

Kristin nods. She has no idea who this person is. But it's best not to argue with them. That's the thing about cops, they can twist anything. Her mum told her that.

'I understand you're expecting,' says the cop. 'Perhaps you'd like us to contact your doctor, or we can find someone locally to come and check you over. See if everything's okay.'

How can everything be okay? What a stupid thing to say?

Kristin gazes at the woman; she looks familiar. She prefers cops to wear uniforms, then at least you know what they are.

The cop is waiting for an answer.

'I don't care,' says Kristin.

'Okay,' says the cop.

'What I want,' says Kristin, 'is for you to take me to jail and lock me up. Now.'

The woman stares at her. 'Okay,' she says again.

Why does she keep saying okay? This must be some kind of cop trick. They pretend to agree with you to shut you up.

'Before you say any more,' says the cop, 'I'm going to caution you.'

'I'm not going to say anymore,' says Kristin. 'I've got nothing to say. I just want you to take me in. Arrest me. Whatever. Now.'

'Kristin, this is for your own protection.'

That's a fucking lie!

Kristin looks at her nails. Small traces of his blood are clinging to the little stars. It's all she has left of him. She licks the nail on her thumb. She wants to taste him. A last taste of him.

Someone touches her arm.

They're stopping her! She can't lick her own nail?

The cop is speaking. It washes over her. She tries to imagine his face. But all she can see is that terrible gaping wound in his neck. She wishes he'd taken her with him. That would be better. Leaving her here on her own. That's the cruellest thing of all.

Ged!

'… do you understand what I've just said, Kristin?' says the cop.

Kristin nods.

'Why do I need to arrest you? Can you tell me?'

Why is she being so bloody dense?

'No,' says Kristin. 'No comment.' That's what her stepfather used to say to the police when they came around.

43

Deirdre Latham is making a shopping list. She's checking the salad drawer in the fridge, when her husband appears in the kitchen doorway.

'Are you off to golf?' she says.

'I've just seen the news,' he replies. 'Bit of a shocker.'

She's examining the cherry tomatoes. 'Well, darling, if you will spend your days checking your phone like a teenager, you'll get sucked in by that nonsense. The world will continue to turn, whether or not you pay attention to the latest atrocity.'

'Ged Sullivan's dead.'

Deirdre turns to face him. 'Good Lord! How?'

'Police are investigating. Sounds like murder.'

'Murder? Oh my God! Do you think Sophie knows?' She replaces the tomatoes and shuts the fridge door with a snap.

Roger shrugs. 'It's a news alert from the BBC. No details. They're saying his body was discovered this morning at his home in Newmarket.'

'We should call Sophie.'

'Hold your horses, Dee. And say what?'

Deirdre is rooting in her bag for her phone. 'Well, I don't know. Find out what's going on.'

'She and Ollie will be concerned for his sister. They may even be on their way to Newmarket.'

'But who do you think killed him?' Deirdre finds the phone, opens it and clicks on her daughter's number.

'Isn't hassling them for information a bit ghoulish?'

'I'm shocked by the news,' she says. 'How is that hassling? It's ringing.'

Roger can be too timid. He always worries about people's feelings. Doesn't want to upset them. She's not as pernickety.

If she's honest, she's excited. Some real life drama to break up their mundane routine. It's why she enjoys being a local councillor; the squabbles, the backstabbing, the secret deals.

Still, she's surprised when Sophie answers.

'Hey, Mum.' Her daughter's voice sounds flat and dejected.

'My God, we've seen the news about Ged.'

'Oh. It's out there then.'

'It's on the BBC. Are you all right, darling?'

Roger is tugging at her elbow. 'Put it on loudspeaker.' She can never remember how. He takes the phone off her. Presses the screen.

There's silence on the other end of the line. A background whooshing. Wind?

'Dad, here,' says Roger. 'You okay, Soph? Where are you?'

'We're in... Aldeburgh.'

Deirdre frowns and mouths, *Aldeburgh?*

'Sounds like you're outside. What are you up to?' says Roger. 'Having a weekend away?'

'Yeah, something like that. I'm on the beach.' Her voice is

lifeless and detached. This is not like their daughter at all. Sophie has always been a live-wire, full of energy, always on the go.

Deirdre and her husband exchange looks. She has a mushrooming sense of dread; an instinctual feeling that comes from nowhere and tells her that her child is in trouble.

She grabs the phone. 'Sophie, what's wrong? You sound a bit—'

'Mum, I've got to go. Ollie's coming back.'

'Where's he been?'

'To get a bacon sandwich from the cafe. I'll speak to you soon, okay?'

The line goes dead.

Deirdre turns to her husband. 'What the hell's going on? His brother-in-law's just been murdered, and they're sitting on the beach in Aldeburgh eating bacon sandwiches? And what did she mean? *It's out there then.* As if she already knew?'

Roger Latham is pondering. 'How far is it from Newmarket to Aldeburgh? Maybe forty or fifty miles.'

'Perhaps they're on their way there?' she says. 'Kristin must've called and told them.'

'Driving from London? No. London to Newmarket, you'd go north. Straight up the M11 towards Cambridge and turn off. Aldeburgh is due east, away from Newmarket in the other direction.

'What are you thinking, Roger?'

'I'm not sure. I reckon it's much more likely that they've come from Newmarket.'

'My God, you think they were there? Is that what you're saying?'

'I don't know. But that was a strange conversation. Sophie sounded upset.'

Deirdre can feel her temper rising. She slams her handbag on the kitchen counter.

'It's him, isn't it? He's done something. That bloody husband of hers.'

'You're jumping to conclusions, Dee.'

'Am I? She should never have married him. We both know that.'

'Ollie's not what we expected. But that doesn't make him a bad person,' says Roger.

Why does he always try to be so reasonable? It's maddening.

She folds her arms and spins around. It's impossible to keep still. She's seething.

'Oh, don't be so naïve,' she says. 'He saw Sophie, he saw her money, and he targeted her. What do we know about him? Nothing. He's a chancer. It's written all over him. She's too besotted to see it.'

'Deirdre, stop! This gets us nowhere.' His tone is sharp, and he's glaring at her. Roger rarely rebukes her like this.

She's taken aback. It's all too much.

She bursts into tears; she can't help it. 'I know my own daughter,' she wails. 'And she's in trouble. You can hear it in her voice. He's got her involved in something. She's scared. What are we going to do, Roger?'

He puts his arms round her and draws her into a hug. 'Calm down, darling. It'll be all right.'

He strokes her hair, but she pulls away from him.

'How will it be all right? We have to do something. What are we going to do?'

Panic is engulfing her.

'At the moment, I've no idea. But I'm thinking about it.'

'Well, think faster! This is awful.'

44

Ollie drives them down the coast. They head south, skirting round Ipswich on the A12. Sophie sits beside him; her body is stiff and her mind numb.

'Let's run through it again,' he says. He's calm and practical. Whatever emotions he has around what happened, he's packed them away.

'Point one,' he says. 'They will come, and they will come soon. We are shocked and horrified, of course we are. We've only just seen the news. Why?'

She sighs. This is like some stupid game she doesn't want to play. Long car journeys as a kid when her parents made them play I spy.

Why did she answer her mother's call? Stupid!

'Come on, Sophie,' he says. 'Answer the question.'

'We went to Aldeburgh and sat on the beach. Our phones ran out of charge.'

'Why did we go to Aldeburgh?'

'Because we were upset. We needed space to think.'

'Why were we upset?'

'We watched Ged get drunk and be horrible to his wife.

Kristin was in tears. We went to bed, but we could still hear them arguing in their room. We discussed it and decided our presence in the house was making things worse.'

'And?'

She looks across at him. This is a surreal nightmare, and she wants to wake up. Her husband is tutoring her on how to lie to the police.

'C'mon, babe,' he says. 'This is important.'

'We packed our bags and left in the middle of the night.'

'What time was it?'

'I'm not sure. It was late. We crept out. We didn't want them to hear us. They were still arguing.' She huffs. 'Ollie, are you sure this is going to stand up to scrutiny? What about the staff? And the chef?'

'They weren't in the house. They live in the stable block.'

'There must be CCTV everywhere.'

'Not inside the house. Kristin's paranoid about her privacy being violated. The CCTV on the gate will've recorded us leaving. But that doesn't contradict the story.'

'You sure?'

'Trust me. If we keep as close as possible to the timeline of actual events, they won't be able to pick holes in it. Detailed and plausible, that's the key.'

She glances at his profile. He's done this a lot. There's a confidence in his attitude. Or even arrogance. It gives her an uncomfortable feeling that he's so good at it.

'Okay,' he says. 'And what's the thing we did that we're worried about?'

'You wrote a note on the whiteboard in the kitchen. We were in a rush and we didn't know what else to do. And we assumed Kristin would see it and rub it off because Ged rarely goes into the kitchen.'

There's a sick irony in that.

'Why didn't I just send her a text?'

'Because Ged is so jealous and controlling. He makes her show him his phone.'

Ollie smiles. 'Actually, that part is true. Wouldn't surprise me if he didn't have a spy app on her phone, so he can monitor her. Read her texts, see who she calls. Everything.'

'If he could do it using an app, he wouldn't have to make her show him, would he?'

He shrugs. 'Well, who knows? A bloke like that, how does his mind work?'

Sophie looks at him. How can he be so blasé? She's queasy. The bacon sandwich was a mistake, but he insisted she ate it.

'This is crazy,' she says. 'Surely, we're pointing the finger at Kristin. Making it look like she did it. How can we let her take the blame?'

He doesn't reply. They drive on in silence. Then he indicates and pulls off the road into a lay-by. He turns the engine off and faces her. He takes her hand and kisses the fingertips.

'Listen to me, you did what you did. And I'm not criticising. But it leaves us in a tricky situation.'

'You think I don't know that! I know it's all my fault. But we can't do this to Kristin. It's terrible. We just can't.' The tears well.

'Then what do we do?'

'I don't know!'

Everything is spiralling out of control. The tears run down her cheeks.

He squeezes her hand.

'Sophie,' he says. 'Think about this. Kristin is an abused wife. He was a monster. She'll get the best lawyers in the business. The very best. The trial will be all over the media. She's famous, and she's pregnant. She acted to protect herself and her unborn child. Everyone will be on her side. And she'll walk. I promise you. She gets his fortune and her freedom. And we stay out of jail. It's the best result all round. Win-win.'

She stares at him. It sounds almost rational.

But it's mad.

How the hell did it come to this?

He smiles and opens the car door. 'Now I need a slash.' He gets out.

She watches him step into the bushes beside the road and pee.

Her phone vibrates. She glances at it. Her mother. Again.

Why did she even answer her mother's call? She's not sure she knows. Desperation, maybe?

All she wants is to go home, curl up on her parents' big old leather sofa, bury her face in one of the velvet cushions, and hide from the world.

45

By the time DS Boden gets back to the office, the place is crammed. Extra officers have been drafted in, plus more civilian analysts.

DCI Hepburn is due to brief the team.

Boden finds a complete stranger occupying her desk. He apologises and moves.

Prisha Chakravorty comes over. She's excited.

'Well, this is a surprise,' she says. 'Kristin Kelly killed her old man. Have you seen how many TV crews are outside?'

Boden has just handed Kristin over to the custody sergeant. She's being examined by the police doctor.

Throughout the drive back to Cambridge, Kristin sat in the back of the car beside Boden and didn't speak a word. She gazed out of the window. She seemed to have a serenity about her. At last, she was free of the man who'd abused her? Was that it? It made sense.

But Boden smiles at the young DC. 'I wouldn't jump to any conclusions,' she says.

'You don't think she did it?'

Hepburn strides into the room, and there's no opportunity to discuss it further. Tom Roscoe is behind him. They make a comic pair. Roscoe towers over the boss by almost a foot.

'Afternoon everyone,' says the DCI. 'For those of you who don't know me, I'm Alistair Hepburn and I'm the Senior Investigating Officer. Tom Roscoe is the deputy SIO.'

Roscoe smiles and nods. Boden finds him annoying, though she can't say why. He seems so determined to be nice.

'I'm sure it's obvious to you all that this is a high profile case,' says the DCI, 'which will attract a lot of scrutiny. For those of you who've not been in this situation before, it means that, outside of official press briefings, no one talks to the media. Ever. If they waylay you in the pub, offer to buy you a drink, you say nothing. This is important, and I won't tolerate any breaches.'

He pauses and lets his eye travel round the room to let the message sink in.

There's a certain amount of shuffling and shifting. They don't need to be told this is a big deal. Prisha is sitting up, back straight, hands folded in her lap, giving her full attention. Mackie is checking out one of the new analysts, who's young and nervous and pretty.

Boden has been here many times before. She lounges back in her chair and folds her arms. She scans Hepburn. He's suited and booted. A maroon silk tie. He knows this is the biggest case of his career so far, and woe betide anyone who messes it up for him.

His gaze settles on Boden.

'Right,' he says. 'Jo. Because of the case of the climate protester, you probably know the victim and his wife better than anyone. What do you think we've got here?'

Boden stands up. Heads swivel in her direction, but she

doesn't mind. Hepburn's not the only one who could get a career leg-up from this case.

'Well, sir,' she says. 'It's difficult to say at this stage. Sir Gerald Sullivan died in his kitchen. His throat was slashed. We're still looking for the murder weapon. His wife insisted we arrest her. She appears to be saying she did it, although she hasn't specifically confessed.'

'But we know, from her sister-in-law, Kristin was abused by her husband?'

'Yes, sir. She reckons Kristin was scared of him.'

'Could be she finally cracked, went for the knife? Now she's in shock. And overcome with guilt. Is that it?' says Hepburn.

'It could be,' says Boden. 'I'd say she's in shock. But Luke Cameron also threatened Sir Gerald over the death of Cary Rutherford. I don't think we should ignore that aspect.'

'Agreed.' says Hepburn. 'That's an obvious line of inquiry. And I am looking at how the Rutherford case and this one overlap.' He turns to Roscoe. 'What's your take on this Tom?'

Boden sits down. Mention Cameron, and she's abruptly dismissed. *He didn't get in touch with the Regional Counter Terrorism Unit then. That could come back to bite him.*

Roscoe is perched on a desk at the front, shoulders hunched. He doesn't want to make the boss look small. He straightens up.

'Yes, boss,' he says. 'You've put your finger on it. It's basically a domestic. Abused wife, who's pregnant, gets pushed over the edge, finds the nerve to fight back. We need to persuade her to talk to us. Jo has already built up a rapport with her. I think she's best placed to do it.'

He's smiling in her direction, and backing her up, which

is a surprise. But for all the nice-guy persona, Roscoe is a player.

'Okay,' says the DCI. 'Lots to do. Kevin is the HOLMES manager; he'll be issuing actions. Let's get on with it.'

Boden looks at Roscoe. He's still smiling. Should she be glad or suspicious? It's hard to tell. But she finds him rather smug.

46

Sophie lay awake for most of the night, but at least she was in her own bed. She didn't want to disturb Ollie. He never seems to have problems sleeping; howling gales, partying neighbours, nothing rouses him. As soon as his head touches the pillow, he's off.

At first light, she creeps out of bed and wanders into the main room. The polished oak floor is cool on her bare feet, and she realises that she's hot, almost feverish. Is she coming down with something?

She goes to the kitchen sink and pours herself a glass of cold water. She drinks half of it down in one go.

Wandering over to the windows, she peers out at the river. It's low tide, exposing a narrow ridge of grey sand littered with debris. She used to love wandering the Thames fore-shore. Weird things were always getting washed up. She wonders if there are many bodies.

A shiver runs through her. Too hot, now too cold. Ged's face is never far from her thoughts.

She's always had a temper. According to her parents, she

was prone to tantrums when she was little. Her brother, Nick, was, of course, the perfect baby and the perfect son.

But she's learned over the years to rein her anger in. At least, she thought she had. Okay, she could rant. But it was always verbal. She's never hit anyone. She and her brother scrapped as kids. But, once they were teenagers, he got bigger and stronger, and their father called time on that. Nick had to learn to be a gentleman and never raise his hand to a girl. She amused herself by trying to provoke him.

She turns and is surprised to find Ollie standing several meters away, watching her.

'Sorry,' he says. 'Didn't want to make you jump. You seem miles away. What are you thinking about?'

'My brother.'

Ollie chuckles. 'Well, it could come in handy, having a lawyer in the family.'

'He does commercial stuff, not crime.'

He's smiling at her, feet apart, hands on hips. This Alpha male stance reminds her of Ged. But he's wearing boxers and a T-shirt. A few days ago, this would've been a turn-on. All she would've seen was her gorgeous husband. Now she's not sure who she's looking at.

'Fancy a coffee?' he says.

She nods.

He walks into the kitchen area.

'How about some breakfast?' he says. 'I've got an early client, so I need to get going.'

She stares at him. 'Are we just going to carry on as normal? Go to work?'

'That's exactly what we're going to do.' He fills the reservoir of the coffeemaker.

'Shouldn't we contact Kristin? Isn't it suspicious if we don't?'

'Already done. I've left messages on her phone. She's not picking up. Plus several texts asking what's going on, is she okay? That sort of stuff.'

He's thought of everything. It gives Sophie a creepy sensation in the pit of her stomach.

'Granola and fruit?' he says.

'I'm not hungry.'

The doorbell rings. This makes her jump out of her skin.

'Who the hell's that at this hour?' she says.

He smiles. He's unruffled. 'I told you,' he says. 'It's what they do.'

'You think it's the police?'

He turns the coffeemaker on. It gurgles.

'Just stick to the story, Sophie. It's good that you're surprised. Makes you look more innocent.'

But she is innocent!

He walks towards the front door.

She's in an old pair of pyjamas, and she feels exposed. What if they want to search the flat? Her new pyjamas, the one's she took away with her, are bundled up in a plastic bag in the wardrobe. They're splattered with Ged Sullivan's blood. She tries not to panic.

A tall lanky man follows Ollie into the room, followed by a small woman.

'Sorry to disturb you at this hour, Mrs Harmon,' the man says. 'I'm DI Tom Roscoe and this is my colleague DC Chakravorty.'

'It's fine,' says Sophie. 'We saw the news. I presume this is about Ged. It's unbelievable. Terrible. I don't know what to say.'

She's gabbling. Speak slower!

'It's awful,' says Ollie. 'We're in shock. Can I offer you coffees?'

'No thanks,' says Roscoe. 'To be honest, I end up main-lining the stuff. But it smells delicious. You go ahead.'

'Won't you sit down,' says Sophie.

The two officers perch side by side on the sofa. He's so large his knees stick right out. She looks like a child beside him.

Sophie makes herself sit directly opposite them.

Act normal, as if it's a normal conversation.

'We wanted to talk to you, Mrs Harmon,' says Roscoe.

Sophie feels the blood draining from her face.

They know!

'It's about a conversation you had last week with my colleague DS Boden.'

Sophie is flummoxed. *Who the hell's Boden?*

'She and a colleague visited your coffee shop in Shoreditch,' he says with a smile.

'Oh,' says Sophie. 'Oh yes.'

That seems like another life.

'You talked to DS Boden about Kristin Sullivan's relationship with her husband. You said Kristin had told you some things about it that concerned you.'

Sophie's brain is in a spin.

What the hell did she say?'

'Well, yes,' she says. 'She indicated to me that Ged was very controlling. Into S and M, which she didn't like. And I got the impression she was scared of him.'

'Did she tell you he'd harmed her in any way?'

'Not in so many words.'

'Did you talk about her pregnancy?'

'Not then. But I'd had lunch with her a few days before. She said she hated being pregnant.'

Ollie places two mugs of coffee on the low glass table between her and the cops. Then he sits down beside her.

'I think I can help you with that, Inspector,' he says.

Roscoe nods. 'Okay.'

Ollie steeples his fingers. 'My sister knew she shouldn't be pregnant again. When she was much younger, she lost a baby. And there were complications. She was told that it would be dangerous for her to get pregnant again. But Ged wanted it. She found it hard to override him. He sent her to private doctors, who said it would be okay.'

Roscoe nods again. His sidekick has got out an iPad.

'You don't mind if we make notes?' he says.

'Of course not,' says Sophie. Her gaze drifts to her coffee. She wills herself to pick up the mug and take a sip.

'Let me get this clear,' says Roscoe. 'Your sister was being forced to go ahead with this pregnancy against her will? And against medical advice?'

The DC taps away.

'...may be taken down and given in evidence.'

A shiver runs up Sophie's spine. But they're not lying, not yet. This gives her confidence.

'The problem is,' she says, 'medical advice can be contradictory and confusing. Ged's doctors were telling her one thing, but she was frightened. Ollie and I were hoping to persuade her to see my gynaecologist and get a second opinion.'

At least this is true.

Ollie grabs her hand and smiles at her. 'My wife and I are hoping to get pregnant ourselves. And she has a very good gynaecologist, who we trust.'

Roscoe smiles.

'When did you last see your sister and her husband, Mr Harmon?'

The cop makes it sound so casual. Sophie's convinced her hand is shaking. The police must know they were there.

'Well,' says Ollie. 'Actually, we were just there. I've been trying to get in touch with my sister, but she's not answering. I'm worried about her.'

'She's in custody, I'm afraid.'

'What!' says Ollie. 'No! What happened? You think she did this?'

'Our investigation is in the very early stages, Mr Harmon.'

Sophie feels as if they've thumped her in the gut.

They've arrested Kristin!

Ollie anticipated it. He knew it would happen.

Her husband jumps up and strides round the room. He rakes his fingers through his hair. 'This is a nightmare,' he says. 'We should never have left. It had just been so awful. He hated us being there. Particularly me. Throughout dinner, he was picking at Kristin, criticising every little thing. Then we could hear them in their room arguing. We decided if we left it'd be better for her. That he'd stop. Now I wish to God, we'd stayed.' He puts his face in his hands.

Sophie is frozen. It seems as if the cops are analysing every word, every gesture. The woman says nothing, but her gaze is fixed on Sophie. It's unnerving.

Ollie removes his palms from his face and it's wet with tears.

How did he do that?

'When can I see her?' he says. 'I must see her.'

'She's still being questioned,' says Roscoe. 'Probably best if you speak to her lawyer.'

Ollie nods. He wipes his nose with the back of his hand, then he turns to Sophie. 'We'll get her through, babe. We'll get her through this, won't we?'

How is he such a good actor?

Sophie nods. She finds it impossible to speak.

'If you can take us through your movements that night,' says Roscoe. 'That would be helpful.'

47

Kristin spent the night in a police cell. Not that uncomfortable. It felt a bit like the pod in a hotel in Tokyo she once stayed in, when she was there on a job. She dozed on and off. Her thoughts drifted. This was the best place to be.

When she arrived, they took all her clothes. She was photographed, fingerprinted and DNA swabs were taken. Then they brought a doctor to see her. He was about Ged's age. He had salt and pepper grey hair and a reassuring smile; in some ways, he reminded her of Ged. He took her blood pressure and asked her some questions. She liked it when he held her wrist and checked her pulse. He was kind.

Ged!

A young policeman brought her tea and a sandwich in the evening. He kept staring at her; he was trying not to. It was like he wanted to ask if he could take a selfie with her. She wouldn't have minded. The tea was disgusting. She didn't even try the sandwich.

After the doctor, she'd spent what felt like hours in an interview room. The cop who'd brought her in wanted to ask her questions. This other girl arrived, who they said was the duty solicitor. She looked like she should still be at school. Kristin ignored them both. Said nothing. She didn't even bother with the no comment rigmarole. She stared at the wall opposite. It was grey and in need of a coat of paint. Pretty soon, she became familiar with all its marks and indentations.

Ged! So unfair.

There were cameras everywhere. She knew there were people watching her. Loads of them, probably. But she was used to that. She knew how to retreat inside her own head, to go to that place where she was physically present but not there. She'd taught herself this trick when she was a little kid. It's the only thing that had saved her from going crazy.

Eventually, they gave up and took her back to her cell. She curled up on the bunk and hugged her tummy. She never wanted to be pregnant. Hated the idea. She'd seen what it had done to her mother; being torn open to produce this thing, this squalling goblin. Kristin was five; the baby died in its cot. She can still see it, cold and waxy and stiff, like a scrunched up garden gnome.

But now this was Ged's baby; and it was all she had left of him. She thought about his daughters. Those bitches would be livid. This would confirm everything they'd always said about her. And they'd want the baby. But she'd fight them tooth and nail. This was her son. She'd never let them take him. If having him didn't kill her, she'd never let him go. He'd grow up big and strong, and he'd protect her. She'd call him Gerald after his father. Maybe Gerry for short.

There's a window high up in the wall of her cell. It allows a grey morning light to percolate into the tiny room. She tries to guess what kind of day it is outside. She can hear the noise of the traffic; they must be near a main road. Hooting, a couple of sirens.

She's registered the fact she's in Cambridge; she came here once to talk to this art history professor who was advising them on a painting they wanted to buy. Listening to him talk was magic. He knew so much. She'd walked around afterwards, full of envy. How different her life might've been if she'd come to study in a place like this. A couple of students stopped her and asked for a selfie. Seemed weird at the time; they wanted to be her, but she wanted to be them. People think models make loads of money. Another myth.

The door to her cell opens and the cop walks in. She has a different shirt on; yesterday it was blue, today pale mauve, which suits her colouring better.

'Morning,' the cop says. She holds out a bottle of mineral water. 'I hear you don't like our tea. But we need to keep you hydrated.'

Kristin takes the bottle. 'Thanks.' She is thirsty. She unscrews the cap and drinks. It's chilled, tastes good.

'What about some breakfast?' says the cop.

Kristin realises she's drunk half the bottle. She shakes her head. 'I don't eat carbs.'

The cop smiles. 'Yeah, the sandwiches here are grim. Tell you what, there's a really good place round the corner. They do lovely little breakfast bowls with yogurt and loads of fruit. We could get you one of those.'

It sounds tempting. 'If it's not too much trouble,' Kristin says.

'It's no problem. I'll send someone out. Would you like coffee too? They do excellent coffee. What sort do you like?'

'Black Americano?' says Kristin.

Why are they being so nice to her?

The cop taps on the door. Someone opens it. She steps outside and speaks to them. Then she comes back.

'All sorted,' she says. 'Shouldn't be long.'

It's awkward, the cop standing there and looking at her.

'What's your name?' says Kristin. If they told her before, she can't remember.

'Jo. Jo Boden.'

'I like today's shirt better than yesterday's. Better colour on you.'

Jo smiles. 'Present from my mum. She's good with colours. She's always on at me about what I wear. Thinks I'm scruffy.'

Kristin smiles. She wishes her mother had cared about what she wore. But there was never any money for clothes when she was growing up. And not much care either.

'We've had a phone call from your modelling agency,' Jo says. 'Julia DeMarco. She says she's your agent.'

Kristin nods. Her heart sinks.

Bloody Jules! What does she want?

The media must be screaming at her. Top model kills her husband. They'll want all the juicy details.

'It's not our policy to name people we've brought in for questioning,' says the cop. 'But there's a lot of media speculation going on, as you can imagine.'

Kristin gives her a rueful smile. 'Yeah, I'll bet. What does Jules want?'

'She's hired a lawyer for you. He's coming from London.'

Kristin takes a moment to digest this.

'Why?' She can't think of what else to say.

'I imagine they want to help you,' says Jo. 'Apply for bail, probably.'

'Bail?'

Jo nods.

No!

'I don't want bail. I just want to stay here.'

The cop is scanning her. She says nothing.

'What happened to the girl that was here yesterday?' says Kristin. 'I thought she was a lawyer.'

'She was the duty solicitor. This is a serious matter. We didn't want to question you without you having access to legal advice. You should have a solicitor present.'

'Okay. I want her, not him. It's up to me, isn't it?'

'Yes. But I would think that the lawyer your agent has hired is a top criminal specialist. He's probably far more experienced. And may be better placed to help you.'

Kristin stares at her nails. When she arrived and they put her in this sweatshirt and trackie bottoms, they scraped the dried blood out from under her nails. Some stars came off too. They put them in test tubes. Now the nails look dirty and disgusting. She wishes she could get them done. But no way they'll allow that. It's the price for staying here. Ragged nails.

Mum always dreamt of having her nails done. Couldn't afford it.

'Kristin,' says the cop. 'Why don't you want bail?'

'I don't want to talk about it!' she snaps.

Why can't they leave her alone?

She looks up at the cop. None of this is her fault. She seems quite nice. 'Sorry, I didn't mean to shout,' she says.

'It's okay. I'm just wondering—'

'I don't want to talk anymore. Please. If I have to have a lawyer, then I want her, the girl from yesterday. Not him. You said it's up to me. That's what I want.'

48

Sophie Latham sits at the end of one of the long tables in her office. Her laptop is open in front of her, but she stares out of the tall windows. The rooftops of Shoreditch are visible against a cloudy sky which is threatening rain.

She realises her assistant, Leanne, is hovering.

'Can I get you anything?' Leanne says. 'Salad? Sandwich?'

It must be lunchtime. How long has she been sitting there, paralysed, gazing out of the window?

Leanne has a concerned expression.

Does she look that bad? Get a grip!

She forces a smile. Her appetite has deserted her and she's queasy, a physical sense of nausea mixed with suppressed dread.

When the cops left, she felt relief. They told their story and seem to have got away with it.

Is this who she is now? A liar. A bad person. A criminal?

But the sense of respite didn't last.

Ollie presented her with a bowl of granola before he left.

She tried to eat and couldn't. But by then, he'd gone. He didn't want to be late for his client, he said.

She followed his instructions. She showered and dressed on automatic pilot. And went to work.

She looks up at Leanne. 'My stomach's a bit upset,' she says. 'I'll pass on lunch.'

Leanne hesitates, then she says, 'Have you seen the stuff online about Kristin Kelly?'

Sophie blinks. Leanne was there when Kristin visited. Of course she knows the connection. They all do.

'What are they saying?' says Sophie. She doesn't want to ask. She certainly doesn't want to know. But she can't help herself.

'Depends who you believe,' says Leanne. 'She killed her husband and the police have arrested her. But other places, they're saying it's all a set-up. Kirstin is innocent, and Ged was murdered as payback for the climate protester he killed.'

Sophie's head is reeling.

'Oh,' she says. 'Well, I don't know the truth.'

The lie catches in her throat. But she's going to have to repeat it. A lot. And to a lot of people.

At that moment, her business partner, Claire, walks into the office.

She met Claire when she was twenty-four. They spent six months travelling and working their way around Australia and New Zealand together. And in that time, they came up with a fledgling plan for their business. Claire is her best friend. They had five years building the business before Claire got pregnant. She followed that by marriage to Danny, an ecologist whose primary ambition in life was to live in the country. Thanks to the success of the business, Claire bought a small farm in Sussex. She has her development kitchen down there, and Danny keeps bees and makes mead. They now have three kids and a menagerie of goats, hens and dogs. Claire only comes to London when she has to.

'Hey, hon,' she says, approaching Sophie with arms outstretched. 'You look like shit.'

Sophie's lip quivers and she bursts into tears.

'Aw, sweetheart.' Claire leans over and envelopes her in a hug.

Claire is as round and soft and squidgy as her cakes. She has settled into the role of earth mother, and it suits her. Sophie has struggled over the years not to envy her happiness.

Sophie says, 'I wasn't expecting you today.'

'I follow the news. We're not Hobbits. What the hell's going on? Ollie must be going spare.'

She nods.

Claire shakes her head. 'It says online that bastard Sullivan abused her, which I can believe, after what he did to the climate protester. I'm assuming she finally snapped. Have you got her a lawyer?'

A lawyer? They've never even discussed that. Yet, it's obvious.

'Ollie's on it,' Sophie says.

More lies.

Claire sits down beside her and takes her hand. 'What about you? How are you doing?'

She wants to tell her, tell her everything, just blurt it out. Claire would get it; she'd understand how something like this could've happened. *She knows what happened back in Sydney, and why Sophie had to defend herself.*

But they're not alone. Leanne is at the adjacent table. The marketing manager is across the room, staring at his laptop and pretending not to listen.

Her phone buzzes. She glances at it, hoping, but also apprehensive that it's Ollie.

An unfamiliar name comes up. And yet it must be in her address book, which is puzzling.

On impulse, she answers.

'Hello,' she says.

'Hi Sophie. It's Jake Evans.'

Her mind is blank.

Jake Evans?

He must twig from the silence that she doesn't recognise him.

'From Fenton Carter. The estate agents.'

'Oh, sorry Jake. I'm swamped today. Head like a sieve.'

'No problem at all. Well, this might cheer you up. I've got an excellent offer for you.'

'Offer?'

Offer for what?

'On your place in Hackney. I thought that because you'd halted the renovation half way, it might be a problem. I told your husband that when he got in touch—'

'When did he get in touch?'

'This morning. First thing.'

'My husband called you this morning and said we wanted to sell?'

'Yeah. After I talked to him, I remembered the other couple. They wanted the property too. When I sold it to you, they were hacked off that they'd lost out. I called them this morning, after I spoke to Ollie again, and they made me an offer right away.'

Spoke to Ollie again?

She feels giddy.

'You're going to be pleased. If you throw in all the plans

from your architect, they're willing to go to two point two. I confess, I was surprised.'

Not as surprised as Sophie. She's aware of Claire watching her and listening in.

'Two point two million?' she says.

'Yep, they'll take it as it stands. By my reckoning you'll walk away with close to half a mil profit.'

She shivers. Then a wave of heat and nausea sweeps over her.

Get rid of him!

'Yeah, thanks Jake,' she says. 'I need to speak to Ollie. And get back to you.'

'No problem.'

Sophie hangs up. Claire is scanning her. 'You okay? You never said you were selling the house.'

Just tell her. Tell her everything.

Sophie stands up and staggers. 'I need to get to the loo. I'm going to be sick.'

49

The bottle of wine on the coffee table is almost empty. Sophie swills the dregs in her glass, drinks them down in a single gulp, picks up the bottle, and pours out the rest.

Outside, the light is fading; a chilly autumn evening of encroaching darkness. It matches her mood.

She took a cab home from the office, walked through the front door, went straight to the fridge and grabbed the wine.

Now she's waiting. She's not sure for what. For her husband to come home? She's called, texted, but, true to form, Ollie is not answering. She's wondering about that too.

Getting drunk in these circumstances is not the best decision she's ever made. She's well aware of that. But she couldn't feel anymore wretched than she does.

After Jake Evans's call, she was quite abrupt with Claire. Came up with a lie. She'd picked up some tummy bug and needed to get home. Claire was worried and offered to come with her. But she fobbed off her friend and fled.

This is who she is now, a person who lies to her best friend.

She hears his key in the lock. Although she's expecting it, she's startled.

He strolls in and dumps his kit bag.

'Why are you sitting in the dark?' he says.

She doesn't answer. She's been churning it over in her mind, what she'll say, the questions she'll ask. But she's immobilised.

He turns on a lamp and scans her. He glances at the bottle.

'Did you leave any for me?'

She shakes her head.

He takes a glass from the cupboard and a bottle of red from the wine rack. He unscrews the top and holds it up.

'Want a refill?'

She manages to speak. 'Think I've drunk enough.'

He pours himself a glass. 'And has it helped?'

He's so cold. So disdainful. Why?

'Not really,' she says.

'Sophie, what's done is done. You've got to pull yourself together and move on.'

He makes it sound like a minor upset; an argument at work, a business pitch that didn't go well.

'Jake Evans called me this afternoon. Remember him? The estate agent.'

Ollie takes a mouthful of wine. He savours it.

He sighs.

'Of course I remember him.'

He walks across the room and settles on the opposite sofa. He unlaces his trainers, pulls them off, and peels off his socks.

She watches him. He's got into the habit of doing this as soon as he comes home. He prefers to be barefoot. But he leaves his shoes and his sweaty, smelly socks on the floor.

Does he expect her to pick up after him? It's a small thing, but it niggles her.

He stares at his wine and frowns. 'I've been meaning to talk to you about the house.'

'When, Ollie?' she says. 'When were you planning to do that?'

'We need an exit strategy.'

'An exit strategy?'

He sighs again. 'Okay, I'm going to come clean with you. I never thought that house was a good idea.'

'Yeah, I've figured that out. I'm not stupid. You told me all that stuff about crappy materials and what a terrible job they were doing. Is any of that even true?'

He's avoiding her gaze. He's irritated.

'Why do you want to live in Hackney?' he says. 'It's a dump.'

'Why didn't you tell me that's what you thought?'

'It was hard. Your money. You call the shots. Anyway, it's all irrelevant now.'

'Irrelevant how?'

'Well, I don't know how much cash you can lay your hands on, but we need to put as much as possible in an offshore account. The money from the house will help. I talked to Jake too. Told him we'd only accept the offer if they moved quickly. He reckons he can get an exchange of contracts by next week. But two point two mil is a start.'

She stares at him. This is unreal, a nightmare she can't wake from.

'What are you saying? We need to leave the country?'

'Hopefully not. But it's best to be prepared.'

Prepared for what?

He's fingering his toes, cleaning between them, picking away at the dried skin. It's disgusting.

'Do you have to do that in here?' she says.

He looks up at her and chuckles. 'Where would you prefer me to do it?'

'I don't know,' she says. 'In the bathroom?'

He laughs. 'I've been on my bloody feet all day. Dragging fat slobs, who make too much money, round the bloody gym. I'm sorry if my habits offend your delicate sensibilities, love.'

Love?

The sarcasm in his voice is like a smack in the face. Why is he using that tone with her? The tears well up.

Pissed and tearful; it's pathetic. Stop it!

She swallows them down.

'I can't leave the country,' she says. 'And I don't want to. What about the business?'

'Sell your share. Claire might buy you out. Tell her you've got itchy feet, want to go travelling again.'

'She'll know that's not true.'

'You're a good blagger. I'm sure you can convince her.'

He's smiling at her, but there's no warmth in his eyes. She's always loved those eyes; icy blue. But now they look aloof and forbidding.

She stands up. Her heads swims. She staggers. A whole bottle of white wine was a bad idea.

'You're pissed,' he says. 'You should eat something. I'll order a takeaway. What do you fancy?'

'I need to go to the bathroom,' she says.

'I fancy Chinese. Is that all right?'

'Whatever.'

It takes all her concentration to weave her way round the furniture and across the room towards the hall. She wonders if she'll make it.

Concentrate! Don't puke!

She pushes open the bathroom door. Her phone is slotted

in her jeans pocket and she feels it buzz. She pulls it out. It's her dad. She sits down on the closed toilet seat. Stares at the phone.

They've been calling all afternoon. Mostly her mother.

She accepts the call. 'Dad!' she says. 'Oh, Dad. I need help!' Her chin trembles and the tears flow.

'My God, Sophie,' says her father. 'What's going on? What's happened?'

From nowhere, Ollie is looming over her, and she doesn't get a chance to say more. He grabs the phone from her and hangs up.

'You stupid bitch. What the hell do you think you're doing?' he says.

'I can't do this!' she sobs. 'I just want to talk to my dad.'

'And say what? You can't tell them about this. Ever.'

She crying now, wailing like a small child. Tears and snot drip from her face.

'All I did was defend myself! It wasn't my fault. You killed him. You just cut his throat, like he was an animal. It's not my fault. I'm not a murderer.'

This is the truth.

She's said it. This is what she's been thinking. He killed Ged, not her. She's not a murderer. His death is not down to her. She wanted to call for help. Get an ambulance.

He looms over her, hands on hips. He shakes his head and huffs.

'Not your fault? You started it. You and your bloody temper. He's a bastard. You knew that. But you thought you could handle him. Cause no one scares big, tough, feminist Sophie Latham, do they? She never backs down. And you lost it. You lost it completely.'

His voice drips sarcasm.

Why doesn't he understand?

'It wasn't like that.'

'Wasn't it? The truth hurts. You're arrogant and you can't control your temper. You put me in an impossible situation.'

He's supposed to be on her side.

'I didn't ask you to kill him!'

'You gave me no choice. I had to clean up your mess. I did it to protect you.'

Why doesn't it feel like that?

He's scowling at her. His jaw is set.

'What do you think is going to happen here?' he says. 'You think you can throw me under the bus? We'll both be charged with murder. They call it joint enterprise. That's a life sentence. For both of us. Maybe they'll let you out on licence in about fifteen years. You'll be in your mid-fifties. No kids, no business. Nothing. The life you have, all this, it'll be gone. Is that what you want?'

She stares at him.

How does he know all this legal stuff? Joint enterprise?

The answer's obvious. *He's been in trouble like this before.*

He folds his arms and glares at her. 'Now you want to go crying to your daddy. Like the spoilt little bitch you are. He can't save you from this. The only person who can save you is me. And that's what I'm trying to do.'

He walks out of the bathroom.

She stands up. Her legs are wobbly. But she has to get out of there, call her parents, get help. Her dad will know what to do.

She staggers down the hall towards the front door, lurching against the wall. She's very drunk.

His voice drifts towards her from the kitchen area. She can't see him.

'You walk out that door, and go blabbing to your parents,

then you're on your own. I mean it, Sophie. You'll take the rap for this, not me. I'll make sure of it.'

He's threatening her!

Her head is spinning. She slumps forward onto the floor. She's going to be sick. There's nothing she can do.

50

A second after she wakes, Sophie is aware of a thumping headache. She remembers being sick in the hall; then it's a blank. She's in her bra and pants. Ollie must've put her to bed. There's no sign of him. She peers at the clock. It's early.

Her mouth is like sandpaper. She finds a glass of water on her bedside table and downs half of it in rapid gulps. Movement is painful, and her head throbs. She gets out of bed and staggers to the en suite bathroom. They keep painkillers in the cabinet, but she discovers the packet is empty.

She avoids looking at herself in the mirror. She doesn't want to know how bad she looks.

How did her life turn into this shitshow?

There will be more paracetamol in the kitchen. She pulls a bathrobe off the back of the door and puts it on.

Ollie is seated at the kitchen counter with a coffee and a microwaved pastry. He smiles at her.

Cold eyes. Why has she never noticed before?

'I can guess how you're feeling,' he says. 'Sit down, I'll get you something.'

She settles on a stool. At least the room isn't spinning.

He gets some tablets from a drawer, lifts a glass from the dishwasher and fills it with water.

She glances towards the hall and front door. There's a faint odour of cleaning products.

'I'm sorry,' she says. 'Was it gross?'

He puts the glass in front of her and shrugs. 'Get this down you. You need to hydrate.'

He opens the packet of tablets and pops two out of the blister pack.

She takes them obediently and drinks some water.

He threatened her. She remembers that.

He sips his coffee and scans her. 'Mind if I use your laptop? I'll need the password.'

It's already on the counter and out of its sleeve.

That's what he's doing. Waiting for her to wake up.

She nods. 'Okay.' She doesn't have the strength to question him.

'Thanks,' he says. 'And I'll need all the passwords for your bank accounts, and also your phone.'

She stares at him. 'What? Why?'

'I told you. We need to get some funds offshore.'

He makes it sound like he wants to borrow a card to pop to the shops.

'No,' she says. 'I need to think about that.'

'Don't you trust me?'

'Last night, you threatened me.'

He sighs. 'Last night, you were drunk and being extremely silly.'

'Ollie, you frightened me.'

'Yeah, I had to. To stop you blabbing to your bloody family.'

Maybe he's right.

They stare at one another. Her head's pounding. She can't think straight.

'I'm your husband, but you don't trust me. Is that it?'

'It's not that—'

'What is it, then? Given what I've just done to protect you.'

That again! He blames her.

'Moving money,' she says. 'Have you thought this through? It's not that easy.'

He shrugs. 'I'm meeting a mate of mine later this morning. He's going to help me.'

'Well, who the hell is he?'

'Used to be a client. He works in financial services. He knows all about this. Moving cash.'

'You can't just go to some random bloke you used to train in the gym.'

'I told you, he's more than that. He's a mate.'

His arms are folded. He has a stubborn frown.

She sighs.

'This is ridiculous. What are we even doing? Going to some dodgy bloke to move money abroad?'

'Dodgy? What're you going to do, Sophie? Phone up your accountant and say I need to shift all this money into untraceable foreign accounts? As quickly as you can mange it, thanks.'

'No, but I need to do some research.'

He laughs, but the tone is bitter. 'Research? I've already said, I've got a mate who can help us.'

'Let's not do anything rash.'

He shakes his head, as if dealing with an awkward child. 'What's your plan, then? Let's hear it.'

'I don't know. I—'

The doorbell rings. They both start.

He gives a cynical chuckle and checks his watch. 'Bright and early again. That's the old bill for you. What were you saying about not needing to panic?'

Sophie swallows down the bile rising in her throat. She forces herself to cross the room towards the front door. She won't be shanghaied, not by her husband or anyone else. It takes all her willpower to track a steady course.

She reaches the front door, takes a steadying breath, and opens it.

Her brother, Nick, is standing beaming at her. He holds up a paper bag. 'Sorry it's stupidly early. But I brought bagels.'

She wants to fall into his arms and sob. But she's aware of her husband keeping an eye on her from down the hall.

'Hey, Nick,' she says. 'To what do we owe the pleasure?'

Her brother rarely came round before she got married. Since then, never.

He follows her into the flat. 'Got a case conference nearby,' he says. 'Thought it was time I checked you guys out.'

Ollie is standing in the kitchen area, hands on hips. His look is hard and unreadable.

But Nick smiles at him. 'How's it going, mate? Has she driven you crazy yet?'

Ollie smiles back. 'I expect you want a coffee to go with those.'

'Cheers,' says Nick. 'That'd be great.'

Sophie gazes at her big little brother. She's never been so glad to see him in her entire life.

51

Kristin is drifting. Her mind coasts in the eerie zone between waking and sleeping. She wishes she could stay like this forever. Then she remembers. The sticky puddle of blood, and him lying there. He wouldn't move. The pain of it catches in her throat producing a sob.

Ged!

She sits up.

The walls are matt grey; it's a police cell. She's been here for a second night.

She refused to see the lawyer that Jules sent. Told them she didn't want bail.

Her heart thuds in her chest. She rests her hand on her belly. But she's all right. They're both all right, and in the best place. She must focus on her baby now, on taking care of him.

She takes some deep breaths. When she's nervy and worried, this helps. She loves yoga; she does loads of online classes. It's got her through some bad times.

But this?

Her eyes close and she settles on her breathing.

Minutes pass. It's impossible to concentrate.

His face! His neck carved open like a piece of raw meat!

She wants to scream.

No! No screaming. Press the nails into the palm. Hard!

She's doing this when the lock on the cell door clanks.

Kristin opens her eyes.

The cop walks into the cell.

Jo something? She can never remember the name.

The cop's holding a small paper carrier bag.

'Morning,' she says. 'Got you another breakfast pot. Quinoa porridge with fruit and coconut yogurt.' She lifts it out of the bag and offers it to Kristin.

Kristin takes it. It's a relief to be distracted from the horrors in her head.

'Thank you,' she says.

'How did you sleep?'

'Okay. Baby was kicking a bit.'

Gerry. His name's Gerry.

'Well, that's good,' says the cop. She has a nice smile. She seems like a girl you could be friends with if she wasn't a cop. But she folds her arms and leans on the door jamb, like she plans to hang around.

Kristin rests one hand on her belly. He's there, and his presence gives her confidence.

Take care. Cops can be tricky.

'I've told you already,' she says. 'I don't want to speak about what happened.'

That's a door in her mind that must remain shut. She has no choice. Priorities. *Gerry.*

'Oh, I'm not here to ask you questions,' says the cop. 'That all has to be done formally, with a solicitor. I just want to make sure you're all right.'

Kristin nods. 'Thank you.'

'In my job,' says the cop, 'you see people when terrible things have happened in their lives. And it makes you realise how easily things can go wrong. We're all more vulnerable than we think. Particularly as women.'

Kristin opens the breakfast pot. 'Are you married?' she says.

The cop shakes her head.

'Do you mind me asking?'

'Not at all,' says the cop. 'I haven't been in Cambridge long. Came for the job. I've made a few friends, but I'm not seeing anyone.'

'Shouldn't have thought you were short of offers,' says Kristin. 'You're very good looking.'

Or would be if she made an effort, did something about her hair, and put on some make-up. But Kristin doesn't want to be rude.

The cop chuckles. 'I don't know about that. Most blokes run a mile when I tell them what I do. How's your coffee?'

Kristin peels the top off the cup. The aroma rises.

'Smells good,' she says.

'The place we get it is round the corner. They're over the moon. They've got a queue of reporters and media crews in and out. You must've tripled their turnover for them.'

Kristin smiles. 'They're all still here because of me?'

'Oh yes. They certainly are. The power of celebrity. I imagine that must be pretty difficult for you sometimes.'

Kristin sips her coffee. 'You get used to it. They build you up so they can knock you down, that's what Ged says.'

Ged says!

It hits her and brings a lump to her throat. Her life with him is in the past. She doesn't know him anymore. She knew him. He's gone.

The tears well in her eyes.

How will she survive without him?

'Must be hard, just walking down the street,' says the cop.

Concentrate. Don't cry.

'Used to be,' she says. 'But once I got married, he protected me. Kept the paps at bay. I felt safe.'

'Who are you scared of now, Kristin?' says the cop.

This comes out of left field.

How does she know? Bloody cops! You can never trust them.

'Who says I'm scared of anyone,' she snaps.

'Sorry,' says the cop. 'I don't mean to upset you. I just get a feeling. People always trying to get to you. These hoards of reporters outside. I can see you need protection.'

Now the tears won't stop.

'It's not fair,' she sobs. 'Ged did nothing wrong, but he was always getting blamed! You don't know what it was like!'

The cop says nothing.

'And bloody Raoul, he's a psycho. Ged wanted to sack him, but he couldn't. And that night he was just worried about the horses. And what Raoul might do. Ged did nothing wrong. Why does no one believe that?'

The cop shrugs, pulls a tissue from her pocket and hands it to Kristin.

She dabs her eyes and struggles to compose herself. 'Sorry. I must look a fright.'

'No,' says the cop. 'You just look like you're upset. And you're entitled to be, don't you think?'

Kristin nods.

That's true, for sure!

She feels desolate and powerless. She blows her nose and stares at the coffee, which is going cold.

The cop sits down beside her on the bunk. Not too close, but near enough to be comforting. For several moments, neither speaks.

'Kristin, are you scared of Raoul? Are you hiding from him?'

Her lip trembles. She tries to focus.

Hiding? She's done that her whole life.

Random thoughts are spinning in her head.

Hold it together!

'I dunno,' she says.

'Well,' the cop says. 'Strikes me you were quite happy with Ged.'

Were! There it is again. Like a knife in the heart. He's gone!

Kristin's tears brim over. She can't help it. 'He kept me safe,' she says.

'Sounds to me like he loved you.'

'Yes! He did. Wasn't perfect, but he was a good husband. He never once raised his hand to me. Not once! And he never would.'

He didn't need to.

'And my guess is,' says the cop, 'that you never would've harmed him. You had no reason.'

She dips her head and shakes it.

'No,' she whispers.

She places her palm over her belly.

Gerry.

They've got it sussed. This won't work.

'You don't need to be scared,' says the cop. 'We can do something about Raoul. And I don't think your baby should be born in prison, do you?'

They've won.

Kristin sighs. 'I just want to be somewhere safe and peaceful.'

'Trust me, jails are neither of those things. And I doubt they serve quinoa porridge.'

Kristin smiles at the cop. 'Probably not.'

52

Nick Latham sits on a high back stool at their kitchen counter. Sophie is opposite him. She's doing her best to appear normal, but it's a struggle.

The bagels are tasty; smoked salmon and cream cheese. It's the first food she's consumed for twenty-four hours. She's hoping it won't come straight back up.

Ollie continues to stand. He sips his coffee and watches. It's clear he has no intention of letting her out of his sight.

He thinks she'll blab to Nick.

If she gets the chance, will she?

Nick is making conversation. But he's scanning his sister. Growing up, they were always scrapping. But she knows that if she's in trouble, he's there for her.

Could she be in any more trouble than this?

'I'd love a place round here,' he says. 'I hate the morning commute in. Sweaty packed trains. Never get a seat, but the season ticket still costs an arm and a leg. But, y'know, you settle down, have kids, you have to compromise.'

'Where you live is nice,' says Sophie. 'I like Hertfordshire.'

Nick chuckles. 'Not sure I do. But it all becomes about catchment areas and good schools. Ava isn't even four, but you have to get them into the right playgroup for the right nursery then the right school.'

'Sounds complicated,' says Ollie.

Sophie shoots her husband a look. There's an implacability about him she's never noticed before. He's going through the motions, but he's totally detached.

Has he always been like this? Is he like this with her?

'You don't know the half of it, mate,' says Nick. 'You've got it all to come.'

Ollie grins. 'Yeah, I know.'

He's playing a game. That's what this is to him.

'But you guys are sticking with Hackney,' says Nick. 'That place'll be amazing once it's done.'

'We hope so,' says Ollie.

He lies with such ease.

Nick turns to his sister. 'You're quiet, Soph. It's not like you. Night on the tiles?'

'No, but I had a bit to drink. Can't hack it anymore. My head's killing me this morning.'

'You look rough,' says her brother. He sighs. 'Obviously, I've seen the news. Tough time for you, Ollie. Feel for you, mate.'

'Yeah, well, it is what it is,' says Ollie. He turns away.

He's pretending to be upset. But he's not!

'I don't know what I'd do if my sister got arrested for murder,' says Nick.

The remark hangs in the air. The irony is not lost on Sophie.

She stares at her half-eaten bagel. There's a moment of silence.

'You're in the right business to help her,' says Ollie. 'Unlike me.'

'Well, I saw on the news she's got Charles Parsons representing her. Top drawer criminal specialist. She can't do much better than him.'

'We're confident he'll do the business,' says Ollie.

'Have you talked to him?'

'Only on the phone,' says Ollie.

Is this true? He hasn't mentioned it.

Her husband puts his cup down. 'Kristin's agent, Julia DeMarco, is organising everything. She's the best person to deal with the press and all that. She's keeping me posted.'

He hasn't mentioned that either.

'It goes without saying,' says Nick. 'If there's anything I can do to support you guys.'

'We're trying to carry on as normal,' says Ollie.

'Sensible.'

'I won't deny it's stressful,' says Ollie. 'Which is why we had a few too many drinks last night.'

'Yeah,' says Nick, studying his sister. 'Think you freaked Dad out last night. He says you hung up the phone on him.'

'She was in the bathroom,' says Ollie.

'Being sick,' Sophie says. At least that's not a lie.

'Truth is,' says Ollie, 'she dropped her phone down the toilet.'

'What a pain!' says Nick. 'Has it survived?'

'Not sure,' says Ollie. 'We hope so. But perhaps you can reassure your dad. Without saying too much about the drunken bit.'

Nick looks directly at Sophie. 'Oh, I will,' he says.

She can't hold his gaze.

'I need to get showered,' she says. 'Get to work.'

Nick stands up. 'Yeah, I should go.' Abruptly, he pulls his

sister into a hug and squeezes her. 'Glad to see you're all right,' he says.

'Yeah, I'm fine. Don't be late for your meeting.'

He nods and smiles.

Was the meeting an excuse?

Ollie escorts him to the door. And he disappears.

Sophie's heart sinks. She stares out of the window.

Ollie returns to the kitchen.

'Well, that was all unnecessary, wasn't it?' he says.

She turns to face him. 'What? I'm under surveillance now, 24/7?'

He comes over and grasps her by the shoulders. 'Don't be silly. Of course you're not. I was just trying to save you from yourself. You can't tell them, babe. However much you want to. You may feel better for about thirty seconds. Then what? What will they do when they know? Do you want to put that burden on them?'

He's right.

'No, of course not.'

He scoops her hair out of her eyes with his finger and smiles at her.

Here's the old Ollie. Is he back?

'You may not think so,' he says, 'but I'm on your side. And you have to trust me. We'll get through this together.'

'Do you love me, Ol?' she says. She feels pathetic.

'Of course I do. I think if any man's proved that, I have.'

She gazes at him. He's smiling at her. But those icy blue eyes are so cold.

53

Jo Boden stands in front of DCI Hepburn's desk.

'She described Raoul Kemp as a psycho, boss. Said Sullivan wanted to sack him.'

Hepburn sighs, turning his pen over end to end.

Tom Roscoe is lounging on a filing cabinet. It seems to Boden that he's always draping himself over the furniture. When he stands up straight, he's just too tall.

The boss swivels his desk chair. 'What are we saying? The two cases are linked. Protesters break in, Kemp bludgeons Cary Rutherford, then somehow he forces Kobe Jackson to take the rap. Sullivan finds out. Threatens to expose him. Kemp slits Ged's throat.'

He glances at Roscoe.

'It's one possibility,' says Roscoe. 'But I agree with Jo. We're barking up the wrong tree with Kristin Sullivan.'

'The other unknown quantity,' says Boden. 'is the brother and sister-in-law. They left in the middle of the night. And it was them that convinced us that Sullivan abused his wife. Their version of the Sullivan marriage and Kristin's don't exactly tally. But now he's dead, Kristin could be in some sort of denial. Or she's complicit in some way and now she's feeling guilty.'

Hepburn steeples his fingers. 'What motive would they have for killing Sullivan?'

'Perhaps they think they're protecting Kristin?' says Roscoe. 'The brother seemed quite upset about Kristin's pregnancy. Claims it's against medical advice and is dangerous to her.'

Boden chips in. 'What if the Sullivan marriage was coercive to a degree, though not physically violent? But brother and sister-in-law believed she was in danger because of the pregnancy.'

'And of course, there's a lot of money here,' says Roscoe. 'Sullivan's mega rich. Don't know what sort of pre-nup they might've had, but Kristin probably stands to inherit quite a bit on his death. Divorce him, she'd get nothing.'

'Pre-meditated or a row that got out of hand?' says the DCI.

'I'd say the latter, boss,' says Boden.

'When do we get the results of the post mortem?'

'Should be with us later this morning,' says Roscoe. 'Might give us a better timeline. We know from the security camera on the gate that the brother and sister-in-law left at ten to four.'

'Okay,' says Hepburn. 'Find Raoul Kemp. Let's release Kristin Sullivan under investigation. At least that'll get the media circus off our doorstep. But you said, Jo, you think she could be complicit. Why?'

Boden shrugs. 'She's scared? She put herself in a jail cell to hide. Why? Because she knows who did it?'

54

Sophie lets her gaze roam around the open plan office. This is all down to her. This is something she's created. She and Claire are partners, but she provided the dynamism and the vision and the organisation that built this business. Claire is brilliant in the kitchen, but Sophie makes it all work.

Now her whole life is teetering on the edge of the abyss. Ollie says she has to persuade Claire to buy her out. They need cash and fast. But where will they run to? She's not sure she even wants to try.

She is heartsick at her own stupidity. How on earth did she allow herself to get in a row with Ged Sullivan? The fool-hardiness only matched the absurdity of it. He baited her. Of course he did. That's the kind of bloke he was. But she's dealt with far worse in her life. Men who've called her ugly, and tried to mock or shame her. Water off a duck's back.

No. It always hurts.

Then there was what happened in Australia. How many times has she told herself to forget it and move on? But she can't. It festers deep inside her, like a sore that won't heal. Oozing through her subconscious and poisoning her thoughts.

She was in a backpackers' bar in Sydney and someone spiked her drink. She woke up in the alley behind the bar. Never even saw his face. But her body hurt, and it was clear she'd been raped. Friends told her there was no point going to the police. She went to the bar owner and asked about CCTV, but they were surly and unhelpful. To them, she was just another stupid girl who couldn't hold her booze.

Claire took her to a special clinic; they checked she wasn't pregnant. She was also tested for HIV and other sexually transmitted diseases. They came up negative, but she still felt violated and unclean. She came home soon afterwards, but never told her parents. The only person who knows about it is Claire. Since then, she's never spoken of it.

Her dirty secret.

And she knows why. She's ashamed of her own naivety. Her stupidity and arrogance. She thought she was in the driving seat and could live life on her terms.

How easily he duped her. A few drops of clear liquid.

The pain of it, the shame of it; she knows these feelings will never leave her. Claire tried to persuade her to do therapy. But what would be the point? Rehashing it? Why? She would never forgive him, her anonymous assailant. And she swore no man would ever trick her or lay a hand on her again.

Never. She'd always fight back.

Since then she's developed a weather eye for danger. She looks over her shoulder, takes a cab home instead of walking, avoids dating apps. As a result, she's never met anyone. She's led the life of an independent woman; career-focused, always busy, but often lonely. That's what it was like until she met Ollie.

The moment she saw him, she knew he was the genuine article. Shy. Funny but self-deprecating. He was made for her.

Did she really get that wrong?

But who is Ollie Harmon? He's not the man she thought he was. What if Ged's slurs were true?

Doubts and fears slither round in her head, like a nest of vipers. Her judgement is shot. She has no idea what to do next.

Leanne is watching her from across the office, and she realises that she's been doing nothing and staring into space for some time. She clicks her laptop on and tries to look busy. She still has a business to run, though it's hard to see where she'll be going with it. Maybe Ollie is right and she should talk to Claire? But she knows her friend's financial situation. Claire and Danny have got everything invested in their farm; they don't have any disposable cash. And selling up seems so drastic. Perhaps it won't come to that.

No, it won't. There'll be another way. There will.

Once she calms down and gets her head straight, she'll figure it out. She has to believe that.

She begins to plough through her mountain of emails. And forcing her brain into this routine, repetitive work helps. It's demanding enough to distract her. Her body remains tense with underlying panic, but she functions. It puts off for a little longer the moment when she has to decide what she's going to do.

She's been working for half an hour when Ollie comes bounding up the stairs and into the room. He rarely comes to the office and only last week an unexpected visit from her husband would've made her heart soar. Now she's filled with dread.

Behind him, and slower on the stairs, there's a man in his forties, in a sharp designer suit, bull-necked with a shaved head and a paunch.

Ollie strides across the room towards her desk with a smile on his face. His manner is breezy.

He leans over and kisses her on the forehead.

Is it an act?

'Hey, babe,' he says. 'This is Vasyl. Y'know, the mate I told you about.' The man joins him, large and unsmiling. 'Vasyl, meet Sophie, my wife.'

Vasyl?

The man gives her a curt nod.

'Right,' says Ollie, taking charge. 'Sit down, mate. Let us get you some coffee.'

Vasyl draws up his sharply creased trousers and sits, but waves his hand dismissively. No coffee. The tie is silk with a gold pin. He has a fist full of rings, which could double as knuckledusters.

Sophie meets his gaze. The eyes are steel hard with a permanent frown. The mouth is set.

Ollie turns to Leanne, snapping his fingers to get her attention. 'Get me a double espresso, will you, love?'

His bouncy manner is false. He's putting on a show for this so-called mate. Underneath, he's jittery and hyper.

She watches her disgruntled assistant get up.

Shooting her an apologetic look, she says, 'Could you, Leanne? Thanks.'

Leanne disappears down the stairs. There's no one else in the office.

Vasyl takes out a packet of cigarettes and a lighter.

'This is a no smoking office,' says Sophie.

Vasyl chuckles. 'Really?' He lights his cigarette and inhales. 'Let's get on with this, shall we? I haven't got a lot of time.'

His accent matches his name. Eastern European? Ukrainian? Russian?

'I don't know what my husband's told you—' says Sophie.

'Just listen,' says Ollie in a peremptory tone. 'Vasyl's taken time out of his busy schedule to come here.'

It is a slap. How dare he!

Sophie erupts. 'Ollie, I'm not going to hand over money to this man I don't know.'

'We've talked about this.'

'No, we haven't.'

Vasyl draws on his cigarette and blows out a plume of smoke in Sophie's direction.

He glances at Ollie. 'You told me you sorted this out. You want my help or you don't?'

'We want your help,' says Ollie.

Vasyl's gaze swivels back to Sophie.

'Thirty per cent commission on all cash transfers, forty on property liquidation. We can handle up to ten mil spread over several transactions.'

Sophie glares at him. 'You're a bloody money launderer,' she says.

He gives her a supercilious smile and flicks his cigarette in the bin. 'From what I understand, I'm your best chance of staying out of jail. For an extra thirty k, I'll provide the passports. Within twenty-four hours you can be on a private jet to the Caymans, or anywhere else you fancy.' He turns to Ollie again. 'I'll need the property transferred into your sole name, Mick. I don't want no hassles. You know how we do business.'

Ollie nods. 'Sophie and I need to talk. But it won't be a problem. I promise.'

Sophie is too stunned to speak.

This man's a criminal!

Vasyl looks at his watch. A Rolex Oyster. He gets up and smiles at Sophie. 'Don't fuck me about, Sophie. I'm not a man you fuck about. Neither are my associates.'

He buttons his jacket and strolls away across the office.

Leanne appears in the doorway with an espresso on a tray. He stands aside to let her enter, then disappears down the stairs.

Sophie has the sensation that all the air has been knocked out of her body. She looks at her husband and wonders who the hell he is.

Mick. Vasyl knew his real name.

You know how we do business.

But Leanne is walking towards them with her tray. She holds it out for Ollie to take his coffee.

He picks up the small espresso cup and downs it in one. His eyes are fixed on Sophie.

Determination. Resentment? But no love.

He turns to Leanne and switches on his best smile. 'Thank you,' he says. 'Sorry if I was rude. Bit of a tense morning. Some pretty heavy stuff going on.'

Leanne shrugs. 'I heard about your sister.'

His manner has flipped. This is all a performance.

Ollie shakes his head wearily. 'Yeah, I'm really worried about her.'

'I just saw a news alert,' says Leanne. 'Cops have released her.'

Ollie stares at her. His eyes widen with surprise and he clenches his jaw.

Another flip?

'Great!' He pulls out his phone and scrolls. 'Did they say where she's gone?'

'I dunno,' says Leanne. 'I saw a clip. She was with her agent and her lawyer. Paps were all over them. But they drove her away.'

Ollie jumps to his feet, phone in hand; he frowns with concentration as he scrolls.

His focus has changed completely.

'Undisclosed location is what they're saying. I've got to see her. Find her.'

He sounds excited.

But there's something else. A strange, wayward look in his eyes.

'Why don't you phone the agent or lawyer?' says Sophie.

He ignores her as he continues to scroll.

Then he wags his finger at her. 'You go back to the flat, and you wait for me. Got it?'

He turns away. She's been dismissed.

With a wag of the finger.

He hurries across the room and disappears down the stairs.

Leanne is watching her. What the hell is she thinking?

Sophie doesn't know what to say.

The two women gaze at one another. Embarrassment on both sides.

'Can I get you anything?' says Leanne.

Sophie shakes her head. Her lip is trembling, but she doesn't want to cry.

'I need to make a call,' she whispers.

Leanne nods and retreats across the room.

Sophie picks up her phone and dials. Her hand shakes as she waits for the call to be answered.

'Mum, I'm in so much trouble,' she says. 'I don't know what to do. I need help.'

55

Kristin scans the room. Spacious, traditional, heavy drapes in russet shades, and a world away from a police cell. It smells of polish and air freshener.

Billed as a country house hotel on the edge of Richmond Park, it's in London, but away from the hustle of the city. The suite has French doors with a balcony overlooking the garden.

Julia DeMarco claps her hands. 'Right. I hope you'll be comfortable here,' she says brightly. 'They're very discreet, used to dealing with the most discerning guests and I under-stand the food is excellent.'

Discerning means filthy rich.

'Aren't you staying?' says Kristin.

'Sadly, darling, I can't. There's a lot to organise. But I will be back as soon as I can. Promise.'

She's hacked off.

Jules is sinewy-thin and darts around like an old broiler hen. She can't keep still. Her hair is a dead straight curtain, somewhere between blonde and white, which grazes her shoulders. But her nails are amazing. She built her modelling agency from scratch, back in the dark ages. In the business, she's a legend. Kristin is petrified of her. But Jules is a zillion times better than her first agent. He was a groper and a sleaze. Best not to think about him.

Kristin sits down on the end of the bed. It's six feet wide and covered with a thick, patterned brocade.

'Now, don't look so glum,' says Jules, in that headteacher tone of hers. 'Charlie Parsons says the police are being ridiculous. They haven't got a hope in hell of making this stick. The CPS won't bring charges.'

Kristin nods. 'Aren't you going to ask me if I did it?'

Jules purses her lips. 'Darling, I'm assuming not. Ged was a lovely man, and I know you were very happy.'

'I wouldn't say very. No one's very happy.'

How is it Jules always makes her feel like the bolshy kid at the back of the class?

Her agent perches on the bed beside her and seizes her hand in a boney claw. 'A terrible monstrous thing has happened, darling. An absolute tragedy. And you're in shock. Who wouldn't be? To find your husband like that. And what the police did to you is unforgivable. Obviously we'll sue. But I've got an excellent doctor coming to see you.' She checks the Chanel white ceramic watch on her wrist. 'In fact, he should be here by now. He'll give you something.'

Jules can't wait to get out the door. All this has pissed her off.

'I don't like taking pills,' says Kristin.

Her mother was a junkie. Jules can't have forgotten that.

'In the circumstances, it'll be fine. You need to rest. And there'll be a nurse, just to keep an eye on you. And the security guys outside.'

'I'm not ill.'

'No, grief is not an illness. But it can have a peculiar

effect. Feelings you're not expecting. And we need to keep you safe and out of harm's way.'

Harm's way! What does a woman like her know about that?

Kristin sighs. 'I'm not trying to be difficult. But it's weird being here. I don't like it.'

'They won't let you go back to the house,' says Jules.

The idea of walking into that kitchen again?

No way.

She's never going back there.

'I know that. But why not the flat? At least I'd have my own things.'

'And the Press camped on your doorstep. No one's going to find you here. You're safe. Isn't that what you wanted?'

'Yes.'

No question of that.

Kristin feels beleaguered and abandoned. Some company would be nice, even if it's Jules.

There's a discrete tap on the main door to the suite.

'Right,' says Jules, standing up. She says *right* a lot. She heads out into the adjoining sitting room and opens the door.

The doctor is thin and balding. His suit jacket is too big for him. The nurse follows him in. In contrast, she wears blue scrubs that are too tight for her. Kristin doubts either of them wants to be there. It's a job for the money. They've come to babysit her. And they will have been well paid for their time and discretion.

Even pregnant, Kristin knows she's one of the most valuable assets in Jules's agency. Ged had once explained to her how it works. He'd compared her to a racehorse. She's more like a prize cow.

She glances at her phone. It's next to her bag on the shiny, mahogany veneer table beside the bed. The phone is silently vibrating.

Getting up, she walks over to it and looks.

Him again.

Her brother has been calling her repeatedly. But there's no way he'll find out where she is. She clicks it off.

Jules escorts the doctor into the room.

'This is Dr Mostafa, Kristin.'

Kristin manages a smile.

'I'm so sorry for your loss, Lady Sullivan,' says the doctor. 'I hope we can make you more comfortable.'

Kristin nods. The phone vibrates again.

56

Sophie sees her parents walking towards her along the riverside walk. They're arm in arm; a solid, dependable unit, and for so many years her bulwark against the world. Relief floods through her body.

When she phoned her mother, she discovered they were already in London. They'd come down the previous evening because they were worried, and Nick's visit was a ploy cooked up by all three of them to discover what was going on.

As she approaches them, Deirdre Latham opens her arms.

'My God, Sophie,' she says. 'What the hell have you got yourself into?'

Sophie can't speak.

She feels like a five-year-old as she lays her head on her mother's shoulder and sobs.

Now it'll be all right, won't it?

A few passersby give them curious glances. But Deirdre holds fast to her daughter and Roger stands next to them, gently rubbing Sophie's back.

They remain like this for several minutes.

Finally her father says, 'Let's find somewhere we can talk.'

Deirdre links arms with her daughter and they continue along the South Bank towards Blackfriars Bridge. The pub beside the bridge is in a mid-afternoon lull and they find a corner table in the empty upstairs bar.

Roger goes to order some drinks.

Sophie faces her mother across the table. She blows her nose and says, 'I don't know where to begin. I've done the most terrible thing.'

Deirdre is watching her with a tense frown.

'Is this about Ged Sullivan?'

Sophie nods.

The worst part of this is the shame. They'll be so disgusted with her.

How can she do this to them?

She hesitates.

'What the hell has that little shit got you into?' says Deirdre.

'Oh Mum, I got myself into it.'

'What do you mean?'

'He's not who you think he is.'

'Ollie isn't? You've finally woken up to that fact?'

Sophie sighs.

How is she ever going to explain?

Roger arrives with a tray of drinks. He places a glass in front of Sophie.

'Large brandy,' he says. 'Get that down you.'

Sophie picks up the drink and takes a mouthful. It burns her gullet as it goes down. She's not a brandy drinker. But her father's right; it's what she needs.

'I was talking about Ged,' she says. 'He's not what you think. He was a monster. And he hurt Kristin. That's what turned him on. Dressed up in a mask and made her play S and M games. Got her pregnant even though they both knew it was dangerous for her.'

'How do you know all this?' says Roger.

'Kristin told me about it. She was trapped. I think she was terrified of him.'

Deirdre sighs. 'And how does this involve you? You hardly know the woman.'

'She's my sister-in-law. I couldn't stand by and watch her suffer. I just wanted to help her. We just wanted to get her away from him.'

'You and Ollie?' says Deirdre.

'Does it seem so unreasonable?' says Sophie.

'That depends on what you did,' says her mother.

'We went to stay. It was in the middle of the night. I suppose we'd had quite a lot to drink. I went down into the kitchen and Ged was there. We got into an argument.'

'Just you and Ged?' says Roger.

'Yes, just the two of us. He was awful. Really vicious. The things he said, I suppose it wound me up. But that was clearly his intention.'

Deirdre shakes her head. 'You lost your temper, didn't you?'

Same assumption as Ollie.

'Mum, he was coming straight for me. He was going to hit me. Which is what he did to that poor girl, the climate protester. And which is how he treats his wife.'

'Why didn't you run away?' says Roger.

'I don't know.'

She does.

'I suppose I didn't want to back down. Didn't want him to win.'

Again.

Her father is looking at her with a mixture of concern and disappointment.

'Oh come on, Dad,' she says. 'It's what people always say. You should've run away. Don't wear a short skirt. Don't take any risks. This wasn't my fault. And it all happened too quickly.' The tears roll down her cheeks. She brushes them away with her hand and takes another mouthful of her drink. 'He was about to punch me. So I grabbed a knife from the knife block on the counter. And I stabbed him.'

There's silence around the table. Her father inhales sharply. Her mother is staring straight at her. She reaches across the table, grabs Sophie's hand and squeezes it. She has tears in her eyes.

'Jesus wept!' she says.

'I promise you, Mum, I had no choice. It was self-defence.'

'Then what happened?' says her father.

Sophie sighs.

It's out. She's said it. The sky didn't fall.

'The next thing was, I realised what a terrible thing I'd done. His phone was on the kitchen counter. And I picked it up and dialled 999 for an ambulance. And then Ollie arrived.'

'From where?' says Roger.

'I don't know. He just appeared. I told him we had to get help. But he ignored me. He pulled the knife out of Ged's stomach. And he used it to cut Ged's throat.'

This is the thing that she can't believe and will never forget.

The coolness of it. The calculation!

Roger and Deirdre Latham look at one another. Sophie can see the horror on both their faces.

'He said afterwards he did it to protect me. So I wouldn't go to jail.'

Deirdre takes a large swallow of her gin and tonic.

It seems an age before her father says, 'What did you tell the police when they arrived?'

'We didn't,' says Sophie. 'We left straight away, in the middle of the night. Ended up in Aldeburgh. That's when I called you. They came to see us at the flat the next day. And we said we left in the night because we'd heard Ged and Kristin arguing and we felt our presence was making things harder for her. They seemed to accept that.'

'And did you?' says Roger. 'Hear them arguing?'

'No. But it gets worse. Ollie thinks we should go abroad. Run away essentially. He wants me to transfer money into an offshore account. And also I found out that Ollie is not his real name. He changed it.'

Deirdre jumps to her feet. She's seething. 'Where is this little shit now?' she says. 'I want to talk to him.'

57

The Lathams take a black cab back to Sophie's riverside apartment. Deirdre sits next to her daughter, although she focuses her gaze out of the window. It's the only way she can stay in control.

Look at the landmarks. Try not to think.

Her husband sits on the bucket seat opposite their daughter and holds Sophie's hand.

They travel in silence.

Deirdre finds her brain dancing between memories. The little blue paddling pool in the garden. Pulling up at the school gate.

Sophie was such an amazing child, bright and energetic, but always wilful. When Nick came along, he was just easier in every way. Sophie had to push everyone and everything to the limit. And Deirdre wasn't one of these laissez-faire parents who let her kids rule the roost. She laid down the law and expected to be obeyed. This meant being at loggerheads with her daughter.

Roger took a softer line. He let her get away with far too much in Deirdre's view. This made Deirdre the bad guy, and she's well-aware that, as a result, Sophie thinks she prefers Nick. But that's not true and never has been.

Sophie breezed through school without too much effort. Of the two children, her daughter had the brains. Nick did well, but needed more help, more encouragement.

When Sophie's business took off, no one could have been more proud than Deirdre. But she has difficulty telling her daughter that.

So many things she should've said, but didn't.

Their relationship is often scratchy, and Sophie avoids confiding in her. They disagree about everything from politics to soft furnishings. Roger says they're too alike, though Sophie would never acknowledge that. *My two Valkyries.* That's what he calls them.

From the outset, Deirdre handled the whole question of Ollie badly. She was aware of it, but couldn't seem to stop herself. Sophie was typically bullish, and, out of the blue, announced she was getting married. She refused to listen to anyone else's opinion.

But Deirdre had to speak her mind. What mother wouldn't? She didn't understand how an intelligent woman like her daughter could be so blindly besotted and not recognise the kind of man he was. She was right. But that's little comfort now.

As they get out of the cab outside Sophie's block, Deirdre scans her daughter. She's pale and shaky.

He did this to her!

Deirdre is furious, and she's in no mood to take prisoners. They head inside.

Roger removes the key to the apartment from their daughter's trembling hand, unlocks the door and enters. Deirdre and Sophie follow.

Ollie is sitting on the sofa, bent forward over the coffee

table and staring at his phone. He glances up at them and a smirk spreads across his features.

'Well, well,' he says. 'Mummy and Daddy to the rescue. Now why aren't I surprised?'

Little shit!

'What makes you think we haven't called the police already?' says Roger.

'Have you?' says Ollie, with an air of unconcern. 'I'm assuming not. Because what your precious daughter should've explained to you is she's in the frame for murder. She could go down for a very long time.' He chuckles. 'How's that gonna play with your posh friends, or your respectable colleagues on the council, eh Deirdre?'

'You listen to me, you little shit,' says Deirdre. 'You don't fool me, and you never have. You're a liar. And now it seems, a murderer.'

'Mum, please!' says Sophie.

But Deirdre won't be silenced. 'I always knew you were a con man. I could smell it on you. And when the police get your real name, and start digging into your record, I'm guessing there'll be a fair few skeletons in the cupboard.'

Ollie shrugs. 'And how do you think that'll help Sophie? Cause here's the thing, Deirdre. How do you know she's not lying?'

'My daughter wouldn't lie. Not about this.'

'You reckon? But what if she is the murderer? It's my word against hers that I was even there. And I've got her pyjamas, the ones she wore when she stabbed him. The ones that've got Ged Sullivan's blood on them. That's forensic evidence linking Sophie directly to the crime. Once the police get hold of those, it's game over. Bye bye Sophie for the next fifteen years.'

Is he right?

Deirdre looks at Roger. He turns to their daughter. 'Is this true about the pyjamas?'

'I don't know,' says Sophie. 'I put them in a bag in the cupboard.'

'But they're not there anymore, Soph,' says Ollie. 'I've put them somewhere for safekeeping. You can check if you like.'

He's grinning at her. She stares back at him, appalled.

'Why,' she says. 'Why would you do that?' Her eyes brim with tears.

'Because, my dear wife, after your little performance with Vasyl this morning, I figured I might need some insurance. And it seems I was right, doesn't it?'

'Who's Vasyl?' says Roger.

'The money launderer he wants to use,' says Sophie.

Ollie stands up, slotting his phone into his pocket. He folds his arms and faces the Lathams.

'Vasyl is your daughter's passport out of this mess, which, I should mention, she got herself into. Because lovely Sophie can't hold her temper, can she? But you know that, Deirdre, don't you? Cause she's just like you. A spitting vixen.'

'What do you want?' says Deirdre, fixing him with a stony glare.

He smiles. 'Now that's more like it. A bit of pragmatism. I'm not unreasonable. I'm prepared to trade your daughter's freedom for cash.'

'I thought you might be,' says Deirdre.

'Hang on a minute,' says Roger. 'I'm not sure I like where this is going. We won't be blackmailed.'

'Won't you?' says Ollie. 'That's very high-minded of you, Roger. But you've had it cushy your whole life, haven't you? All served up on a plate. Stepping into your daddy's shoes.

It's easy to be moral when you're sitting pretty and you've made your stash.'

Sophie steps forward. 'Ollie, stop this. You don't have to attack them. This is about you and me.'

'I agree. But you should've thought of that before you ran wailing to them. I told you before Soph, there's only one person who can get you out of this, and that's me.'

'I haven't had it cushy my whole life,' says Deirdre. 'The house where I grew up, there was little love and less money. But, I didn't use that as an excuse to become a criminal.'

'Yeah,' says Ollie. 'Like me, you did the smart thing. You went out and married someone rich enough to keep you in style. Worked for you, didn't it? And it would've worked for us. If Sophie hadn't been such an arrogant tosser and picked a fight, she was too stupid to know she couldn't win.' He turns to Sophie and shakes his head. 'You thought you could tell Ged Sullivan off, and he was going to be the perfect gent, like Daddy, and stand there and listen to your feminist crap?'

Deirdre watches her daughter. She's shaking.

'I know this is my fault,' she whispers. 'I started it, but—'

'It is your fault,' says Ollie. 'No buts.' He stabs his index finger in Deirdre's direction. 'So don't bring that vicious old cow round here to slag me off. I've told you how we get out of this. Why won't you listen?'

Sophie's shoulders hunch. She crumples and sinks to her knees. Sharp sobs shake her with each intake of breath. It's what she used to do when she was a child and got herself into a mess. It rips at Deirdre's heart.

Stay calm. Don't lose it.

Roger goes and kneels beside her.

'You're right,' says Deirdre. 'I am a vicious old cow. But I am also pragmatic. Let's get down to business and talk about what you want.'

'What I want?' Ollie says.

'Yes. In exchange for those pyjamas.'

Roger shoots her a look. But she won't be deflected. They must save their child.

'What's it going to cost us? Name your price.'

58

Sophie sits on the end of the bed. The hotel room is small and boxy, with a balcony and a view of the Tower of London. It's been dark for some time, but she hasn't turned on the light. Her parents are in the adjacent room. There's a connecting door. Like childhood holidays again. She can hear them moving about.

Close enough to keep an eye.

She'd watched in stunned silence as her mother and her husband horse traded over a bloodstained pair of pyjamas. Ollie wanted three hundred grand in cash, transferred into his account immediately. *A gesture of good faith,* that's what he called it. Then the title to the house in Hackney made over to a shell company nominated by him.

Vasyl.

'That will take time,' said Deirdre.

'I suggest you get Nick on it then,' Ollie replied. 'I want to see paperwork by the end of the day tomorrow. Once it's signed and sealed, I'll tell you where you can find the pyjamas.'

'How do we know you won't renege?' said Deirdre.

Ollie smiled. 'Don't you think I want to be out of this shitstorm as much as you? It's in all our interests to move fast. You do this, in twenty-four hours I'll be gone. Isn't that what you want?'

'Yes,' said Deirdre.

Throughout, her father said nothing. He just watched his wife with a frozen look somewhere between pain and astonishment. His moral compass was spinning.

Poor old bear.

It wasn't the money that bothered Sophie. She could cover it. And Ollie was canny. Didn't ask for a ridiculous amount. He knew what was doable at speed. And he'd made a deal with Vasyl.

Was fleecing her always the game plan? Was he always going to dump her?

As they were leaving, Roger broke his silence. 'What about the police?' he said. 'You'll be on their list. They're not stupid, y'know.'

'Front it out,' said Ollie with a shrug. 'They've got no evidence. Stick to the story. They can't prove anything.'

As they travelled to their hotel in a cab, none of the Lathams spoke.

A numb despair engulfed Sophie. Her life has slipped its moorings. All her hopes and dreams have been washed away in the flood, together with her dignity and her self-confidence.

He set her up. He played her. She was his mark. She was duped.

How!

She glanced at her parents. Both had blank expressions, thoughts turned inwards, facing their own anguish.

She wondered what impact all this would have on their relationship. They've been married for forty-two years, but you never know how a partner will react in an extreme situation until it happens. Roger must wonder what kind of woman he married and what kind of child they bred.

The effect on them only magnifies Sophie's pain.

Her father sorted out a room at the hotel for her; he insisted on paying. They agreed with Ollie that she'll stay away from the flat until he's gone.

And that's it. He walks away.

She closes the door, and at last she's alone.

The mini bar is full of the usual array of miniatures. She considers downing them all until she sinks into oblivion. But it won't make her feel any better. She opts instead for a bottle of mineral water.

She sips it, and she sits.

The sky is an orange-tinted grey. London is never dark. Red dots wink on the cranes. Someone's always building something in the City; bigger, higher. It's a panorama she loves, but tonight it fails to distract her.

There's a demon inside her brain and he's laughing at her. At her monumental stupidity. She wonders what would've happened if she hadn't got in a fight with Ged Sullivan. How long would her marriage to Ollie have lasted? The shenanigans over the house in Hackney? Making her sell it, was that always his plan? His secretiveness. The phone messages he never answered. Lies piling up. That should've told her something. But she believed his story. Every word.

What a pathetic fool?

She's read about women like this. Gullible. Desperate. An easy mark. She didn't think she was one of them.

But her mother saw him for what he was. Perhaps

everyone did? Was she the laughing stock of all her friends and acquaintances? She remembers a conversation she had with Claire. Even her best friend said, 'This is all a bit sudden, Soph. Are you sure you don't want to slow down a bit?'

But that's not how Sophie Latham operates. Oh no. She goes for it! Gets what she wants.

If she's honest with herself, how good was it? Was she always fooling herself? The sex was okay; sometimes he was more into it than others. And it was always on his terms. She told herself they'd get better. Perhaps he was nervous. The closer they became, the more intimacy between them would flow.

It didn't.

Once the honeymoon was over, it started to drop off. He was tired, or worried about his sister. His moodiness kicked in. She didn't want to push him.

Through the adjoining door, she can hear her parents' voices. Deirdre's is raised. They're arguing.

It fills her with dismay.

'She's our daughter!' says her mother. 'She's my baby! My child! I won't abandon her, Roger. You can't make me.'

Her father's reply is quieter. She can't make out the exact words.

Tension twists in her gut. Guilt. She did this to them. It's unforgivable.

Is this who she is?

Stupid certainly. But not this.

She stands up and goes over to her bag, which is on the narrow table under the wall-mounted TV. She picks it up and empties it out, dumping the entire contents onto the bed.

Where did she put it?

She rakes through her belongings until she finds it. The card the cop gave her. The corners are dog-eared.

She holds it between her fingers. There's an official crest. Underneath it says: Cambridgeshire Police. Detective Sergeant Joanna Boden, followed by a mobile number. She stares at it.

59

Jo Boden's day has been long, and it isn't over. Lunch was at her desk, dinner was a takeaway pizza that the boss ordered in for the troops. Running two murder investigations in tandem is putting a severe strain on the team, even with extra help drafted in.

For most of the afternoon, Mackie was out with uniformed back-up searching for Raoul Kemp. They ran him to ground at his boyfriend's flat in Ipswich.

Boden and Chakravorty have been digging into the backgrounds of Lady Sullivan's brother and sister-in-law. They've had two analysts to help them. Sophie Latham appears to be an open book. The net is full of articles about her, interviews with her and videos of her at live events. She's a rising star in the business world.

Boden has spent several hours watching her online. She's a confident performer, relaxed in front of large groups of people, articulate and insistent that business can be ethical. Boden has listened to her speak about her efforts to create a carbon neutral company, her feminism and her commitment to tackling the climate emergency. She's combative, likes an argument, and doesn't have much patience for other points of view.

Would she and Ged Sullivan have got on?

No way.

There's nothing to suggest she knew Cary Rutherford or Luke Cameron, or belonged to any specific groups.

Ollie Harmon is a different proposition to his wife. They can only track him back eighteen months; before that, Harmon doesn't exist. But Prisha has discovered that Kristin Kelly had several siblings, including a brother, Michael Kelly, who's the right age. It's a common name and they've been trying to drill down and match it to him. He didn't change it from Kelly to Harmon by deed poll. And there are loads of Michael Kellys with a record on the PNC.

Boden turned to Chakravorty. 'How on earth did these two get together, Prish?'

The DC shrugged. 'He's a looker, she isn't? She's older. With money. A cougar in need of a mate?'

A cougar? Boden chuckled to herself. She doubted Sophie Latham would like that.

Boden wanted to have a crack at interviewing Raoul Kemp herself. But the boss vetoed it. She feels sidelined. Hepburn is under severe pressure from all sides, and his underlying biases are coming out. He's more comfortable relying on Roscoe, and, her guess is, he's niggled by her failure to extract a confession from Kristin Sullivan. That was her chance; she blew it. His priority is a result and a case that will fly with the CPS.

Late afternoon, a shout had gone up from across the office. Boden and Chakravorty went over to investigate.

Roscoe, DCI Hepburn and Mackie were all gathered round the main computer screen watching a grainy piece of footage; some sort of altercation with a lot of shouting. It didn't look that different to the footage they'd already seen.

'Wind it back. Let's see it again,' said the DCI.

As they joined the group, Boden whispered to Mackie, 'What's going on?'

Tom Roscoe answered. 'This appears to be footage of Sir Gerald Sullivan losing his rag and attacking Cary Rutherford with a baseball bat.'

'Wow!' said Boden. 'Where did you get it?'

'Raoul Kemp,' said Mackie. 'When we arrested him, he admitted he persuaded Kobe Jackson to take the rap for his boss. But when Cary died, he got worried. Sullivan wanted him to offer Kobe more money. But Raoul said that wouldn't work. He also knew Sullivan wanted to get shot of him. So he kept all the CCTV footage of what happened as insurance. Icing on the cake, he also gave us the bat. It's gone to the lab.'

The DCI cracked his knuckles. Boden sensed he'd like to wrap this up. A quick result was beckoning.

'Okay,' he said. 'Seems to me we might be looking at a blackmail attempt that went wrong. Raoul Kemp tried to put the screws on his boss. Sullivan wasn't having it. Fight ensued. Post Mortem shows one stab wound in the victim's belly. Sullivan was a nasty bastard. Video proves that. That first stab might've been Kemp defending himself. Then he realises he's stuffed. No going back. He finishes it by slashing the jugular.'

There was general nodding of heads in agreement.

'The bat's metal so if it's got Sullivan's fingerprints and Cary Rutherford's blood and DNA, that'll pretty much confirm he killed her,' said Roscoe.

'Good work, Mackie,' said the DCI.

Mackie grinned like the cat who got the cream. 'Thank you, sir.'

Boden and Chakravorty returned to their desks.

'Now he's going to be insufferable,' said Prisha. 'Mackie solved the case.'

'Mackie solved both cases,' said Boden.

She watched the live feed from the interview room on her computer as Roscoe put the accusation to Raoul Kemp.

The suspect got upset. A chair was thrown.

Predictable.

Why would Raoul demand money from his boss in the kitchen in the middle of the night? And if he did, and Sullivan got angry and tried to hit him, how would he defend himself? A tough little bruiser like Kemp would've used his fists. He's younger than Sullivan. Fitter. He could've stopped him in his tracks.

Boden notices Prisha scanning her.

'You reckon DCI Hepburn's got it wrong, don't you?' she says.

Boden shrugs.

'I think what he has got right is how it happened. A row that turns into a fight. Someone grabs a knife to defend themselves. Then there's no going back. Question is who?'

'Who do you think?'

Boden shrugs again.

The Harmons? But where's the evidence?

Then she sees Raoul Kemp is back in his chair and speaking.

On screen, he's shaking his head. He looks like a whipped dog. 'You think I'm stupid?' he says. 'A man as powerful as that. He blackmails government ministers for Chrissake. More than my life's worth to cross him. I did his bidding. Kept my mouth shut. And I was well paid for it.'

'Why didn't he leave the climate protestors to you to sort out?' says Roscoe.

'I dunno. He could have. But he came stomping down to the stables, and he was already well wound up.'

'You know why?'

'His wife was freaking out, he said.'

'About the protestors?'

Raoul frowns. 'Not just that. Her brother had come to dinner that night. Ged was ranting about it. Said the brother was, well, a word beginning with c. It wasn't happy families.'

'Did he say what it was about?'

'No.'

'But you think Ged was already angry?'

'Definitely. And when the protestors came round the corner chanting, he just lost the plot, grabbed the bat and waded in.'

Boden turns to Chakravorty. 'Interesting,' she says. 'Back to the brother.'

The phone on her desk vibrates. *Unknown Caller.*

She answers it. 'Jo Boden.'

There's a moment of silence, then a female voice says, 'This is Sophie Latham. I wonder if I can talk to you. In person. I have some things to tell you.'

Boden glances at Chakravorty.

'What sort of things, Ms Latham?'

'I need it to be face to face.'

'Are you at home?' Boden says.

'No. I'm at a hotel in London. Near Tower Bridge.'

Boden picks up a pen. 'Give me the address.'

60

Sophie Latham hangs up the phone. Was she expecting to feel relief? It doesn't come. But she's stepped back across the line, and returned from the dark side. The police are on their way.

She was obtuse in what she said to DS Boden on the phone. But the cop didn't need persuading. All she said was it would take her a couple of hours to get there.

This leaves Sophie in a strange limbo. Her thoughts continue to race. It's as if she's been running at full pelt on the treadmill. She's about to collapse and slaps the emergency stop. She's no longer running, but inside she's still hurtling forward.

When will it stop!

She's tempted again by the mini-bar. One drink to help her relax. But it wouldn't be one. She sorts through the packets of tea beside the kettle and makes herself a camomile infusion.

Opening the door to the tiny balcony, she gazes out. It's nothing like the amazing view from her own apartment. This is a tourist hotel and riverside real estate is at a premium. The apartment with its expensive river frontage is part of the life that she takes for granted. Like her business. Her wardrobe of designer clothes. Her friends. Dinners out in high-end restaurants. Trips abroad. Her freedom. All the things she's worked so hard for. But now she could be about to lose it all. Is she being stupid?

Stick to the story. Pay him off. Move on.

The demon again. She's fighting to order her thoughts, and to hang on to her resolution. When they get here, what will she tell them? The truth? But what is the truth?

Was it self-defence?

She slapped him first. He came back at her with unbounded fury. He could've killed her.

Don't mention the slap.

She had no choice.

Round and round it goes on a loop. Doubt. Guilt. Fear.

There's a tap on the door. Too soon for the cops.

Sophie opens it. Deirdre comes in. She looks as if she's been crying. Her hands grasp a tissue. She has something she wants to say.

'Your dad and I have been talking—'

Sophie cuts her off. 'Mum, I've called the police.'

'Oh,' says Deirdre, opening her eyes wide with surprise.

'The DS who first came to interview us about the death of that protester, she gave me her card. I called her. She's coming to see me.'

'What are you going to say?'

Say nothing!

'I'm going to explain what happened, all of it. I've committed a crime. A serious crime. And I've covered up a worse crime.'

Deirdre inhales. She seems perplexed.

'Your dad's been talking to Nick on the phone. They've

been discussing lawyers. Who we can get to put your case. They think giving Ollie what he wants will just dig you in deeper. If it comes out, as it will, you'll look bad. It'll make everything worse.'

Sophie feels deflated.

No escape.

But she says, 'I know. And they're right. I've lied enough. I don't want to do it anymore. It's not who I am.'

Deirdre flings her arms round her. 'Oh Soph, I just wanted to protect you. Save you. Maybe it was the wrong thing.'

'I know you did, Mum.'

They cling to each other.

Then Deirdre says, 'Nick is worried that if the police get hold of Ollie, he'll blame it all on you. Deny he was ever there. And there's no way to prove it. Your word against his.'

His threat. And he'll carry it out.

'I would hope I'm the more credible witness,' she says.

Deirdre's features are scrunched. She seems in pain. 'But what if he says to the police yeah, okay, I'm a bit of a conman? I married her for her money. But I'm not a killer. She's the crazy feminist who argued with Ged, went ballistic and killed him. When I got there, he was dead.'

Sophie stares at her. 'Nick thinks they'll believe him?'

No!

Deirdre is frowning. Her family has discussed this.

'He charmed you, didn't he?' her mother says. 'You think he can't charm a jury? Those looks. Those eyes. This is what he does, Soph.'

Sophie dips her head. They're right.

'I'm so ashamed,' she says. 'You must think I'm a complete fool.'

Or worse.

Deirdre strokes her daughter's hair out of her eyes. 'My darling girl,' she says. 'You've always been a risk taker. It's what I most admire about you. You're a shooting star.'

'I thought that was Nick. He's your favourite.'

Deirdre shakes her head. 'No. You're wrong. He's my lovely boy. But he's not you. He never could be. You've always been the one who astounded me.'

'Have I really, Mum?'

Deirdre grasps her hand and squeezes it. She has tears in her eyes.

'Absolutely,' she says. 'And I'm sorry if you've ever doubted it. But it's made me fear for you, and what the world could do to you.'

'I can't understand how I was so easily manipulated by a man. How on earth did you know about him?'

Her mother sits down on the bed. She sighs and shakes her head. 'I suppose elements of him remind me of my old man. That wary look, always trying to assess the situation, work out his next move. Never open or relaxed. He was always hustling, my dad. I don't think he ever did anything criminal. But that may be about lack of nerve. There's a stee-liness about Ollie. You get a hint occasionally. Feels to me he's got bags of nerve.'

'Oh Mum, I don't know what to do.'

'Well, the police are coming now. Trust your dad and Nick. They're trying to come up with a way of catching him off guard.'

'What do you mean, off guard?'

'Nick's firm uses private detectives to gather evidence. We could hire one. They might find a way to monitor Ollie's phone, record an incriminating conversation. Somehow catch him out. They have all sorts of other gadgets nowadays.'

'Sounds a bit hit and miss.'

'Well, Nick says we just need to cast doubt on his story. Prove he lies.'

Nick says!

It still grates on Sophie. She shouldn't be irritated. Especially after what her mother has just said. Her brother is only trying to help. She should just be grateful. She's dragged them all into her mess.

More guilt.

But she can't suppress her annoyance. What she hates most is her sense of impotence. Is she just going to sit round feeling sorry for herself like this? Let Ollie or Mick, or whatever the bastard's called, win?

Fuck no!

'Listen Mum, I've got an idea. When the police arrive, can you talk to them?'

'What?'

She picks up her jacket and bag and heads for the door.

'Sophie, where are you going?'

'I'm going to play my bastard husband at his own game. I'm going to get some evidence against him.'

'Oh, my God, Sophie, no! Stop! Think about this. What about this police officer that's coming?'

'Talk to her. Tell her I'll be back soon.'

61

As soon as Sophie lets herself into the apartment, the aroma of curry spices hits her. She walks down the hall. The source of the smell is a pile of Indian takeaway cartons on the kitchen counter.

Ollie has his back towards her, sitting on the sofa, bare feet up on the coffee table, shovelling curry into his mouth from a foil carton. He's watching the television: motorbikes screaming round a race track.

He turns his head in surprise, fork halfway to his mouth.

'Thought you weren't coming back 'til I was gone,' he says. 'Isn't that what we agreed?'

Cool indifference.

She's nothing to him. Less than nothing. A means to an end. Every touch, every gesture, every kiss, all a sham.

Such casual cruelty.

'I need to get some stuff,' she says. 'Is that a problem?'

'Not for me,' he says with a shrug. 'Just thought it was easier for you.' He adds as an afterthought, 'Want some Indian? There's loads.'

Sophie watches him as he turns his attention back to the television.

Now he doesn't need to pretend, he's ignoring her. Was he always pretending? Did he feel nothing for her? She takes a deep breath.

Get a grip!

'Okay,' she says. 'I am a bit hungry.'

'Help yourself,' he says. Then he sniggers. 'You paid for it.'

She takes off her jacket, hangs it over the back of one of the high back stools in the kitchen area. She gets a plate from the cupboard and spoons a small amount of rice and curry onto it. The kitchen is a mess, surfaces sticky, a clutter of empty beer bottles next to the sink. No more Ollie, the house-husband.

Here he is, in his true colours. Beautiful on the surface. Ugly inside. She wants to throw him out of her flat, and out of her life.

Calm down.

Carrying her plate over, she perches on the opposite sofa.

He picks up the remote, clicks the television off, and drops the handset on the floor. It clatters on the hard wood.

He's making a point. He can do what he likes, because he has the power.

Thinks he has.

He plonks his foil carton on the table and wipes his fingers on his jeans.

'Where's the money, then?' he says. 'No sign of it yet in my account.'

'I don't have three hundred grand in ready cash. My accountant's sorting it out. You'll have it.'

'Tick Tock, Soph. And what's Nicky up to?'

'He's spoken to a colleague who specialises in conveyancing. They're doing it.'

Can he tell she's lying? Hopefully not.

He grins. 'Wonder if he knows how much you hate him, your brother?'

'I don't hate him. That's not true at all.'

All those tiny confidences and insecurities shared. Betrayal happens on so many levels.

He's staring straight at her. Those amazing blue eyes. They make him almost angelic.

Wasn't Lucifer an angel?

'Brothers and sisters, eh?' he says. 'What a mindfuck.'

He belches loudly and grins.

On the table in front of him is a half drunk bottle of red wine. He picks it up, takes a swig.

'Get yourself a glass. Looks like you could do with a drink.'

'I'm fine, thanks.' She pushes the food round her plate.

He chuckles to himself, shakes his head, and takes another drink. 'I know you're pissed off. Who wouldn't be? But we had a bit of fun, didn't we? You can't say I don't give value for money.'

He makes it sound as if they went on a couple of dates, and it didn't work out.

'What's that supposed to mean?' she says.

'You shouldn't take it too personally. It's not personal, it's just business. As Michael Corleone once said.'

Is that who he thinks he is? The Godfather?

'You mean you've done this before?'

'What can I say? Women like me, Soph. They always have. And a boy's got to eat.'

'What was the plan? You siphon off as much money as you can. Then you dump me and disappear. Change your name again. Or even divorce me and claim half my assets.'

'You're the one insisted we get married. It's not my usual game plan.'

She can feel herself tearing up.

Don't cry!

He laughs. 'But I didn't expect you to lock horns with Ged. That was an unexpected bonus. I've been trying to figure out how to get Kristin free of that scumbag for months. And you gave me the opportunity on a plate.'

'And you took it? You cut his throat?'

'Come on, it's not like he didn't deserve it. Look upon it as my contribution to saving the planet.'

'You said you did it to protect me. Is that even true?'

He stands up, knocking the carton of curry on the floor. Now he's irritated. He huffs. 'What do you care? You've got money. Plenty of it. You were desperate. I targeted you. Let's just move on.'

Desperate?

The word stings.

She fell in love with this man. Gave him her heart. Would've given him anything.

She bites back a retort.

He takes another drink of wine and paces. 'It's a shitty world,' he says. 'Dog eat dog. Most people don't have a lot of options.'

She watches him swig from the bottle. Were those eyes always this stony and full of hate? His sullen moods, his unexplained absences, the fact he rarely answered his phone; the pieces of the puzzle are slotting into place.

Keep it light.

'You could've used your looks differently,' she says. 'Become a model like Kristin.'

He laughs again. The sound is hard and mocking. 'Bloody hell, you know the hours they work? Nah, work is for mugs. Live off your assets, that's the smart way.' He thrusts his pelvis forward. 'And we both know what mine are, don't we, Soph?'

Who's he kidding? More often than not, he avoided sex.

There's no way she's feeding his ego. She shrugs. 'What would your dad've thought?' she says. 'The soldier who fought for his beliefs?'

His shoulders shake. He bursts out laughing and takes another drink.

'Ah, that one got you, didn't it? Everyone loves that. Tough guy hero, faced danger, but for a noble cause.'

'He wasn't in the IRA?'

'Who the fuck knows what he was? All I know is the bastard left us high and dry.'

Sophie puts her plate aside. 'Where will you go now?' she says. 'Spain? Further afield?'

He gives her a side-eyed glance. 'Too many questions, Soph. We need to wrap this up. I got stuff to do. And you need to chase up that money.'

She stands up. 'Okay. I'm just going to pack a suitcase.'

She walks into the bedroom, lifts a case down from the top of the cupboard and opens it on the bed.

As she gathers underwear from the drawer, she hears him speaking. He's talking to someone on his phone. She creeps to the doorway to eavesdrop.

'I told you, mate,' he says. 'If you know where she is, I'll get in there and get you your interview. It's her bloody agent that's got her under wraps. Stupid bitch thinks she's helping Krissy, but she's not. It's not what Krissy wants. She's just scared of the old biddy. Trust me. I can persuade her.'

There's a pause. His voice changes. He's excited. 'Awesome. Text me the address. Tell your editor he won't regret this. You can trust me to deliver.'

He hangs up. Sophie peeps round the edge of the door. She can see him staring down at the screen. The phone beeps with an incoming text. He grins.

He's found Kristin.

Now he's heading straight for her. She jumps back from the doorway and gets over to the chest of drawers by the time he sweeps into the room.

He glares at her.

'Listen,' he says. 'Things are moving on. I need that cash. In my account tonight. Or the deal's off.'

'I'm trying to arrange it,' she says, scooping underwear from the drawer and taking it to the case.

'Try harder,' he says, glaring at her. 'And don't think you can play me, Soph. I'm better at this game than you. I know all the angles.'

Really?

She cowers and says, 'Don't worry. You'll have it. I promise.'

'Make sure I do. You won't survive too well in jail. And fifteen years is a long time.'

She keeps her head dipped as she continues to pack the case.

'I know,' she says.

Make him believe he's won.

He gives her a curt nod.

Then he goes over to the long row of cupboards that run along most of one side of the room. He opens the end one, reaches down under his gym bag and pulls out a backpack.

It's dark blue; she's never seen it before. The one he uses is black. This one's hidden away at the back of the cupboard.

She tries not to seem too interested. But he doesn't seem to care.

He carries the backpack out of the room. She creeps to the door and watches. He dumps it on the kitchen counter.

Sophie's brain is racing. Is this where he's hidden her blood spattered pyjamas?

Must be.

He opens a drawer and takes out his electronic tyre pump.

What's he up to? He's going somewhere on his bike?

He keeps his Trek road bike out on the balcony under a special cover. It was her wedding present to him and cost thirteen grand.

Taking the tyre pump, he heads for the balcony door, opens it, turns on the outside light and goes out.

She can glimpse him through the window, uncovering the bike.

Her heart is thumping. This is her opportunity. If the pyjamas are in the backpack….

Go for it! Grab the pyjamas from the bag and get the hell out!

She knows she must be fast. She scoots out of the bedroom, round the corner, and into the kitchen area.

He's bending down to pump up the tyres.

She unzips the backpack. Her pyjamas are wrapped in a plastic carrier bag. She searches inside, keeping one eye on the balcony door. Her fingers connect with what? Not plastic. Her pyjamas? No, not as soft. This is ribbed and knitted.

She pulls out a black, full-face balaclava and stares at it.

WTF!

She reaches back inside the bag and brings out a pair of metal handcuffs trimmed with red velvet.

An avalanche of realisation crashes through her.

Kristin's question about S and M!

She asked Sophie if she and Ollie ever did anything like that. And when Sophie said no, she seemed disappointed.

It was him!

Now it makes sense. Total sense. She was talking about him. Her brother, not her husband. The person who did these terrible things to her was Ollie, not Ged.

Shock reverberates through Sophie. The balcony doors opens. She drops the items in the bag, zips it and flees to the bedroom.

62

Thoughts tumble through Sophie's head. A mixture of shock and panic.

Can it be true?

Her brain recoils. What does any of this mean? He has a balaclava and handcuffs in his bag. Maybe the balaclava was for riding his bike?

But handcuffs? Trimmed with red velvet?

It's him. It has to be.

He was having sex with his own sister. Forcing her? Hurting her.

And was Kristin trying to tell her this?

She can hear him in the other room. What's he doing? Sounds like he's lifting his bike through the balcony door? The faint tick of the wheels turning as he pushes it across the room.

She skips back out of sight. He's in the hallway. The sound of rotating wheels stops. He's propped the bike against the wall. The soft thump of a shoe? Is he putting his trainers on?

Adrenaline is surging through her veins. She has no idea what to do.

His footsteps are approaching; she ducks into the en suite just before he walks into the bedroom.

'You done yet?' he says.

He can't see her.

But through the crack in the door, she can see him. Hands on hips. Keyed up. Impatient. He's been like this ever since his phone call.

'Just talking to my accountant,' she calls. 'He's setting up the transfer now.'

Will he buy the lie?

No reply. He turns and leaves, his whole body humming with tension.

He's excited.

She moves back into the bedroom. There's a crash and clatter of saucepans from the kitchen.

She has to risk it.

She tiptoes over to the bedroom door and peers round it.

He's in the kitchen, leaning over the large drawer below the hob, where the heavy pans and the cast iron casseroles are kept. He's lifting them all out and dumping them on the floor.

She peeps round the doorjamb and spies on him.

He kneels down, unhooks the drawer and removes that, and reaches his arm right into the space at the back of the cabinet.

This is his hiding place?

He pulls out a plastic carrier. The bag she put her blood-stained pyjamas in? Then he reaches in and brings out a smaller wrapped object.

The knife!

And then something else. A phone? Wrapped in clingfilm.

He stuffs all three items in the blue backpack. Hoisting it on his shoulder, he strides across the room. He's on a mission.

Sophie dives back into the bedroom and bends over her suitcase.

But he passes the door without entering.

She hears the front door opening, the bike wheels turning. The door slams behind him.

Has he gone?

Silence.

Sophie collapses on the bed and puts her face in her hands. Her heart is drumming in her chest. She takes a couple of deep breaths.

Focus!

She gets up and peeks out into the hall.

It's empty.

She hurries to the front door, bolts it and puts the chain on.

Then she goes into the kitchen area. She glances at the pans strewn on the floor. Not the most original hiding place. But effective.

She skirts round the kitchen counter to her jacket, which she hung on the back of a bar stool. She dips her hand in the pocket and takes out her phone.

Yes!

It's still recording.

She stops it, winds it back and presses play.

Her own voice comes out of the tiny speaker:

'Okay,' she says. 'I am a bit hungry.'

'Help yourself,' he replies. 'You paid for it.'

The recording is clear. His voice is audible and identifiable. She clicks it off. No time to check it all now. She must phone the cop.

As she dials the number, she paces.

It's answered on the second ring. 'Ms Latham. We're on our way to you. Just at King's Cross.'

Not at the hotel yet. Good!

'Listen,' says Sophie. 'I'm back at my flat. But first I need to tell you a couple of things.'

'Okay,' says the cop.

Sophie takes a deep breath. 'I'm worried about Kristin. My husband has gone after her, and I think he means to harm her. I can explain it all when you get here. But I don't know where she is. Ollie has been trying to find her. I think he has. And I think we should warn her.'

There's the sound of a hand over the phone. Muffled voices. The cop is speaking to someone else. Then she comes back on the line.

'Why do you think this, Ms Latham? I need a reason.'

'He's taken the knife he used to kill Ged, and he's gone after her.'

'You're saying he killed Ged Sullivan?'

'Yes. I was a witness.'

There's a pause.

'Okay,' says the cop. 'Leave it with me. But we need to speak to you urgently.'

'I know,' says Sophie. 'But I'm at my flat. Your colleagues came here before.'

'Yes, we have the address.'

'Well, I'm not going anywhere.'

'Wait for us there.'

'I will.'

Sophie hangs up.

She walks over to the sofa and slumps down on it. A carton of congealing curry is upended on the floor. A bottle of red wine, with a few dregs left in the bottom, is on the coffee table. Sophie stares at them. This is her life thanks to him: a messy wreck.

He's used her and discarded her. Much like her unknown assailant in Sydney all those years ago.

It seems she learned nothing.

But now the anger has drained out of her. She's too tired to rage. Too suffused with misery.

How did it come to this?

She needs to be honest with herself. He can't be blamed for what she did to Ged.

That's down to her.

63

Boden and Chakravorty pick up an Uber outside the station. But the traffic on Euston Road is backed-up; a burst water main flooding the road. The journey to the South Bank and Latham's posh riverside flat seems to take forever.

After their conversation on the phone, Boden called Tom Roscoe and repeated what Latham had told her.

Kristin Kelly had been released under investigation and taken by her agent to a hotel near Richmond Park in order to avoid the media.

Boden caught the urgency bordering on panic in Sophie Latham's voice, and it bothered her. It also confirmed what she'd thought for some time: Latham and her husband were at the heart of this. They made much more plausible suspects than Raoul Kemp.

But she knew the bosses didn't agree.

'You want me to ask the Met to go mob-handed into some posh London hotel on the say-so of someone we already know has lied to us?' said Roscoe.

'I don't think she's lying now.'

'You don't *think?* And you've only talked to her on the phone?'

'Yes.'

She heard him sigh.

He's not buying this.

'The DCI's already pretty peeved I let you and Chakravorty go swanning off to London on what he sees as a fool's errand.'

'He still reckons it's Kemp?'

'Okay, I'll tell him you've received an allegation that it was the brother. But he's going to take some convincing.'

'Chrissake, Tom, that's what we're doing. Going to question Sophie Latham and find out if this holds water.'

'Yeah well, this end things aren't going so well. Ged Sullivan's eldest daughter is married to some MP, who's mates with the Home Secretary, and they are making waves. They want Hepburn off the case and someone brought in from another area to replace him. They're accusing us of incompetence.'

The boss is running scared. Great!

'They just don't want it to come out that Ged beat a climate protester to death,' said Boden.

'You're probably right. And Hepburn has said that to the Chief Constable. But these are powerful people.'

'If the Chief's doing his job, he'll protect the investigation from that sort of pressure.'

'I'll tell him you said that, shall I?'

Feels like he's laughing at her.

Boden sighs. 'Just saying.'

'And I agree. But, Jo, we need to be realistic here. And proportionate in our response. You know that. You need to get a proper statement from Sophie Latham, then we can act.'

Proportionate? Harmon does something bad to his sister and they'll all be running for cover.

Boden sits slumped in the back of the cab. Roscoe and Hepburn are the same. They just don't want an IOPC investigation to ruin their brilliant careers.

'What's up?' says Chakravorty. 'You look pissed off.'

Boden sighs. 'What if Latham's right, and there's some weird shit going on here between Kristin Sullivan and her brother? What if he has gone after her?'

'I don't see what can we do,' says Chakravorty. 'If the DI won't call the cavalry.'

'Think about it. If he killed Ged Sullivan, if he's already got blood on his hands, he's likely to escalate. She could be in real danger.'

'Why would he want to kill his own sister, if he killed Ged to protect her?' says Chakravorty.

'I agree,' says Boden. 'It doesn't make a lot of sense. But I've got a bad feeling about this.'

'Perhaps Latham can explain it.'

Boden stares out of the window at the crawling, fuming traffic.

'Yeah, if we ever bloody well get there.'

64

Kristin's slipping away now. Losing consciousness. Her lungs are screaming for air. She can't breathe. His forearm is across her throat, bearing down and compressing her windpipe. Her body jackknifes with terror.

No! This is not happening.

But the fear is real. Adrenaline is flooding her veins.

No. She's dreaming; it's the fever dream again.

Her heart pounds. Trapped in the instant before waking.

She gasps.

As she surfaces, the horror ebbs and recedes.

Just a bad dream. It will pass.

She opens her eyes. A shiver runs through her; goose-bumps, although she's bathed in sweat. The dread never goes. It's visceral.

Embedded in the memories; the tracks left in her brain. No way to scrub them out. They're etched too deep.

Ever since she can remember. The same recurring dream.

She inhales. Deep breaths to slow her thumping pulse.

Dark outside.

A faint orange glimmer edges between the curtain and the wall.

She places a hand on her heart to soothe herself.

Relax. Breathe. All fine.

But something's not right.

A smell?

There's definitely a smell. The musky scent of male sweat?

Someone's in the room.

A shadowy spectre glides in front of the curtain. Or did she imagine it?

Panic shoots through her.

It's not part of the nightmare.

This is real.

He's here in her bedroom.

It's him.

If she moves, she'll betray herself.

She waits.

He creeps closer. A silent wraith. He leans over her.

Shallow breathing, but she can feel no breath. Of course not. A balaclava covers his mouth.

Now she's sure it's him. It's been a while, but she knows this game. She must pretend; play her part.

It will be over quickly.

He pulls back the covers. He knows she's naked. It's her vulnerability he wants. To possess, to dominate, and to leave his mark. That's what the game's about.

It will be over quickly. No need to panic.

Something soft brushes her cheek. Not skin. Plastic?

He thinks she's asleep. She exhales and pretends to wake. His hand goes over her mouth.

He's wearing gloves. Vinyl gloves. Why? He's never done that before. There's a tension. She's blocked him ever since her marriage; he couldn't get to her. Now she can sense his impatience.

Then she feels a sharp edge graze her chin.

A knife! The blade of a knife?

He strokes her throat with it. There's never been a knife before.

Raw fear twists her gut.

Now she understands. Of course she does. She's upset him, and he's angry.

It's the last game.

This is how it ends.

But it was always going to be like this, wasn't it?

No!

Instinct kicks in. The will to survive. Save herself. Save her baby.

Gerry!

Terror jolts her into action. She moves swiftly, which surprises him. Clenching her fist, she lashes out toward his face. Her punch meets bone. He yelps. Falls back.

A sharp sting!

The point of the blade nicks her skin, but she rolls from beneath him, off the bed and onto the floor.

She can hear him scrabbling in the darkness. He always needs it to be dark to hide his shame. So he can pretend.

Scooting across the floor, she scrambles to her feet, gets to the bathroom and turns on the light.

He's on the bed, one hand clutching his nose, trying to get his bearings.

Call him out! Do it! Break the silence. Break the spell.

'Take off the mask, Mickey,' she says. 'You wanna kill me? First, I need to see your face.'

She's naked. She can sense his eyes crawling over her flesh.

He jumps to his feet. He's holding a long, slender knife in his right hand. She recognises it. It's from the knife block in the kitchen.

Scream!

The nurse or one of the dozy security guards will hear her.

No point. It'll be too late.

If she dies here tonight, does she even care?

He hesitates. They're hardly a metre apart. He's big; taller than her and broader. But his whole body is quaking.

What now?

She could run, try to make it to the door. But she stands her ground.

Tonight it ends, one way or another.

'Take the mask off,' she says. 'At least have the guts to show me your face.'

He's dithering. Can't decide what to do.

A stand-off. Only for a second or two, but it feels longer.

Then abruptly, he tosses the knife on the bed and rips off the mask.

'Why did you fucking hit me!' he says, dabbing his nose with his finger tip. 'I'm fucking bleeding! Why would you do that? You know it's only a game.'

A game he's made her play since she was a kid. Except it's not a kids' game.

'Then what's the knife for?' she says. 'Why bring a fucking knife, Mickey?'

'This is your fault, not mine,' he says. His hair is ruffled. He pouts like a peeved child. Blood trickles from his left nostril. Tears well in his eyes. 'Look at you. Your belly's huge. With his baby! HIS FUCKING BABY! Why did you do it? I can't believe you did this to me. You betrayed me. Aren't I entitled to be angry?'

She's trembling, but he mustn't see it. She must front this out, talk him down.

The knife is behind him on the bed. The cut on her chin smarts. It's bleeding. That's how close it came.

'You killed our baby,' he wails. 'But you'll have his. Why would you do this to me?'

'Listen to me Mickey,' she says. 'It wasn't like that. You know it wasn't. It was an abortion. I had an abortion because I was thirteen and you're my brother.'

He plonks down on the bed. His shoulders hunch. The knife is inches from his hand.

'Don't you love me?' he says. 'I've always protected you.'

What a sick joke that is!

'And we're only half-brother and sister, aren't we? It's not the same.'

She's scared; he's unpredictable. But she's also exasperated. Reaching round the bathroom door, she grabs the towelling bathrobe and puts it on.

He looks up at her. *Those crazy blue eyes.*

He seems to stare without ever blinking.

'I've always loved you,' he says in a tearful voice. 'You should be with me. You know you should. But you married him.'

She takes a deep breath. She's weary. Bone weary and sick of living in fear.

Fuck it! Fuck all of it!

All she wants is for it to end. She doesn't care how.

She folds her arms and stares right back at him. 'Is that why you killed him?' she says.

He frowns. He seems puzzled. Suddenly, the tearful little boy is gone. He stands up, straightens up. Shakes his head and laughs. He's morphed into someone else.

'What? That's ridiculous,' he says. 'You think I killed Ged? I didn't kill him, Krissy. I swear to you on all that's holy. It wasn't me. It was Sophie.'

Sophie? That makes no sense.

'The bitch is completely mad. I told you.'

'Why would Sophie kill my husband?'

'I dunno. She's got a temper like a fiend. Spouts all this feminist shit about no man's going to intimidate her. She stabbed him.' He points to the knife. 'That's the knife she used. I kept it to show you.'

Kristin is speechless.

Could it be true?

'I wish to God I'd never met her, let alone married her,' he says. 'But when you got together with Ged, I was just so sad. And desperate.'

He's smiling at her now, as if this is all some trivial misunderstanding. This is what happens after one of his *games.* Once it's over, he pretends nothing has happened. When she was a kid, he'd buy her sweets or an ice cream, for *being a good girl.*

Be a good girl. It's what they all say.

Kristin's brain is in a spin. She was sure it was him. As soon as she walked into the kitchen, she knew. He was so wound up when he discovered she was pregnant. She told Ged not to invite them. She knew it would all go wrong.

He steps forward and grabs her hand. She flinches. But he holds on.

'Hey,' he says. 'I'm not going to hurt you. I'd never hurt you. I love you. And you've got to listen to me. We belong together. We always have.'

She tries to pull away. 'Let go, Mickey!'

He releases her; raises his palms. He has tears of frustration in his eyes.

'This is all Ma's fault,' he says. 'She just filled your head with all that Catholic crap about sin. We love each other. How can that be a sin? And now I've got money. We can go away together. Abroad somewhere.'

He's mad. Obsessed.

He wants to drag her back into his fantasy, force her to submit again, and be part of his lie.

Not this time.

'It's all in your head,' she says. 'It's always been in your head. I got pregnant because you raped me. I don't love you. And even if Sophie killed my husband, I can't believe you weren't involved somehow.'

He's shaking his head, trying to erase her words.

He grabs her wrist. His grip bites. He squeezes his eyes shut and the tears roll down his cheeks as he pulls her towards him.

'Don't say such horrible things, Krissy. You know it's not true. I've only ever—'

'Let go!'

She tugs hard but can't get free.

'Krissy, just listen. I've got a plan.'

No. She's cowered and placated. Walked in fear her whole life.

Enough is enough.

She knees him in the balls, takes a deep breath, opens her mouth and screams.

65

Boden and Chakravorty are being escorted down the hall by the hotel manager, when they hear the scream. The sleepy security guard sitting on a chair outside the door to the suite looks up abruptly from his phone.

'Oh shit!' says Boden, as she and Chakravorty start to run.

After talking to the DI, she debated in her own mind what to do about the information Latham had given her. She hesitated for about thirty seconds.

Then she turned to Chakravorty and said, 'You asked what we can do, Prish. We're on the ground, in the best position to assess the situation. I say we do our job. Which first of all, is to preserve life.'

Chakravorty had agreed. They'd instructed the cab driver to change direction and head for Kristin Kelly's hotel.

As she runs, Boden pulls out her warrant card, she shoves it in the security guard's face and says, 'Police!'

He's more than willing to let the two cops go through the door instead of him.

The main door to the suite opens into a sitting room. It's

empty. A ball of wool with some knitting and a half drunk cup of coffee on the table.

Three doors open from the room. Two are shut, one ajar. An eerie light seeps out.

The bedroom?

Boden glances at the DC, and points at the door.

What's behind it? You can never tell.

She knows all the procedures she should follow. The precautions she should take.

'Call for back-up,' she whispers to Chakravorty.

She steps forward and flings open the door.

The room is in semi-darkness, illuminated only by the light from the en suite bathroom. Kristin Kelly is standing beside the bed in a bathrobe and a man is in front of her, bent double, clutching his groin.

'Police,' she says. 'I'm DS Boden. Are you all right, Lady Sullivan?'

Kristin blinks at her several times, then she smiles. 'The cop with the porridge. I wasn't expecting you.'

'Are you all right?' says Boden, turning on the main light.

The man's nose is bleeding. Kristin has blood on her chin. There's a knife on the bed.

Some kind of fight.

Kristin shrugs. 'Not really. Do you know my brother?'

The man struggles to his feet. Boden recognises Ollie Harmon.

He wipes his nose with his sleeve and smiles.

Standing next to Kristin, the family resemblance is obvious. He has the same spectacular good looks as his sister, but with paler skin and those stunning blue eyes.

'She kneed me in the balls,' he says. 'And I deserved it.'

'Why?' says Boden.

'Because it was my wife, Sophie, who killed Ged.' He shakes his head and frowns as if he still can't grasp it.

'And how do you know this, Mr Harmon?'

'I walked into the kitchen after she'd done it. She was standing there with the knife in her hand. Okay, I helped cover up for her. I admit that. But I panicked. And she is my wife. She begged me. But I've still got the pyjamas she wore that night. They're covered in his blood.' He turns to his sister and shakes his head sorrowfully. 'I'm so sorry, Krissy. I should've called the police and turned her in.'

Boden scans him. The tears brimming from his eyes are real enough.

He dips his head and whispers, 'I'm so sorry, Krissy. Sorry I brought this mad woman into all our lives.'

It's quite a performance. Boden studies Kristin. She seems detached. Numb? In shock? She says nothing, just turns away, pulling the bathrobe around her.

'Okay,' says Boden. 'We'll have to look into this. But I am going to caution you, Mr Harmon.'

He gives her a dazzling smile. It's almost seductive. 'Of course, I quite understand,' he says. 'You're just doing your job.'

66

Sophie Latham waited ages in an anxious purgatory for the police to arrive. She didn't recognise the officers who turned up at her flat. They cautioned her and told her she was being arrested in connection with the death of Sir Gerald Sullivan. She'd be taken to Cambridge to be interviewed.

She tried to explain, to show them the recording she'd made of Ollie as good as admitting it. But they weren't interested. They did let her call her parents.

She asked the officers what had happened to DS Boden, but they knew nothing about that. They put her in the back of an unmarked police car.

It's after midnight as they leave London. A wet night, but hoards of people are still out and about. The East End is buzzing with pub goers and clubbers, Ubers picking up, revellers straying into the road.

How much is she going to miss all this!

She wonders what sort of sentence she'll get. There'll be a trial, with the total humiliation of having her life and marriage, not to mention her character and her stupidity, dissected in open court. The media will be there in force. She'll be in the dock in more ways than one.

And it's what she deserves.

She stares out of the window as they hit the M11 and the urban fringes of London give way to open countryside and darkness. She's read about people going on trial and insisting they committed their crime in a moment of madness.

What a lame excuse! What a cliché!

Now she knows what that means. The woman consumed with rage and fear, the woman who grabbed that knife, this is not the real Sophie.

Except it is.

Maybe there are many Sophies? Good, bad, ugly, kind, cruel, smart, angry? Facing Ged that night, her better self failed her. Her father was right. She should've turned tail and run away. That was the right thing to do. She chose not to. She slapped him.

Bad choice!

The journey to Cambridge takes an hour and a half. Her escorts hand her over to other uniformed officers. Everyone is polite and professional as they process her through the system. Fingerprints, DNA swabs, mugshots.

She ends up in a locked cell; more waiting. She loses track of time. It must be the middle of the night.

The door opens.

It's Nick!

She stands up and falls into his arms. He holds her tight.

Finally he says, 'Hey, you're not supposed to hug your lawyer.'

Her lip trembles. 'I'm just so glad you're here. Thank you.'

'Okay,' he says. 'The police have your phone. And their

digital forensics people will examine the recording you made of Ollie.'

'Still doesn't alter the fact that I stabbed him, does it?'

'No. But they'll interview you. Not sure when. And just tell them what you did and why. What you were thinking at the time.'

'I didn't think. That's the problem.'

'No. You reacted. Thing is Soph, don't let your massive sense of guilt overwhelm the facts. People get into fights all the time. And we're all entitled to defend ourselves when threatened with serious harm. What Ollie did is a separate issue.'

'Where is he?'

'They're not saying.'

'Is Kristin all right?'

'I think we'd know if she wasn't.'

'I phoned Boden. Tried to warn them.'

'And I assume they acted on your warning. All of which is in your favour. I know this is an awful situation. But just try to keep calm, okay. And I'll be with you all the way.'

Sophie wipes the tears away with her hand.

'When did you get so smart, little brother?'

Pulling a tissue from his pocket, he hands it to her.

He smiles and shrugs. 'I'm the plodder, you're the brains.'

'Yeah, and look where that's got me.'

67

Boden stands next to the boss's desk, sipping a mug of coffee. She and DCI Hepburn are watching the live feed from the interview room on his computer screen.

It's been a long night. But the case has moved on in leaps and bounds. The evidence is stacking up. Hepburn is a pragmatist. He doesn't seem to hold it against her that she disobeyed Roscoe's explicit instructions.

All he said was, 'Fast moving inquiry. You were there, you made a judgement call. I hope I always allow my officers the leeway to take the initiative when necessary.'

Nothing more had been said. Roscoe apologised to her.

In the interview room, he and Mackie are facing Ollie Harmon across the table. They've been at it for some time.

Harmon is a pro; charming and helpful. But now they know why. His real name is Michael Kelly, and he has a long rap sheet with convictions for drug dealing, fraud and GBH. He's served two prison terms. But he's also been to court on three other occasions and was found not guilty. The psychiatric report from his last prison places him high on the psychopathy scale.

Nightmare. A charming psychopath who can work the system.

On screen, he lounges back in his chair. He's playing the innocent man who's just trying to be helpful.

'Look,' he says. 'I'm not pretending to be a good boy. I'm not. I married her for her money. I mean, you've seen her. Bit of a dog. But, y'know, serves me right, you could say. Once the ring was on her finger, I discovered what a complete, vicious bitch she is. And she hated my sister Kristin. Absolutely hated her from the word go.'

'Why do you think that was?' says Roscoe.

'Jealousy. Pure and simple. Kristin is everything she wants to be. Beautiful. Famous. Admired by men. Sophie's just got a couple of coffee shops.'

'And how did this jealousy manifest itself?'

'Well, she was always making sarcastic remarks. About Kristin just being a clothes horse. And stupid. Frankly, some of it was bordering on racist. Black model with no brains, that sort of thing. I called her on it on several occasions. That's when we started to fight. But the big thing was that Kristin's pregnant, and that's what she wanted to be.'

'Were you trying to get pregnant?'

'I knew to start with that was the deal. But the more I got to know her.' He grimaces. 'The idea of that woman having my kid? No way.'

'Were you always planning to leave her?'

'I didn't really want to marry her. It's not my usual MO. But she was insistent.' He grins. 'Couldn't resist my charms, I guess.'

Boden turns to Hepburn.

'He's a piece of work,' she says.

Hepburn sighs. 'Narcissist certainly. But also very plausible. If I was sitting on a jury, I might well buy it.'

Boden frowns. 'It has to be him, boss.'

They turn back to the screen.

Roscoe is speaking. '… and I'd like you to listen to this and tell me what you think it is.'

'Okay.'

Boden watches him. That smile. But the eyes, and more particularly the stare, tell another story. In another life, with those looks and performance skills, he might've made it as an actor.

The recording from Sophie Latham's phone is playing: it begins with a laugh.

'But I didn't expect you to lock horns with Ged. That was an unexpected bonus. I've been trying to figure out how to get Kristin free of that scumbag for months. And you gave me the opportunity on a plate.'

'And you took it? You cut his throat?'

'Come on, it's not like he didn't deserve it. Look upon it as my contribution to saving the planet.'

'You said you did it to protect me. Is that even true?'

'What do you care? You had money. You were desperate. I targeted you. Let's just move on.'

Mackie turns the recording off and Roscoe says, 'Two voices here, male first, then female. Can you tell me who they are?'

Michael Kelly runs his hand through his hair and shrugs. 'Not really.'

'Could the female voice be your wife, Sophie?'

'I dunno, maybe.'

Boden turns to Hepburn and says, 'It's rattled him. He didn't know she'd recorded that.'

'What about the man?' says Roscoe. 'Is that you?'

He chuckles. 'Okay,' he says. 'It sounds a bit like me. I'll give you that. But if you're asking whether this conversation took place between me and Sophie, then the answer is no. I mean, I'm no expert, but nowadays stuff like this is easy to fake. A good sound engineer could put something like this together, no problem.'

'How?'

'You use AI. Bots can imitate a voice. It's expensive. But Sophie could afford it. And her brother's a lawyer. You can't tell me that his firm doesn't use private security companies who've got access to all this. You should question him.'

'So you're denying that this is you?'

'Sophie and I never had that conversation. So, no, it can't be me. And I'm telling you, mate, this all comes back to the same thing. I'm a wheeler dealer. And, okay, a bit of a gigolo. I don't deny it. Women like me, and I take advantage of that fact. But I'm not a killer. No way. And this is my sister's husband we're talking about here. I liked him. I was a guest in his house. Why would I want to kill him? I've got no motive.'

He opens his palm and grins at Roscoe and Mackie.

Then he adds, 'I've told you who did it and why. And I've given you her bloodstained pyjamas.'

He adds a shrug.

Case closed, he appears to be saying.

Arrogant shit.

But the boss is right. He's plausible.

Hepburn rubs his face. 'This is going to be: he says this, she says that. What about this call to the emergency services on Ged's phone she says she made?'

'No sign of the phone. But Prisha's on it, talking to the ambulance service. They should have a recording.'

Hepburn nods. 'You look knackered. Go home, get some kip.'

'I'm fine.'

'You're not. Do what you're told.'

He's right. She smiles.

'Yes, boss.'

68

Sophie Latham sits up straight and looks her interrogators in the eye. Two men, well, it would be. The one asking the questions is a DI. He has a supercilious smile. She feels judged before she's even spoken. No sign of DS Boden.

Treat it like a business meeting.

As she waited in the cell, she kept telling herself that. But, if she's honest, it's impossible. Her confidence is shot. She's never been this wretched. Or ashamed. How did she get into this mess? This is the question tormenting her, and it's turned her into an emotional wreck.

They've been through all the preliminaries. Her gaze flits round the room. Cameras everywhere; it's very formal. She wonders who's watching.

The DI fidgets; he's tall and seems to have trouble getting comfortable in his chair. His sidekick is large too and a foot tapper; he looks more like a bouncer than a police officer.

The DI clears his throat. 'The thing I'm not clear about Mrs Harmon—' he says.

'Actually, it's Ms Latham,' says Nick. Her brother is

there, beside her, solid and reassuring, and he's sticking up for her.

'Ms Latham,' says the DI, with a dip of the head. 'Why did you go down to the kitchen in the middle of the night?'

Breathe. Take it slow.

'I couldn't sleep. I didn't want to disturb Ollie. So I got up. Went downstairs, saw the light in the kitchen. I thought it might be the chef. Or the staff.'

'In the middle of the night?'

'Well, I can't remember exactly what I thought. It could've been someone cleaning up. The meal was good. I just thought it'd be nice to tell them that. But it was Ged, eating a bowl of cereal, which I didn't expect.'

'What were you expecting, wandering round a house where you were a guest, in the middle of the night?'

They've already made up their minds. They think she killed Ged.

Her hands are shaking. She keeps them in her lap.

'I'm not sure,' she says. 'It'd been a funny evening.'

That sounds so lame!

'Funny in what way?'

'Awkward. And um, well, awkward.'

This is going badly.

She's panicky. Butterflies in her stomach. They gave her a disgusting cheese sandwich; she ate it because she was hungry.

Both the cops are staring at her, waiting for her to say more.

'The discussion over dinner was difficult,' she says. 'We knew why Ged had invited us. This thing with the climate protester. He said he was in London at the time, and we knew that wasn't true.'

'Although when you spoke to DC Mackie here, you said

you and your husband had been there that night with just Lady Sullivan, and Sir Gerald wasn't there?'

Of course. He was the bruiser who came with Boden.

Sophie nods.

'Could you answer, Ms Latham, for the record?'

'Sorry. Yes.'

'And that was a lie?'

'Yes.'

'Which you subsequently maintained?'

'Well, yes.'

She lied then, so they'll think she's lying now.

'And were you asked to lie?' says the cop.

'Yes. Kristin asked Ollie. He told me she'd phoned him.'

'And you agreed to this. Why?'

'Well, it's complicated. He was worried about her. What Ged might do to her. Her pregnancy. But, y'know, it was all a fairy story. I can see that now. I don't know what her relationship with Ged was really like.'

Slow down!

She knows she's gabbling. She glances at Nick; he smiles.

'Look,' she says. 'You have to understand that all along my husband was feeding me a pack of lies. And I talked to Kristin and what she said seemed to confirm it.'

'Tell us about that.'

'Kristin asked me to meet her. And we had this discussion. About sex. And she asked me if Ollie and I did S and M stuff. Played games with masks. And I thought she was trying to tell me she did that stuff with Ged. That he hurt her and abused her. At the time, I thought that's what she was saying. But then, much later, I found this balaclava and these handcuffs in Ollie's backpack. I realised then she was talking about her brother. She was trying to warn me, I suppose. It was her brother who'd done this to her, not her husband.'

It sounds ridiculous.

She takes a deep breath. Her body's shaking. The two cops have impassive looks on their faces. Do they even believe her? It's impossible to tell.

The DI steeples his fingers. 'Let's go back to the night of Sir Gerald's death. You said you couldn't sleep. But you didn't want to disturb your husband. So you got up. And he was fast asleep, was he?'

'He seemed to be. He'd drunk quite a lot.'

The door of the room opens, a woman in uniform comes in and whispers in the DI's ear.

'Let's take a short break,' he says.

The two cops get up and leave.

Relief floods through her as the door shuts behind them.

Nick pats her hand. 'It's going well,' he says.

'Is it? Doesn't feel like that.'

Her heart is thumping. Ollie was right; she'll be going to jail...

69

The police poked around for ages, talking to staff. Kristin refused to say what happened.

She stood up to him. She did it! Finally!

Afterwards, she was numb. She couldn't speak. And they didn't push it.

More uniforms arrived. They took Mickey away. The nurse appeared, wrapped a blanket around her and fussed over her. She wanted to call the doctor, but Kristin told her no. Poor woman was shitting herself. Thinking she'd get blamed, which she probably would.

The cops discovered her brother had charmed his way past the security guard. He said Jules had phoned him and asked him to come over and take care of his sister. He fed the same line to the nurse, and despatched her to the hotel kitchen to get some hot milk to help his sister sleep.

Vintage Mickey. Plausible and utterly convincing.

The nurse insisted on bathing the scratch on her chin and putting a plaster on it. After that, Kristin said she wanted to be alone. She banished the nurse to the corridor with the useless security guard.

Now, they're all gone. And she's alone.

She wanders round the room, pours herself a stiff drink, and wonders what the hell will happen next.

Could Sophie have killed Ged?

That's bullshit. Has to be.

But she faced her brother down! Stood up to the bastard. She did it!

Why has it taken all these years?

Without warning, the tears come. The dam inside bursts. She ends up crouched on the floor, sobbing.

After the abortion, Mum threw him out. She was a messed up junkie, but once she discovered what had been happening, she did the right thing.

The problem was, after that, wherever Kristin went, eventually he'd turn up. Always full of charm to start with. He was a changed man. He'd turned his life around. Then he'd want her to play the game again.

Sick!

But there was no escape. She was too scared to say no to him. She'd seen what he was capable of; look what he did to Mum.

Marrying Ged wasn't the ideal solution, but it worked. He couldn't get to her. She never told Ged the full story, just that her brother was a pest and a con man, and always trying to tap her for money. Which was also true.

As she thinks about Ged, she stops crying. But a strange lethargy creeps over her. The booze. She's not used to drinking. Her body is limp. Wrung out. She settles back in the armchair, pulls the blanket around her and lets her thoughts drift.

Ged was a selfish sod who expected to get his own way. But he could also be fun. Okay, he had a temper, but she'd grown up around enough angry men to know how to dodge the flak. And he was old school, liked to see himself as a gentleman. Wife beating was against the code; although a couple of times he'd come close. The sex was pedestrian. What mattered to him most was how things looked. How she looked, and the envy in other men's eyes when he walked into a room with her on his arm. She was just one of his assets. But when she got pregnant, everything improved. He was so excited. She got treated like a queen.

It wouldn't have lasted. In her heart, she knows that. Like his horses, once she'd lost her youth and speed, she would've been dumped. But he protected her. She misses that feeling.

God, how she misses it!

Her limbs are heavy; she can't move. Now Ged's gone, what will she do? How will she cope? Left on her own, with a baby. Just like Mum. Her worst nightmare.

She lets her eyes close; she's shattered. All she wants is to sleep forever and never wake up.

Jules shakes her shoulder. Those boney fingers.

Light is seeping into the room.

'Kristin,' she says. 'Darling, you need to wake up. The police are here.'

Of course. It was obvious they'd be back.

The nurse faffs around, trying to help her dress.

They're waiting for her in the sitting room.

She's smiles when she sees it's 'quinoa porridge' again. She can never remember her name.

'How are you doing, Lady Sullivan?' says the cop. 'Are you okay?'

That pitying look.

She refused to talk to them last night.

What the hell could she say? The idea of speaking about it. About him.

No way. Not now, not ever. She faced him. It's done.

She feels bolshy. Why can't they leave her alone?

Be polite.

'Didn't have a proper chance to thank you last night,' she says. This is her Lady Sullivan persona. Be formal. Put them in their place. Ged taught her how to do that.

But the cop just smiles. 'I'm glad we got here when we did,' she says.

Jules claps her hands. 'Can I offer you and your colleague some coffee, DS Boden?'

Jo Boden. That's her name!

She has the young Asian girl with her again; the one with the eyes that don't miss a trick, who records everything on her iPad.

The cop scans Jules.

Probably figuring if this is this best way to get rid of her?

'Thank you,' Jo Boden says. 'That would be nice.'

Jules scurries out. The cop turns to her. Their eyes meet. But it's not challenging. She seems concerned.

'Never trust the filth,' Mum said.

But then look what happened to her.

'Okay,' says the cop. 'The reason we're here is we don't have a clear picture of what happened last night.'

Clear? What the hell do they think, then?

Kristin shrugs. 'I didn't want to see anyone. Media and all that. Which is why I came here. Security was useless. Well, you know that. My brother talked his way in. He was being an arse.'

They've got him. Why can't they just put him in jail where he belongs?

'Can you tell us what happened? We recovered a knife.

Vinyl gloves. And there was a backpack hidden behind the sofa with various items in it.'

Kristin realises her heart is thumping. It comes from nowhere. She can't breathe. A sense of crashing down. Her knees buckle. The cop takes her arm and guides her to a chair.

'Take some deep breaths,' she says.

Kristin does. Everything's swimming. Is she about to puke? But it works.

Jules returns to the room. 'That's all sorted,' she says. She frowns at Kristin. 'You look awful, darling. Are you all right?'

'She felt faint,' says the cop. 'Bit of a panic attack.'

'And are we surprised?' says Jules in her poshest voice. 'Kristin is anxious to help in any way she can. But I have to say that your previous treatment of her was completely unacceptable. She's a grieving widow, and here you are back again to harass her. Well, I'm here to tell you that won't wash.'

Jules is ready to do battle.

But the cop smiles. She's not fazed. She's not intimidated by Jules.

Kristin likes that about her.

'I understand your concerns,' she says. 'But this is a murder inquiry. And I'm sure Lady Sullivan is as anxious as us to ensure that we bring the right person to justice. That is our sole aim. And we don't always get it right first time. For that, I apologise.'

'Did he kill Ged?' says Kristin.

The cop looks at her. 'He insists he didn't. Says it was Sophie.'

'What do you think?'

'Our job is to find the evidence that leads us to the truth.

And you can help us do that, if you're willing to. I know that means speaking about your brother. And I can see that's going to be hard.'

She has no idea. Or does she?

Kristin sighs. Everyone's looking at her; waiting. She can see Ged's face. All that blood. It's her fault he's dead. She lied to him. Let him think Mickey was a pain, but no more than that. She knew her brother would go ballistic about the pregnancy. Ged took care of her. He didn't deserve to end up dead in his own kitchen. But if she speaks? She can't.

Then Mickey will think he's won.

'What do you want to know?' she says.

'Tell us about Mickey,' says the cop. 'He conned his way in here last night. Can you tell us what happened?'

She takes a deep breath.

'I think he came to kill me. Well, rape me first, then kill me.'

'Good grief!' says Jules.

'And was this the first time he's tried to attack you?' says the cop.

'No,' says Kristin. 'It started when I was ten.'

70

DCI Hepburn has called a briefing to update the team. Jo Boden sits on a desk at the back, dangling her feet. Roscoe smiles at her.

'Okay,' says the boss. 'First, we have a recording, which we believe is Latham's attempt to get help after she stabbed Ged Sullivan. Play it Prisha.'

The recording plays:

'Emergency. Which service do you require?'

'Ambulance,' says a female voice. 'It's a stabbing. We need help urgently. The address? Oh my god, Ol what's the address? Tell them the address.'

'The call ends there,' says Chakravorty. 'We've been looking for Sullivan's phone. It wasn't in the kitchen. But then we found four phones in the backpack recovered at Kristin's hotel. One belongs to him. It's smashed. His prints are on it, also Latham's and Michael Kelly's.'

'Tom, would you like to summarise?' says the boss.

Roscoe stands up. 'Latham's account of events appears to hold water. She says she rowed with Sullivan, thought he was about to hit her. He did attack Cary Rutherford, fracturing her skull and causing her death. So he was prone to uncontrolled anger, leading to violence. She stabs him. Realises what she's done, tries to call an ambulance, using his phone. This is when her husband arrives on the scene and the call ends. Latham says her husband smashed the phone with a meat mallet. We found one in the kitchen. It's a utensil used to tenderise meat. This one has Kelly's prints on it.'

'Which would confirm Latham's version of what happened up to that point,' says the boss.

'Yes,' says Roscoe. 'Jo and Prisha got a detailed statement from Lady Sullivan this morning. And that gives us background and motive for what we think Kelly did next. Jo?'

Boden stands up.

'According to Kristin, Michael Kelly began to sexually abuse his sister when she was ten and he was sixteen. When she was thirteen, she became pregnant by him and had an abortion. He appears to have never forgiven her for this. His fury at the time was directed against their mother. She died of a spiked heroin overdose. Kristin says he was responsible. That he murdered her. For this reason, she feared him. After this, the pattern of abuse changed. For years, he stalked and threatened Kristin and subjected her to sadistic sexual punishments. When she became pregnant by another man, her husband, he regarded this as a betrayal. He broke into her hotel suite, she believes, intending to punish her one last time, then kill her. We recovered a knife at the scene, which was the same knife used to kill Ged Sullivan.'

The room is silent. Boden looks round. Her summary was clinical. It has to be. But they're as stunned as she was when she heard Kristin's account.

'It's quite horrific. She says she's never shared it with anyone else before. And it feels like the truth.'

'Okay,' says Hepburn. 'That's great work, both of you. Well done.'

'Thank you, sir,' says Boden.

Prisha smiles.

The boss paces at the front of the room. 'There's a lot to unpack here,' he says. 'I'll need to speak to the CPS to discuss how we'll approach this. There'll be additional charges against Michael Kelly, and he needs to be interviewed about these matters. Given Kristin Kelly's celebrity, bringing it all to court will not be easy. And the issue is further complicated by the fact Ged Sullivan killed this climate protester.'

Roscoe folds his arms. 'We're going to need loads more help, boss.'

'Agreed. I need to brief the Chief. I'll raise that. Anything else at the moment?'

'What about Sophie Latham?' says Boden.

'Cut her loose,' says Hepburn. 'Release her on bail. But I'm fairly sure the CPS will buy her claim of self-defence. In the context of Sullivan's angry assault on Cary Rutherford, the claim he was threatening would probably convince a jury.'

Hepburn heads for the door, with Roscoe in his wake.

Boden turns to Chakravorty.

They exchange exhausted smiles.

'Do you reckon that's fair?' says Prisha. 'She gets off.'

'I don't know. But what would you do faced with a bloke like Sullivan? What would any of us do? I'm glad it's not my call.'

71

Sophie insists on returning to her own flat. Her father unlocks the door, and she follows him in. Deirdre and Nick bring up the rear.

A police forensics team has been through the whole place. Cupboard doors are open. Furniture is skewed. There's an odd chemical smell, which Sophie can't identify.

'Looks like it's been turned over by a bunch of burglars, who then tried to tidy up,' says Roger.

'We'll soon have things shipshape again,' says Deirdre.

Sophie glances around. The sense of intrusion and invasion, and not just by the police, jumps out at her from every corner. It's not her home any more. Her life has been laid to waste.

'Don't worry, Mum,' she says. 'It doesn't matter.'

'It does matter,' says Deirdre. 'We should get a firm of industrial cleaners in.'

Sophie is too drained to argue.

Nick sticks his head in the bedroom. 'Do you want me to get some bin bags and clear out all his stuff?'

She turns to face her brother. Practical and to the point. He's been brilliant. The last thing she expected.

Without him...

She tears up again.

Stop crying! Will she ever? Probably not.

'What happens now?' she says. She wants to sound businesslike, and prove, at least to them, that she has some control over her emotions. Even if it's an illusion.

He shrugs. 'The wheels grind slowly. But I'd say they'll accept it was self-defence. The full file will go to the CPS and they'll decide if they want to charge you with anything.'

'I won't have to go to court?'

'You won't be in the dock. But you'll be a witness to what Ollie did. You'll have to testify about that. But listen, it'll take months before we get to that. Months and months. Maybe even a year.'

They will still rip her to shreds.

And she deserves it.

Sophie walks over to the sofa, sits down, and puts her face in her hands.

Roger comes and sits beside her. He puts his arm round her shoulders.

'Nick's right,' he says. 'You're going to have time to recover. You won't always feel like this.'

'No, Dad. You're wrong. I will never forgive myself for what I did. I wish they would charge me with something. In a way that'd be easier. I should be punished. I should go to jail.'

Her mother comes and sits on the other side of her. 'Listen to me,' she says. 'No one had any inkling of the kind of man Ged Sullivan was. All the papers are saying that he attacked that poor girl with a baseball bat. The police have a video. Fractured her skull. And he expected you to lie in order to cover up his crime. I don't know how you deal with that sort of man.'

Sophie clutches her mother's hand.

'Not the way I did. I was stupid and arrogant. I let him provoke me when I should've just walked away.'

'It's easily done,' says Deirdre.

She's being nice. They're trying to make her feel better.

Sophie shakes her head. 'I wasn't prepared to back down. That's the problem. I was so convinced I was right, and nothing mattered more than that. It blinded me. I've spent my whole life thinking how smart I am.'

'You are smart,' says Deirdre.

'No, I'm not. If I was, this would never have happened. I jumped to conclusions. I read everything wrong. There's a line between being determined and being bloody-minded. I cross it all the time. Come on, you don't have to be nice to me. You all know it's true.'

Deirdre sighs and smiles.

'It's sometimes true,' says Roger.

'What you're missing here,' says Nick, 'is Ollie's agenda. You thought he was asleep. You go downstairs. It kicks off with Ged, and suddenly there he is. He must've followed you.'

'And what we now know about him,' says Roger, 'is he's an opportunist. How long was he there, watching what was going on? It's likely he could've intervened earlier, stopped Ged from threatening you. But still the outcome might've been the same.'

Why are they being so kind?

She doesn't deserve it.

'How about a cup of tea?' says Deirdre.

'A stiff drink might be more in order,' says Roger. He gets up and goes to the kitchen area.

Nick is checking his phone. 'Well,' he says. 'According to the BBC, Michael Kelly will appear in court tomorrow morning, charged with murder, attempted murder, and various counts of sexual abuse. I think we can assume he won't get bail. He'll be held on remand.'

Thank God for that.

Sophie has been trying not to think about him. He played her with such skill, knew where she was weak, and how to manipulate her. She thought she was in control. He outmatched her at every turn. He knew what she wanted, what her perfect man would be like. And he became that character. The perfect husband. She bought it. She bought the complete package and refused to listen to the doubts of her family and friends. Their opposition only strengthened her resolution to have what she wanted.

She realises her mother is watching her.

'Are you all right, Soph?' says Deirdre.

She shakes her head. 'I'm sorry, Mum. You tried to tell me what a fool I was being, and I just attacked you for it.'

Her mother shrugs.

Roger has found a bottle of scotch and is lining up glasses on the kitchen counter. 'We're your family,' he says. 'We should've done a better job of protecting you.'

'I should've done a better job of listening,' says Sophie.

But when he was Ollie, he was perfect. Wasn't he?

She pushes that thought away. It's an illusion. She has to let go of it.

Soon! Soon she will. But not yet.

He's a monster. That's who he really is. And he set out, without compunction, to destroy her. She hates him. She hates Mickey Kelly. But in her heart, she still carries a torch, just a small torch, for Ollie.

EPILOGUE

It comes as a bolt from the blue to Sophie. A text from Kristin Kelly pops up on her phone.

She stares at it in disbelief.

In the last few months, she's watched from a distance as the media circus has reported on and chewed over every aspect of *the shocking Kelly case,* as it's now known. Kristin's every move—her battles with Ged's daughters, the progress of her pregnancy—has been dissected. Her face is everywhere. There're rumours of a film deal.

Sophie's been far too ashamed to attempt any contact with Kristin.

How do you say, sorry I stabbed your husband?

The trial date is creeping closer. But Sophie has stayed out of sight. Nick has constructed a legal ring of steel around her. All approaches to answer questions, give interviews, *tell her side of the story,* have been rebuffed.

She spent some time hiding away in Sussex on Claire and Danny's farm until a dogged reporter ran her to ground. She fled from there to a cottage in Cornwall. But her face has become famous. She was spotted out walking, videoed, and it was posted online. She now knows what it's like to be Kristin.

Defiantly, she returned to London. She decided to stop feeling sorry for herself and go back to running her business. Several times a day, she's snapped and people even ask for selfies. She knows of at least two Facebook groups dedicated to campaigning to free Mickey Kelly. They've dubbed her *the real murderer.* Even from a jail cell, he has the power to charm. She's dreading his trial. Only when it's over will she have a chance of getting her life back.

No, be honest, that'll never happen.

DS Boden came to tell her that no charges would be brought against her. She acted on Sophie's warning and went to Kristin's hotel that night. The police are satisfied it was Ged Sullivan's attack on Cary Rutherford that led to the climate activist's death. This has weighed in the decision not to prosecute Sophie. The CPS accept she acted in self-defence, and that her response was proportionate to the threat. But her lawyers have made it clear to her it won't prevent her soon-to-be former husband from trying to implicate her in Ged's murder.

Sophie knows from the army of reporters camped outside the hospital that Kristin's baby was born a week ago. The legal battle over the Sullivan estate is fierce and ongoing. But public sympathy has swung in Kristin's direction. Attempts by his daughters to discredit her and proclaim their father's innocence have fallen flat. Caught between a crazy brother and an angry husband, two PR companies have been working to present Kristin as both vulnerable but unvanquished. Her testimony in court at her brother's trial will be followed globally.

Sophie reads her text:

Wondered if you fancied coming over for a coffee? Probably about time we had a chat.

There's a smiley face and two kisses.

Two kisses?

Sophie is nonplussed. What does she want?

Only one way to find out.

She's petrified.

Kristin is living in an exclusive apartment block overlooking Hyde Park. On the morning of Sophie's visit it's cold and wet, so a hood and scarf don't look out of place. She enters the building unrecognised.

A security guard, at the door to the fifth-floor apartment, checks her ID against her driver's licence.

A maid opens the door.

Kristin is sitting on the sofa cradling her baby. The new mother is looking radiant. There's a serenity about her that surprises Sophie.

She looks up and smiles. 'Come and meet Gerry,' she says.

Her tone of voice is amicable; like they're old friends.

Weird.

Sophie has a cascade of emotions as she walks across the room. Guilt is the uppermost. Shame, embarrassment, awkwardness; they're in there too, creating a toxic mix.

She can't help noticing the panoramic view of the park. The room is spacious; the furnishings are colourful and the walls are hung with contemporary art. But it feels like a home; a very different vibe to the Newmarket house.

Sophie manages to smile. Inside, she's quaking. Kristin used to be the anxious one. Now it's her.

'Congratulations,' she says.

Should've brought a present.

'Thank you. And thank you for coming. This can't be easy for you.'

Their eyes meet. Kristin's gaze is steady, but there's no anger.

She looks like him. And that's still hard.

Sophie shrugs. 'I thought I'd be the last person you'd want to see.'

Kristin shakes her head. 'Why? The police said you phoned them, warned them that Mickey was coming after me. That's true, isn't it?'

Sophie nods.

The maid enters with coffee on a tray. She places it on the table between them. More awkwardness.

'Sit. Please,' says Kristen.

Sophie perches on the edge of one of the sofas. Being here, having coffee, is surreal.

'Thank you, Solange,' says Kristin.

The maid retreats, leaving the two women to face each other.

Kristin seems different. Well, she's just given birth. But it's more than that. To Sophie, it always seemed that, despite her beauty, Kristin was never happy in her own skin. Perhaps that's what's changed?

Say something.

'He's very calm,' says Sophie.

Kristin chuckles. 'That's because he's just been fed. Want to hold him?'

What!

It seems rude to refuse. She stands up, comes over. Kristin hands her the baby. He's heavy for a newborn. A dark, silky down covers most of his head.

Sophie rocks him. He's lovely; brand new and innocent.

'Eight pounds, five ounces,' says Kristin.

'Wow,' says Sophie.

What can she say? The usual platitudes seem inappropriate.

He's got his father's eyes? Maybe not.

'It's been on my mind for some time,' says Kristin. 'I've wanted to apologise to you. But I didn't know how. You must be furious with me.'

'You apologise to me?'

'Yeah. I should've told you about my brother, warned you. I knew what he was doing to you. And I wanted to tell you. When I asked you to meet me that time. I really thought I could do it. Then I bottled out.'

Would Sophie have believed her?

Be honest. No.

But instead she says, 'you must've been scared of him.'

'I find it hard to talk about. And I'm going to have to. In court. Actually, I'm terrified. But I want him to go down. I need to do it for my mum. He killed her too, y'know. Though it'll be hard to prove that now.'

'Must've been a nightmare for you, living all these years, knowing that.'

Kristin nods. She seems close to tears. The baby dozes.

Will she mention Ged?

'I've got a favour to ask,' says Kristin. 'Don't know where you stand on religion.'

Religion?

She continues. 'I'm having Gerry baptised. I was brought up Catholic. Not that I believe in Jesus and all that. But I believe in the devil. I want my son to be protected. I want him to have people who'll watch out for him. Teach him how to be strong and a good person. Jules has agreed to be a godmother. But she's getting on a bit. I was hoping you might be his other godmother.'

'Me? You want me?'

To protect Ged Sullivan's baby?

Sophie shakes her head in disbelief. 'After what happened? They must've told you the details.'

There's a moment of heavy silence.

Kristin sighs.

'Yes,' she says. 'They did.' She hesitates, then she adds, 'but I know what Ged was like when people crossed him. He was scary. And you really pissed him off that night.'

'Yeah, but I should've walked away. Run away even. What I did was wrong.'

Kristin sighs. 'Perhaps. I never risked confronting him. I always backed down. That's how it worked with him and me. I had to be the kind of wife he wanted. The bimbo model.' She chuckles. 'I'm quite good at it. But then I've been doing it since I was a kid.'

'Did you love Ged?'

'Yeah, mostly. In a way. But the important thing was he protected me from Mickey. I could keep my brother at arm's length. Well, thought I could.'

'Why did you even invite us that first time?'

Kristen shrugs. 'Stupid, I guess. I was trying to be normal. I thought, well, if he's married too. But then I saw how angry he was when he found out I was pregnant, and I knew nothing had changed.'

'How has it been for you?' says Sophie.

'Hard when I was still pregnant. Ged's daughters tried to cut off the money. Now I'm inundated with offers of work. The fragile victim. The industry loves it. Jules says I'm totally hot.'

'Isn't that a bit sick?'

'Completely. But I need the cash for the lawyer's bills and to fight Ged's daughters. So the game goes on.'

Sophie stares down at the small bundle in her arms.

'You sure you want me to be his godmother?' she says.

'Yes.' says Kristin. 'And when it comes to the trial, I think we should make it clear to everyone that we're facing it together. You had my back when it mattered. I want to make things right and do the same for you.'

Is this forgiveness? Sophie Latham isn't sure.

'I'd like that,' she says. 'That would really help.'

NEXT IN THE SERIES

LIE DENY REPEAT

A marriage gone bad...

When Cheryl met Xan, she was a struggling single parent with a five-year-old son. Now they have two children, and he's hell-bent on turning her research work into a business that could make billions. But does he still love her?

A dangerous affair...

A business deal brings Hannah into Xan's life. She's a young woman driven by ambition. He can't resist her. But the lies they tell soon spiral out of control, as a toxic mix of lust, ambition, and greed drags them all into dark waters.

A deadly outcome...

When the police recover a body from the river, Detective Jo Boden must ask the question: is it an accident or could it be murder?

Order your copy now from Amazon.

Scan QR code to buy Lie Deny Repeat.

LEAVE A REVIEW

If you feel like writing a review, I'd be most grateful. The choice of books out there is vast. Reviews do help readers discover one of my books for the first time.

Scan QR code to review Her Perfect Husband

A MESSAGE FROM SUSAN

Thank you for choosing to read *Her Perfect Husband*. If you enjoyed it and would like to keep up to date with my latest book releases and news, please use the address below.

susanwilkins.co.uk/sign-up/

*Your email address will never be shared, and you can unsubscribe at any time.

Scan QR code to go to Susan's sign up page

Do get in touch and let me know what you thought of *Her Perfect Husband*. I love hearing from readers. You can message me via my susanwilkins.co.uk/contact/

BOOKS BY SUSAN

The Informant

The Mourner

The Killer

It Should Have Been Me

Buried Deep

Close To The Bone

The Shout + The Right Side Of The Line (Free when you sign up to Susan's newsletter)

A Killer's Heart

She's Gone

Her Perfect Husband

Lie Deny Repeat

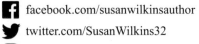

ACKNOWLEDGEMENTS

Huge thanks to Colin James and Graham Bartlett for their expert advice on how the police would proceed. Some things have been altered slightly in the interests of drama.

Thanks to the independent publishing community, the Alliance of Independent Authors, and the many indie authors out there, who are so generous with their time and advice.

Big thanks to my Reading Team for their invaluable feedback. If you're interested in joining this, sign up to my newsletter and you will get the chance to take part. Go to my website: susanwilkins.co.uk/sign-up

Last, but never least, my enormous gratitude to Jenny Kenyon for her sharp editorial eye on the manuscript and all her marketing advice.

But getting the books out into the world would be impossible without my partner in crime, Sue Kenyon. I just write the books. She does everything else.

Published by Herkimer Limited in 2022
Summit House
170 Finchley Road
London NW3 6BP

Scan QR code to go to susanwilkins.co.uk

ISBN 978-1-9169012-7-8

Made in United States
North Haven, CT
30 October 2022